I0597016

Also by *Karla Brandenburg*

The Epitaph Series

Epitaph

The Twins

The Mirror

The Northwest Suburbs Series

Cookie Therapy

Return to Hoffman Grove

Living Canvas

Touched by the Sun

The Mist Trilogy

Mist on the Meadow

Gathering Mist

Rising Mist

Other Novels

Intimate Distance

Heart for Rent, with an Option

Epitaph 3: The Mirror

Karla Brandenburg

Epitaph 3: The Mirror

Karla Brandenburg

Copyright 2017 © Karla Lang

ISBN 978-0999121320

For questions and comments about the quality of this book, please contact Karla@KarlaBrandenburg.com

Cover art by The Killion Group

Acknowledgements: As always, thanks to my critique group, Terry Odell and Steve Pemberton, and my editor, Kelly Lynne. Thanks to my good friend, Jennifer LeClaire, who is an expert brainstormer. Special thanks to my sister, Doctor Ruth, and to Joy Demme for helping me test my shorthand.

Chapter 1

SANDRA MEYER LEANED AGAINST THE counter behind the register and glanced around Morning Joe to make sure the café was empty before she re-read Nick Benedetto's text. He was coming home, on leave from the Army, and he wanted to talk to her. In person. Her stomach churned. Why did he want to talk to her now? After all these years?

As she tucked her phone into her pocket, Garth Benson walked into the café and her mood improved. His jeans were covered in dirt. His shoulders strained the seams of his flannel shirt and he'd rolled the sleeves. An image of Paul Bunyan came to mind and made her giggle. He cocked an eyebrow and gave her a silly grin before he glanced around. "Hey, beautiful."

A thrill ran through her at the compliment. She couldn't take him seriously, but a girl did like to have her ego stroked. "Cup of coffee?" she asked.

He sauntered to the counter and leaned over. "Yes, please. Sweet. Like you."

"You know your compliments are wasted on me," she said as she poured his coffee. She flipped her ponytail over her shoulder and leaned toward him while she handed him the cup.

Garth passed a five dollar bill across the counter and she rang up the sale.

"When are you going to let me take you away from all this?" he asked in the same joking manner he always used.

"Let's see," she said, laying a finger to her jaw and staring off into space. "Where shall we go today? A villa in the south of France? Maybe Rome? Or we could live in a hut on a beach in Hawaii." She focused in on his light brown eyes and raised her eyebrows.

"And what's wrong with Illinois? You don't really want to leave Edgarville, do you?" He leaned close. "Our lives are here. My family. Your mother. You don't want to leave all this glamour, do you?"

She snatched the towel from the counter behind her. "First chance I get," she told him. Not for the first time. She sashayed into the dining area and proceeded to wipe down tables.

"Let me take you to dinner and we can talk about it some more."

Sandra chuckled. "Nice try, big guy."

He took hold of her wrist and she gasped. That's how Nick had tried to persuade her that fateful night. Funny how his text brought the memories to the forefront.

She fought down the flash of panic. Another man, another time. This was Garth. Not Nick. Garth would never hurt her. Sandra pulled her wrist free of Garth's grasp and swallowed down her alarm.

"You deserve a break," Garth said gently. "Now that you're moving into your own place, I can save you cooking one night. Unless you still plan to make dinner for your mom."

Sandra kept working, ignoring his attempt to change her mind. The question had been asked and answered.

She'd been taking care of her mother since she was sixteen, since the car accident that killed her father and disabled her mother twelve years ago. Sandra had taken her mother to and from the doctor's appointments and the physical therapy that followed each of the seven surgeries she'd endured. If Sandra was honest with herself, her mother had been independent for at least half of those years. She was able to drive herself the five miles to and from work every day, the job that had always been more important to her than her family.

There would be no more surgeries, and her mother's final physical therapy appointment had been last month. Sandra had a plan, starting with moving into her own place.

Her own place.

The advantage of having a real estate agent for a mother, she had a lease on a fully-furnished duplex. The agreement was that if her mother could manage on her own and stay healthy for a year, Sandra was out of here. Out of Edgarville. Finally.

"Sandra?" Garth asked, waiting for her to change her mind.

"I need time on my own," she said, moving to the next table. "I'm finally going to get a life. My own life."

Garth set his hands on her hips and she straightened. He was fun to joke around with, but she'd learned her lesson with Nick. Once you let a man touch you, it was too easy for him to overpower you.

Sandra brushed his hands off and smiled. Yeah, he set her stomach fluttering, and he had muscles on muscles with all the heavy lifting he did setting tombstones in the cemetery. While one night with Garth stuck in her subconscious like the last piece of cherry pie, that same piece of cherry pie would weigh her down.

Garth held up his hands. "I know. You don't want to spoil a perfectly good friendship. But you know what? Friends have dinner together sometimes."

He was nothing if not persistent. Sandra cupped his face with her hand, tipped on her toes and kissed his cheek. "You're sweet."

"I've been called a lot of things," he said in a gruff voice that sent ripples across her skin. "Sweet isn't one of them." He crossed his arms. "Rumor has it Nick's back in town."

Going for nonchalant, she moved to the next table and wiped it down. "So I hear."

Garth followed close behind. "Think he'll look you up while he's home?"

Sandra straightened. "Small town. He'll probably be hard to miss."

"You deserve better than what he gave you."

Jealousy didn't suit Garth. "That was over a long time ago." Sandra folded the cloth. "Did you want something to go with your coffee?"

Garth stepped inside her personal space. The man was far too potent. "Don't want to see you get hurt."

Her voice cracked. "Been taking care of myself for a long time."

He nodded, turned and left the café. Of all the people in town she might confide in, Garth would be her first choice, but she didn't dare.

~ ~ ~

Garth Benson strode down Center Street on his way to the cemetery. He knew Sandra wanted out of this small town, but Edgarville was home.

He waved at people on the street, familiar faces. Garth was acquainted with every store owner on the main drag, most of them since he was a kid. The stores had changed hands over the years, mostly to the next generation. People had your back in Edgarville. They looked out for one another.

The world could be brutal. People in the city were always in a hurry, not to mention the shootings that were reported every day. They didn't have time to stop and talk or ask about the family on the way by. Likely, that was part of the problem. Sandra had a rough family life. The strain showed in her eyes when people asked about her mother.

He preferred the way her eyes sparkled when she joked with him, that gorgeous shade of sky blue, the way she flipped her blonde ponytail. On those rare occasions she let her hair down, he wanted to finger comb the thick waves that hung to her shoulders. Between all the work she did at Morning Joe and taking care of her mother, he was sure she skipped meals. She had a cute little body, but she was too thin.

He could help, if she'd let him. Even if it was only a shoulder to cry on. But Sandra was strong. She'd weathered what Nick did to her on her own, and that took no small amount of courage.

Garth ground his teeth and then took a sip of his coffee. Nick was back. One could only hope his years in the Army had taught him a thing or two about how to be a decent human being.

The business district turned residential. Trees overhung the street. Victorian houses adorned with gingerbread trim were interspersed with brick ranch houses and bungalows, each with well-manicured lawns. This was a tight-knit community. Surely Sandra saw that, and yet she'd never spoken about what Nick did to her, and most people didn't know. She'd hidden the bruises well. Garth wouldn't have known if Tammy Calhoun hadn't pointed them out.

Garth continued past the iron fence of the rolling cemetery, turned between the gateposts, his boots crunching on the gravel parking lot beside the office. His brothers sat under a tree, drinking their coffee from a thermos and chomping on cookies their mother had sent along in a Ziploc bag.

His younger brother, Brian, rose to his feet and dusted off his jeans. "'Bout time you got back."

Garth gave him a playful shove. "Slacker."

"Hey," Brian complained. His eyes went from the cup of coffee in Garth's hand to Garth's face and he smirked. "Got shut down again, did you? When are you going to give up on that one?"

Garth fixed him with a murderous glare and Brian laughed.

"You tell her you saw Nick?" Thad, his older brother, asked.

"Didn't have to."

Garth spotted their sister Amy. She wandered through the headstones, her face turned toward the rays of sun beaming through the trees. Nick had charmed Amy once, and Garth had introduced Nick to his fist for kissing her, but Amy had seemed more embarrassed than mad at Garth for stepping in.

What did women see in Nick Benedetto? Garth set his stride and intercepted Amy by the cremation niches.

"Yes?" she asked, brows up.

He slowed his pace. No, he couldn't ask her. "You know what? Never mind."

She folded her arms. "Too late."

Garth cupped the back of his neck. "You remember Nick Benedetto?"

Color pinked her cheeks. "Yeah?"

"Well, he's back in town."

"And why do you care?" Amy took a step closer, watching him closely. "You're worried he's going to stake a claim on Sandra. You know, Kevin tried to tell me there was something between you and Sandra, the way she flirts with you, the way you flirt back."

"You're not still mad about the Crazy Amy thing, are you?"

Amy's eyes flashed. "Technically, she only said it the one time, but it doesn't endear her to me, if that's what you're asking."

There were things about Sandra and Nick that Amy didn't know, things nobody else knew. Except Tammy Calhoun. If Nick hadn't left for the Army, Garth might have done more than punch his lights out when Nick made a play for Amy, might have encouraged Sandra to go to the police, but he figured she had her reasons for keeping quiet.

"Garth," Amy said in a dangerously low tone. "Of all the women in town who want a piece of you, she's the one you give it to?"

"Sandra and I have never dated, and you know it." Although if he had his way, they definitely would.

Amy closed her eyes and shook her head. "Kevin's right. How did I miss it? Honest to God, you gave me grief over every man I even looked at, and you're sulking because the one woman in town who doesn't deserve you won't go out with you?"

He winced.

"She's going to break your heart, and I refuse to feel sorry for you," she told him, hands on hips. "Nick can offer her a ticket out of town, the chance she's been waiting for. You know that, right, Garth?" She lifted to her toes, nose to nose. "Right?"

Wrong. Sandra wouldn't go anywhere with Nick, not based on what Garth knew. "You ever consider maybe she was trying to protect you when she told me Nick kissed you that day? That maybe it wasn't because she was jealous?"

Amy flapped her lips.

Yeah, he didn't figure she'd understand. Garth grunted, turned on his heel and headed for the family's monument shop.

Amy caught up with him before he hit the sidewalk outside the stone gateposts. She shoved him, the way he'd shoved Brian moments ago. Well, maybe not as hard. She stared at him, waiting for him to tell her the rest of the story, but he'd already said too much.

She took a step back. "You really care that much about her?"

He wasn't having this discussion. Not with his sister. "What about you?" he asked. "You going to look up Nick now that he's back in town?" He couldn't help baiting her, even though she was punch-drunk in love with Kevin McCormick and a month from her wedding. Thank heaven for that.

She rolled her eyes. "It was one kiss." She held up a finger to emphasize her point. "One. Even if I wanted anything more from him, which I didn't, you took care of that when you gave him a black eye." She stormed into the cemetery, fists swinging at her sides.

All this drama because Tammy Calhoun had had a crush on Garth. She'd been the one to tell him how Nick was threatening her girlfriend, Sandra, the one to send Sandra to Garth when Nick cornered Amy. Thanks to Tammy, he'd seen the bruises Sandra tried to hide under her makeup, and he had a good idea how she'd gotten them. While the high school kids figured Sandra was jealous, Garth knew she was trying to protect Amy.

Sandra was a year behind Amy in school. That made her somewhere around sixteen at the time of her parents' accident, about the time he'd noticed the bruises she'd tried so hard to conceal. Thank heaven Nick graduated that year and wasn't around to inflict more damage. Most people had looked at Sandra with pity when, at such a young age, she'd suffered not only the loss of her father and then her grandmother, but she'd taken on the care of her mother, who'd been injured in the car accident. It was a wonder Sandra graduated high school.

Sandra was a fighter. A survivor. No, as much as she liked to talk about getting out of Edgarville, she wasn't going anywhere with Nick.

# Chapter 2

SANDRA GLANCED AT THE CLOCK. Almost seven, closing time, and then she had the weekend off to move.

A place all her own. Why was she so nervous? Most people her age had been on their own for years.

Most people hadn't spent most of their adult life caring for a parent.

The original plan had been she and Tammy Calhoun, her best friend, would get a place together when they graduated high school, but Tammy never graduated. The rite of passage somehow didn't feel right without Tammy, but Tammy had died before they got their chance.

The bell over the door rang. Amy Benson.

"Hi, Sandra."

Sandra still cringed when she saw Amy. She'd never forget the glazed look in Amy's eyes. The eerie sound in her voice when she'd repeated Sandra's grandmother's words: "when life gives you that piece of cherry pie, sometimes you just have to eat it." There was no way Amy could have known Sandra's grandmother had passed away before Sandra knew, but she did. Sandra's frightened response, "that's crazy, Amy," had taken on a life of its own.

And why was she thinking about that today? Sandra forced a smile, pushing the ghosts of the past away.

"When's the wedding?" Sandra asked.

Amy's cheeks flushed with color and her pale brown eyes sparkled. Sandra felt a pinch of envy that Crazy Amy had found a husband. Not that Sandra wanted to get married. She hadn't even had a date in years.

"June 12," Amy told her.

"That's only another couple of weeks, a month?" The sooner she got Amy out of the café, the sooner she could finish updating the Morning Joe webpage for the specials for when she was off and close out the sales for the day. "What can I get you?"

"Actually…" Amy's nostrils flared and a different sort of shine lit her eyes. Was she nervous about something?

Amy wanted to talk to Sandra now? "It's closing time. If you could get to the point?"

The bell over the door chimed again, and there he was. Nick Benedetto. One more person she didn't want to see right now.

His dark hair was cut short, a sharp contrast from his high school days of shoulder length waves, but he hadn't outgrown his love of leather jackets. The harsh light in his eyes hadn't softened. If anything, he looked more threatening now that Sandra knew what he was capable of.

"Hey, Amy," he said, maintaining a distance from her.

"Nick," Amy replied.

He took off his jacket and hung it on one finger over his shoulder. The white muscle t-shirt he wore displayed a sleeve of tattoos of heaven only knew what. Sandra didn't care to examine them.

"Listen, I need to talk to Sandra," Nick said. "I don't want to rush you. I mean, I'm not interrupting anything, am I?"

"I was just passing along a message from Garth." Amy took a step closer to Sandra. "He wanted me to let you know he's running late for your date tonight." She opened her eyes wide to invite Sandra to play along.

Nick turned toward Sandra. "You and Garth?"

And look at that. A flash of uncertainty crossed Nick's face. The run-in Nick had with Garth years ago had clearly left an impression, but would he want revenge now that they were older? Sandra checked the muscles Nick had covered with tattoos, mentally comparing his bulk with Garth's. Nope. Garth still had the advantage. Not that Garth would stoop to schoolyard brawls now.

"Look at that," Sandra said. "Seven o'clock. Hate to push you guys out the door, but I need to close up."

Nick huffed. "Amy, can you give us a minute?"

"I'll wait for you outside?" Amy asked.

Did Sandra look as frightened as she felt, seeing Nick after all these years? Didn't matter. She'd take whatever moral support she could get, even if it came from Crazy Amy Benson. "Thanks." She locked the door behind Amy. Amy leaned beside her car in the parking lot, where Nick could see she was watching.

"You and Garth Benson?" Nick repeated.

"I'm kind of busy right now, if you could get to the point?" Sandra asked sweetly. *Don't piss him off.*

"You don't expect me to believe you're friends with Crazy Amy. And I don't believe you're dating Garth."

The man had some nerve. Sandra laughed. "I don't care what you believe." She pulled her phone from her pocket and tilted it toward him. "So what do you want to talk to me about? Because the café is closed."

"I haven't seen anything on your Facebook about Garth."

"You and I aren't friends on Facebook, are we?" She'd have to double check her privacy settings. Was he cyber stalking her?

He shrugged. "I like to keep up with my old friends."

They weren't friends. "What do you want, Nick?"

He sidled up beside her and ran a finger down her arm. Sandra's skin crawled at the touch. "I'm getting stationed in Munich and I thought you might like to come with. See the world. Isn't that what you've always said? I heard your mother was better."

A way out? But not with Nick. "I just signed a lease on a place. Bad timing," she told him. He didn't need to know her mother was the leasing agent and she could get out of the lease if she wanted to.

"I'm giving you the chance to get out of this town." His eyes flashed with the same danger she'd seen in high school, the danger she'd experienced firsthand and tried to protect other girls from. As much as she wanted out of this tired town, there was no way she was going anywhere with Nick.

"I can't," she said with a forced smile. If she was nice to him, he wouldn't hurt her, right? "Thanks for thinking of me." She walked to the door, turned the lock and held it open. "I need to close the café."

He leaned too close, his breath on her cheek. "Trying to help out a friend and hoping we could re-live the fun times we had in high school."

Fun for him maybe. Sandra shuddered. She cast a glance at Amy and found an ounce of courage. "High school was a long time ago. I'm with Garth now."

Nick followed her glance.

That's right, we aren't alone.

"Well, if you change your mind, you'll let me know? Don't think too long or I might have to ask someone else."

"I appreciate the offer, but I'm going to have to pass. Go ahead and ask someone else." *Please go.* She didn't want to antagonize him, didn't want to rile his temper. If she pissed him off, she might not survive this time.

Amy took a step toward them. "Sandra? You want me to call Garth?"

Nick waved to Amy. "No need to call big brother. I'm leaving." He lowered his voice again. "You've always understood me. You don't want to cross me, Sandra."

He'd said the same thing to Tammy way back when, the day Nick had nearly killed her. Did Nick kill Tammy?

So much for being nice. Sandra's knees buckled and she reached for the doorjamb to steady herself. "You have to go now."

Amy took a step closer. "You okay?"

"I'll be in touch," Nick said.

Sandra breathed a sigh of relief as he walked away.

Did Amy know how Tammy had died? If her family had done the headstone… Sandra shivered. The rumors about Amy's conversations with the dead scared the bejesus out of her. She didn't want to know. "You didn't have to stay," she told Amy. "Look, I appreciate what you did in there, but I can handle this."

"Okay," Amy said. "I guess he doesn't bother you the way he bothers me."

Amy had no idea. No one did. Sandra glanced at the sky and laughed. "Oh, he bothers me." She leveled her eyes on Amy. "And now Garth is going to be mad at me, too."

Amy grinned. "I doubt it. Garth might be the one person who scares Nick. Won't hurt having Nick believe he'd have to answer to my brother. Unless you want to be with Nick."

"No, I don't want to be with Nick." Sandra cringed at the snotty tone of her voice. "Look, I know Garth has a crush on me, but he wouldn't play games, nor would I ask him to. He might have stepped in when he was worried Nick would hurt you, but he wouldn't do that for me."

"Wouldn't he?"

"No." Sandra's eyes stung. "It's all about the chase. I'm unobtainable, and that's what Garth likes about me."

"If you say so." Amy said. "I'm going to call him and tell him what I told Nick. The two of you can decide what to do about it."

Sandra's shoulders sagged. "Do you know how Tammy Calhoun died?"

Amy tilted her head. "No."

A fresh knife of pain stabbed at Sandra's heart.

"Her funeral was private," Amy said. "No one was there other than her parents, but I watched from a little way off. I didn't think it was right, but parents sometimes have a hard time coping with the loss of a child."

Tears stung Sandra's eyes. Amy touched her arm, a look of sympathy in her eyes.

"Why are you being so nice to me?" Sandra asked.

"Nick might have been mysterious and exciting in high school, but maturity has a way of changing your perspective." She lowered her voice. "He scares me, too."

Sandra managed a smile. "He doesn't scare me."

Amy laughed. "If you say so." She waved and returned to her car.

They'd never spoken about that day in high school, when Sandra had found Nick backing Amy to the wall in the stairwell and demanding a kiss to let her pass. She hadn't known how to warn Amy about Nick's temper. No one would have taken her seriously. They all thought she was trying to protect her interests, that she was jealous. Except Tammy. Tammy told her to tell Garth. Big brothers protected their little sisters.

Sandra didn't have a big brother.

"So I'm going to call Garth," Amy called before she ducked into her car, "and when he gets done screaming at me, you should probably expect a call from him."

Or not. Sandra waved as Amy drove away and locked the door once more.

She had the weekend off for the first time in she couldn't remember how long, but first, she had to count down her drawer and balance the ledger. She'd leave the deposit in the safe for Darrell to take to the bank with the morning proceeds tomorrow. The café should be in good shape until Monday.

~ ~ ~

"You said what, now?" Garth held his phone out to check the number and make sure he was speaking to his sister.

"You are the one man Nick Benedetto won't want to mess with," Amy said. "Having already experienced your displeasure once in his life. Have you showered?"

He stood in his bedroom wearing nothing but a towel, his hair dripping onto his shoulders. "Yes," he answered testily.

"Put on some nice clothes and go talk to her," Amy said.

"I know what you're trying to do, and it won't work."

"Not if you don't take a stand. What's the worst thing that could happen? She shoots you down? Not like you haven't been there before. Besides, from what Kevin tells me, the way she flirts with you means she's interested."

Sandra was the champ when it came to flirting, but every time he'd tried to turn from kidding to something more serious, she backed off. "No, Amy."

"Consider stealing Nick's girl the grown-up version of bashing his face in," Amy said. "Much less violent and equally effective. She needs someone to buffer her from Nick. Who better than the man who slugged Nick in high school? You were my champion back then. You can be her champion now."

Garth was well aware of the danger Nick presented, more so than his little sister. "She and Nick have a past," he said. Sandra wouldn't want a buffer. In fact, she'd been the buffer more than once, including for Amy.

"Then do it as a favor to me. Whatever he said rattled her pretty good, and I've rarely seen Sandra Meyer rattled. Call her, and make sure you wear something nice. You don't look like such a troglodyte when you're not covered in dirt."

"Ha ha." And yet she'd gotten him to his closet, where he sorted through his shirts. The least he could do was apologize for his idiotic sister. "I'll see you tomorrow," he told her, and disconnected the call.

His hands were sweating. Garth wiped them on the towel before he yanked it off his waist and toweled his hair dry. He stepped into the clean boxers he'd left on his bed and pulled on his comfy jeans. The concert t-shirt he'd set out went back into the drawer in favor of a white one.

He tugged a button-down off a hanger from his closet and stood before the mirror while he slid into it. Garth dragged a comb through his hair and reached for his phone.

"It wasn't my idea," Sandra said when she answered.

"I know."

"You don't have to help me."

"I don't have any problem twisting that scumbag's shorts."

"I can handle Nick."

Was she a glutton for punishment or did she believe that lie? In all the years Nick had been gone, Garth hadn't seen Sandra hook up with other dangerous men. In fact, he hadn't seen her hook up, period. And now that her mother was better…

He opened his dresser and considered pulling the concert t-shirt out again. "All right," he said, grinding his molars. "Just checking, as a favor to my sister."

Sandra sighed. "Listen. I told Nick I wasn't interested and I don't want to play games with that maniac, but since Amy told him you and I were dating…"

He chuckled. "We would be, if you ever decided going to dinner with me wasn't a death sentence."

"You know I don't think that," she said, a smile in her voice. "I have so much going on, and you know that…" Sandra paused again. "Look. Nick said something that gave me an idea. It would be pretty easy to pull off, if you're game, and it wouldn't require you to do anything you don't want to, except take a couple of pictures."

Sandra wouldn't be considering Amy's wild idea if she wasn't scared. "Pictures?"

"He invited me to go to Munich with him," she said hesitantly.

There it was. "Your ticket out of town."

"Not with him. I told him no. I'm just leaving Morning Joe. Mind if I stop over? Then I can tell you the rest of my idea."

A smile tugged at the corners of his mouth. He liked the thought of her in his house. The smile evaporated when he considered why she wanted to come over.

"Garth?"

Pictures. She said she wanted to take pictures. "How about we go out and get something to eat. I'm willing to bet you haven't had dinner yet. Then you can tell me about this idea of yours."

"Okay," she said softly. "Riccardo's?"

"Sounds good. Half an hour enough time?"

"I'll meet you there. And Garth? Thanks."

He disconnected the call and stared at his reflection in the mirror. The nice shirt wasn't such a bad decision after all.

He was past the age of schoolyard brawls. Punching Nick now meant assault and battery, not to mention Nick had spent most of his post-high school career in the military. Nick likely had new tools in his arsenal.

Hopefully, Sandra knew what she was doing, but if she needed Garth's help, she'd get it.

Chapter 3

SANDRA LOOKED AROUND HER BEDROOM, the same bedroom she'd grown up in, reduced to a pile of boxes. All her clothes were packed. Or most of them, anyway.

She took inventory of the sweater she had on and the blue jeans she'd worn all day at work. Was she presentable enough to go out for dinner? Garth wouldn't care if she didn't dress up. In fact, he'd seen her look much worse. He knew she was moving this weekend, he'd even offered to help her move—and she'd declined. Certainly he'd understand if she didn't dig through the boxes for a change of clothes.

Why was she so nervous? Oh yeah, she was having dinner with Garth. Would he expect something in return? She'd make sure she paid her half of the bill. Yes, she was attracted to him, but she was within a year of breaking out of this one-horse town. Garth Benson had his feet firmly planted in Edgarville. He didn't fit into her plan.

She didn't want to involve Garth in her drama, but until Nick went back to whatever hole he'd crawled out of, it wouldn't hurt to have muscular support. Once she recorded photographic evidence she and Garth were a couple, Nick would give up on her.

A couple. She paused to put a hand to her flip-flopping stomach. She'd avoided thoughts of being

Garth's girlfriend—and all that went with it—for so long she'd convinced herself it could never happen. Between her mother and her job, Sandra didn't have the time or the energy to date. She had enough complications in her life without adding unwanted emotions to the mix. A level head was more important now than ever.

She'd tone down the flirting, be careful not to lead Garth on. And under no circumstances would she kiss Garth.

Except she wanted to kiss Garth.

If things got too cozy at his house, she could leave. Speaking of which…

Her new place was on the way to the restaurant. Might as well take a load with her. Sandra gathered a couple of boxes and tottered to her car. She clicked her key fob and backed up to open the trunk, loaded the boxes, and went back for her laptop and camera. Tonight might be fun as long as Garth didn't read too much into her plan.

With everything she needed, Sandra slid behind the wheel and started for the real estate office to get the keys from her mother—and passed Nick's black Trans Am. Good timing. He didn't know where she was moving. She could stay the night at the new place and move more things tomorrow.

Sandra pulled into a parking spot on Center Street. As she walked past the plate glass windows of the real estate office, her mother waved from behind her desk. Forearm crutches leaned against the wall behind her. Even after the accident, her mother spent more time at work than anywhere else. This was where she was most at home.

"Hey, baby," her mother said when Sandra walked in. "You here for the keys?" In spite of her disability, she continued to dress in power suits and heels. As her mother reached for her crutches, Sandra held up a hand to stop her.

"You don't need to get up. If you don't have the key with you, I can get it for you."

Her mother gave her an assessing glance. "Everything okay?"

If Sandra showed any sign of weakness, her mother would swoop in and insist Sandra abandon her plan to move out. "Fine. Why do you ask?"

Her mother opened the desk drawer and shuffled through a small box before she came up with a keyring. "Have you seen Nick Benedetto?"

Of course her mother knew he was back. They lived in a small town, after all. But even her mother didn't know what Nick had done to Sandra. Oh, she knew about the attempted rape, but her mother had been in the hospital when Nick took his revenge for being thwarted. "I have. And I'd appreciate it if you don't share my new address with him." Sandra's mouth went dry. "I thought I'd stay at the new place tonight. You'll be okay on your own?"

"Of course I will." Her mother sighed. "I wish I didn't rely on you so much. You deserve your own life."

Amen to that. Sandra's previous attempts at having a life had been forestalled by medical episodes or new surgeries and follow-up physical therapy. While her mother might not have planned to keep Sandra close, a small voice inside told Sandra otherwise.

An odd expression crossed her mother's face, something between nostalgia and regret. Was she going to invent a reason to prevent Sandra from moving out? Her mother held out the key. "We've had a hard time keeping renters in that duplex, but I'm sure you'll be fine."

She waited until now to mention that? "Is there something wrong with the duplex?" Sandra asked.

Her mother shrugged. "A couple of the on-site property agents seemed to think the place was haunted. Can you imagine such a silly thing? I mean, the complex isn't old enough to have those kinds of stories circulating." Her mother shrugged. "Disgruntled employees. I think they wanted to create problems for the agency. Still, the rumors are out there, and people are nervous about renting the place." She smiled at Sandra. "You'll put a stop to those rumors once they see you living there without any problems."

Which made Sandra feel like a pawn in her mother's scheme. Was that why she agreed to let Sandra move out without threat of a medical episode? Giving her a deal on a furnished place? Or was she trying to frighten Sandra into running back home?

Sandra snatched the key from her mother's hand. "I'm sure everything will be fine."

"You call me if you need anything?" Her mother had a wistful note to her voice.

"Sure." Sandra backed toward the door. "I will. Gotta run. I'm late." She waved and dodged out.

In the relative safety of her car, Sandra closed her eyes and gathered her thoughts. She knew from talking with people at the café that mother-daughter relationships were often strained, and those people didn't have to deal with disabled parents.

She took a look down the row of storefronts along Center Street as she drove to her new home, feeling the eyes of the entire town focused on her. She'd always be "that Meyer girl," the subject of pity after her father died, along with speculation, thanks to the rumors about her mother. No matter how much she'd kept to the straight and narrow, people were waiting for her to screw up, to make a mistake.

A few minutes later, she steered into the parking spot in front of the duplex. Her new home.

Sandra got out of the car and retrieved the boxes from her trunk, the keyring her mother had given her hanging from her finger. Juggling the boxes, she managed to slot the key into the lock and opened the door.

A light brown, brushed leather sofa decorated with throw pillows dominated the living room, a low coffee table in front of it. No dust. Who kept the place up? This unit had been the model, so the real estate office probably hired a cleaning service.

She flipped a light switch and a hanging lamp reflected on the white acrylic dining table. Sandra set her boxes down.

"Come out, come out, wherever you are," she said quietly. She waited a minute, and then smiled at her own imagination. Haunted? Sandra flapped her lips at the thought. Her mother no doubt meant to frighten Sandra so she'd change her mind about moving.

A conveniently placed clock on the far wall of the galley kitchen showed she was short on time to get to the restaurant to meet Garth. She retreated, locked the door behind her, and got into her car, but she sat for a moment, assessing the duplex.

So many old memories had resurfaced today, memories of the worst night of her life. The things her father had said. The rumors about her mother. Her parents had slept in separate beds as long as Sandra could remember. She hadn't wondered why until that last argument.

Her heart ached, the grief as fresh today as it had been then. Sandra's bad decisions had been the cause of her father's death. If she hadn't been so stupid, if Nick had simply stopped when she'd asked him to.

She knew Nick was dangerous, but back then, danger was alluring. She'd naively believed Nick loved her. With her mother always at work and her father driving his truck over the road, an empty house provided all sorts of opportunities for a teenager. Sandra had never considered Nick might expect more from her when she invited him over that night. She'd planned to watch a movie, maybe a make-out session, but Nick had other ideas. Everything had started well, until he'd gone from coaxing her for more to insistent in short order. She didn't remember hearing her father walk in.

And then her father grabbed a handful of Nick's shirt and pulled him off her.

He escorted Nick out the door with a few choice words, then phoned her mother and told her to "get the hell home." Before Sandra could thank her father, he'd stormed into his bedroom and slammed the door.

And then her mother had arrived. Her mother raised her eyebrows to ask where her father was, and

Sandra pointed. All without speaking a word. Her mother disappeared inside his bedroom and closed the door.

"Where the hell were you?" her father shouted.

"Working."

"Is that what you call it? How much does Aaron pay you for the extracurriculars?"

"How dare you!"

"Really?" Something hit the wall and broke, an alarm clock Sandra discovered later. "While you were out working, Nick Benedetto nearly raped our daughter."

"Raped? Or was she experimenting, like young girls do? She and Nick are dating, you know."

"She very clearly told him no, and it wasn't soft and sweet, she said it loud and crystal-clear." Her father paused, as if he wanted to let the weight of his words sink in.

"God dammit, Phyllis, you're her mother. You need to take care of her. Another man might not be so understanding. Hell, her own father isn't stepping up to the plate. That girl deserves a parent who'll look out for her."

"And aren't you the saint of a man who took on that burden," her mother shouted.

Their voices went quiet, too quiet to hear through the closed door, but Sandra had heard enough. Too much. Was he saying he wasn't really her father?

Spots danced behind her eyes and Sandra struggled to breathe. Her parents made it a point never to argue in front of her, and yet she'd heard them several times. This time she needed to know what they were saying. She crossed to her father's bedroom door and laid her ear against the cool wood. She heard the soft tones of her mother, but couldn't make out the words.

"We can't talk about this here," her father's deep voice replied. "Not in front of her."

Sandra jumped away from the door. He couldn't say something like that and leave. She wouldn't let them.

They emerged from his bedroom together, her mother with her arms folded and her father looking grim.

"We're going for a ride," he told Sandra. "We'll be back in a few minutes."

She tried to argue, to tell them she had a right to hear the rest of their argument, but her throat constricted and she couldn't get the words out.

Her father cupped Sandra's chin. "Lock the door and don't let anybody in."

The last words she'd ever hear from him.

Sandra refused to believe Cal Meyer wasn't her biological father, and yet it would explain so much. The separate bedrooms, the late hours her mother kept.

Was this duplex where her mother had been 'working' that night?

She shook her head to clear it.

Sandra started the car and drove to Riccardo's.

Garth's pickup wasn't in the lot when she arrived. She folded down the visor and checked the mirror, applied fresh lipstick and fluffed her hair. It would have to do.

Lights flashed in her rearview mirror as another vehicle pulled into the lot. Garth. Sandra got out of her car and waited for him to park. A minute later, he strolled to meet her, wearing a black button-down shirt and buttery soft blue jeans, not the tattered, dirty ones she usually saw him in. The man cleaned up nice, so much so that she checked her own clothes a second time. She should have taken the extra time to find something nicer to wear.

"Been waiting long?" he asked.

"Just got here."

He took her elbow and led her to the door. When he opened it to let her pass, she caught a woodsy scent, not like the fresh air and earthy smell she was used to around Garth.

"Table for two?" the hostess asked Garth, pointedly ignoring Sandra.

"You got a quiet corner we can hide in?" he asked.

The hostess spared Sandra a hostile glance, and then walked them to the back of the restaurant. She left their menus, told them their server would be right with them, and stalked away.

"One of your admirers?" Sandra asked.

"Who?" he asked.

Was he that clueless? Rather than point the hostess out, she leaned over the table. "A quiet corner? This isn't really a date, is it?" Part of her hoped it was, but another part of her was frightened. It had been a long time since she'd been on a date.

He leaned across the table to meet her. His jaw was clean-shaven, his voice quiet, with a deep sexy undertone that sent a ripple of pleasure through her. "Keeping up appearances. We don't want anyone overhearing our conversation, and if the point is to convince Nick that we're a couple, it's important for other people to see us together." He sat back. "Unless you've changed your mind."

Oh. That. She straightened and smoothed her sweater.

"You said you had an idea. Something about pictures," he said.

The server appeared beside their table. He ran through the specials, took their drink orders, and left Sandra to fill Garth in on her idea.

"Nick mentioned he hadn't seen anything about you and me dating on Facebook, not that I'd share that much of my personal life with him. We aren't even Facebook friends, but it got me to thinking." Sandra wiggled in her seat. All the times she'd flirted with Garth, they'd only been kidding around, hadn't they? And yet the way he looked tonight…

This was a mistake. She knew Garth wasn't afraid of a confrontation, and she'd had her share. Was she inviting trouble?

She licked her lips, which had gone dry, and cleared her throat. He hadn't agreed to her idea yet, but it was only a couple of pictures. What harm could come from that? She ventured forward. "One of my jobs at the café is to keep the website updated, and I've learned Photoshopping along the way. I thought if I doctored some photos to show places you and I might have gone out together…"

"I'm listening."

"I post the photos to a Facebook album and Nick sees the evidence." She lowered her voice, the afterthought meant for her own ears. "Maybe then he'll leave me alone."

"You don't think he will otherwise?" Garth asked, narrowing his eyes. "Did you try telling him you weren't interested?"

A surge of anger shot through her. Her hands curled closed as she remembered beating against Nick, pushing him away while he clawed at her clothes. *Telling him no.* "Yes, I told him I wasn't interested." She glanced around the restaurant, wondering who might still be judging her for her bad choices. Yes, she'd dated Nick Benedetto, and she'd nearly lost her life as a result.

She didn't need Garth's brawn. She needed a restraining order. Nick was still the same asshole. The look in his eyes when he'd walked into the café proved he hadn't changed. Those eyes were hard and cold, the same way they'd been when he'd stopped trying to coax her that awful night, when he'd cornered her a few days after the accident using his fists to get what he wanted.

Sandra let out a breath. "This is a bad idea," she said. "I shouldn't have dragged you into this." She slid out of the booth and Garth rose to his feet.

"Relax. Sit down. You haven't eaten yet," he said softly. "You can at least take advantage of a free meal."

"I'll pay my half of the bill."

"We'll fight about that after we've eaten."

He didn't muscle her, didn't demand. It was a request. Garth's light brown eyes didn't telegraph suppressed rage the way Nick's did.

The server returned and set a glass of red in front of Garth, a glass of white at Sandra's place. She slid back into her seat and Garth followed suit. She'd never pictured the physical, rough-and-tumble Garth Benson with a glass of wine in his hand, and it did something funny to her insides when he offered a silent toast.

And speaking of funny, she heard laughter a couple of tables away. A couple of Nick's friends. One of them, Jordan Greenbaum, raised his glass to her. Of all the people she might have run into tonight… She lowered her head, letting her hair fall across her face.

Garth rose from his side of the table and slid into the booth beside her. "Pictures, huh?" he said.

His body heat warmed her. His voice stroked her. Sandra was playing with dynamite. She tried to ignore the way Garth made her feel. Safe. Protected.

"You don't need to hide from anyone," Garth said quietly, tucking her hair behind her ear. He raised his glass to Jordan. "We could take a selfie—for Jordan's benefit. It sets the stage for more pictures later."

Garth's nearness caught her off guard. His clean scent filled her nostrils. This close, his size overwhelmed her, his muscles more defined since his days with Central High's football team. Physically, he was far more intimidating than Nick had ever been, and yet she wasn't afraid of Garth. He rested an arm across her shoulders and her insides melted.

"All for show," he said quietly, giving her a wicked smile. Garth pulled out his cell phone and held it out, poised to take a selfie. "Cheers?"

She touched her glass to his, her head to his, and smiled for the camera.

~ ~ ~

Jordan had been a flashy quarterback with a lot of talent and an ego to match when Garth coached the high school team. If Jordan had kept his nose clean, he might have done something with that talent, but his choice of friends, one of whom was Nick, got him into trouble more than once.

The server set their food on the table, asked if they needed anything else. Garth tapped the rim of his empty wine glass.

Sandra was frightened. Amy had noticed it, and he'd seen Sandra try to hide behind her hair.

Keep it light. Flirting was their language. He'd tease her out of her fear.

"So what kind of pictures did you have in mind?" he asked, wagging his eyebrows.

Mission accomplished. She chortled at his innuendo and nudged him with a shoulder.

"I've always wanted to go to Paris," she said. "I could put us in front of the Eiffel Tower, or in front of the Louvre."

"We want this to be believable, don't we?" he said, nodding at the server who brought him a fresh glass.

She scowled. "Okay, then I guess Rome is out, too. How about Hawaii? Some nice beach photos."

Her cute little body in a bikini? Garth choked on his sip of water.

She smacked him on the back and he grabbed hold of her hand. "Not a beach person," he told her. "You want iconic? How about hiking the Grand Canyon?"

"Won't work," she said. "I don't do hiking."

Her cell phone chimed a message and she checked it, then tucked the phone into her purse.

"Something important?" he asked.

"Facebook notification," she told him. "Remember Andrea Gaylord?"

"Can't say that I do."

"I went skiing with her family over winter break one year. Before…" Her voice trailed off and she bowed her head.

Right. Before the accident. Before Sandra became her mother's caretaker.

"Skiing," Garth said, holding onto that idea. "We used to go skiing in Wisconsin. That might be something we could pull off, something people would believe."

Sandra's eyes lit up. "Andrea posted the most beautiful pictures from Breckenridge a month or so ago. I could hijack her shots and put us in them."

"Wouldn't somebody recognize her pictures?"

"They'd have to go back to compare them, and I doubt anyone would." She grinned and clinked his glass. "I think it'll work."

"What about the fact it's spring?"

"The pictures don't have to be recent. We can tell people we've been keeping our relationship on the down low." She took a bite of food and washed it down with a sip of wine. "We put on our parkas and stand in front of a blank wall. Cut, paste, and no one knows the difference."

He wasn't quite sure how that was going to work, but Sandra was smart. She practically ran the café in town, and he'd seen examples of her Photoshopping skills on the Morning Joe webpage, the way she superimposed images of the Justice League over people eating in the café along with the slogan, "Where superheroes start their day." Seamless.

He toasted her once more. "Here's to our pretend skiing adventure."

Chapter 4

SANDRA FOLLOWED GARTH INTO THE driveway that ran alongside his house. Why hadn't she known he owned a house before now? She'd only pictured him at his family's monument shop, or mounting headstones in the cemetery.

She turned off her car engine and shaded her eyes against the porch light. The first floor had a wall of windows, surrounded by stucco and wooden beam trim. His house had an old-world feel on the outside, although three blocks off Center Street, traffic noise reminded her they were "in town."

Garth opened her door. "Can I get that for you?" he asked, pointing at the laptop bag.

She stepped out of her car, catching another whiff of his clean scent. "I probably should have brought a change of clothes. It might look suspicious if we're wearing the same thing in every picture."

"Maybe you should run home and grab an overnight bag," he suggested with a lift of the eyebrows.

Sandra swallowed hard. She stared at his front door. They'd be alone inside his house. Just the two of them. She closed her eyes and reminded herself to breathe. They'd flirted so often it was easy to forget they'd never done any of the things they joked about.

Did she dare? "I'm not sleeping over, if that's what you're asking."

"For the record, I didn't ask. You mentioned a change of clothes?"

Right. And why would she assume he wanted to get in her pants? Because it had been that sort of day, a day for remembering that if she hadn't invited Nick over, if her father hadn't gotten home early from his long haul, if her mother had been home instead of... where?

A scruffy-looking tortoise-shell cat dashed down the driveway, stopped in front of the garage and sent a wary glance at them.

"Yours?" Sandra asked.

"Not sure he belongs to anyone, but I give him a free meal now and then."

Garth waved her inside, and she stepped into a foyer, which opened to the right, one step up to the living room decorated in bargain basement chic. A switchback staircase on the left rose to the second story. Beyond the living room, another room lined with windows suggested a sunroom. An oil painting hung on the living room wall, a Benson family portrait. They looked so happy, even Amy. A twinge of remorse made Sandra flinch.

"Something to drink?" Garth asked.

"A cup of coffee? That would go well with skiing pictures," she said.

He turned left and she took one more look at her escape route, the closed front door behind her. With a deep breath, she followed him toward the back of the house, to the kitchen.

Garth carried a saucer out the back door, crouched low and set it on the porch. The cat slinked out from beneath a bush and crept up the staircase. It sniffed at the saucer, decided the food was edible and took a bite. Garth scratched the cat behind the ears and it leaned into his hand, giving him a broken rumble of a purr in appreciation.

An island with a cooktop marked the center of the kitchen. The oven was mounted with the cabinets, a microwave above it. No old world inside.

Garth stepped inside and closed the door behind him. "Powder room right there," he told Sandra, pointing to a door behind her. "For when you need it. I'll put on a pot of coffee."

She set her laptop on the kitchen table. "Last chance to back out. You sure you want to do this?"

He gave her a sideways grin. "We've already been seen together. Might as well play out the charade. You can break up with me when Nick leaves." He took a step closer, and he was inside her personal space, waking up her nerve endings. "Unless you decide you like being my girlfriend."

The way he looked tonight, the way he smelled—being Garth's girlfriend definitely wouldn't be a hardship. And the way he made her feel? No, the thrill running through her wasn't fear.

She'd seen Garth with his family. He shoved his brothers around, but he also grabbed them into big bear hugs for no apparent reason. And then there was the way he treated Amy, like she was something special. Amy had family who loved her. Valued her. Sandra would never have that. Sandra's parents had always been distant, even with each other.

Garth cocked his head, his brow furrowed. "Something wrong?"

Sandra forced a laugh and pushed against his chest—his rock-solid chest—which released a cloud of butterflies inside her. She glanced at the living room behind her. "That wall looks like a good place to take pictures. A plain background is easier to cut out."

He backed away, eyeing her suspiciously. "Then let's get to it."

~ ~ ~

Sandra set her computer on his kitchen table and opened a page of photos with snow and people on skis. Garth stooped down and rested his chin on her shoulder.

"So how does this work?" he asked.

She reached behind and patted his cheek before she pointed at the screen. "Something like this." She opened one of the photos to full screen, clicked around, opened a smiley face and superimposed it onto one of the people in the photo. "We pose like they did in their pics, then put our faces on their bodies."

Impressive.

"I downloaded backgrounds of the slopes we can insert ourselves into so we have our own, original shots, but we should wait until we have our winter coats." She closed the smiley face picture, picked up her camera and rose to stand beside him. "Ready?"

Garth straightened and held out an arm inviting her into the living room. "I'm all yours."

"I wish we had some snow. Would give the pictures a little more realism."

"Snow?" he asked. "Would freezer frost work?"

When she blinked several times, he shrugged one shoulder. "I'm not good at keeping my chest freezer clean. When I added the venison from my last hunting trip, I made a mental note which, unfortunately, is about as far as I usually get to defrosting."

"Perfect," she said. "We don't need much, enough to make a snowball? But let's try a few other shots first."

Garth held out his arms. "Use me how you will." He cocked an eyebrow and Sandra laughed. At least half the desired effect.

She took him by the shoulders, a gleam in her eye as she did so, and turned his side to the wall, then she stood in front of him—hesitantly at first—and positioned his arm around her waist, holding her camera in her other hand.

Nice.

"Smile," she told him in a breathy voice as she lay her head against his chest.

He wrapped both his arms around her, held her close, and gave the camera a big, cheesy grin.

She pulled away and checked the photo, laughing as she did so. "These are going to be great pictures. A couple more like this? Then if you get the frost, we can make those snowballs."

Whatever had been causing the shadows in her eyes earlier seemed to have disappeared. Sandra was having way too much fun cuddling him, teasing him, all in the name of taking pictures. Not for the first time, Garth wondered if Amy's fiancé was right, that Sandra was more interested than she was willing to admit.

Things had definitely heated up between them. He was ready for that frost.

"After the snowballs, we can take headshots that I can fit into the other pictures," she said. She reached for a table lamp and took off the shade. "But we need more light."

"Whatever works." He retreated to the kitchen, questioning his sanity. Garth's crush on Sandra had grown over the years. Would she let him inside her carefully cultivated isolation?

He carried a bowl and a metal spatula to the basement, opened the chest freezer and harvested a full bowl of frost.

When he returned to the living room, he dug into the frost and formed a snowball, then extended it toward Sandra.

"Wait," she said, holding up her camera. "Now, do that again."

He held the snowball out to her and she took the picture, then turned the camera for him to see. Yeah, he looked like a sap. His feelings were written all over his face. He took the snowball and shoved it inside the back of Sandra's shirt.

With a shriek, she twisted and giggled, trying to dislodge the ice. She reached for a handful of frost and came at him, managing to get some down the front of his shirt. Garth grabbed her hands and pulled her close. She tensed, a moment of panic in her eyes. Was she afraid of him?

He held her gaze, her eyes the beautiful blue of a cloudless sky, and she relaxed. The way she'd focused on his lips made him smile. Maybe she wasn't immune to him. He fought the urge to kiss her.

"Enough snow?" he asked, his voice low.

She nodded and her eyes flashed with something else. Desire?

She cleared her throat. "We should get those headshots now."

They needed a moment of levity. "Headshots?" He checked his fly. "Not sure they allow that sort of thing on Facebook." He had no intention of dropping trou, but he needed to see her smile. She took a step back. The color in her cheeks heightened as she fought to keep the smirk from her lips.

"Goofball." She framed her face with her hands. "This head."

"Ohhh," he said, as if he'd needed the explanation to understand. "Gotcha. You'll let me know if you need any shots of the other head, won't you?"

She took another step backward and glanced at the door. For a way out? "You're so bad," she said with a giggle.

No, if he was bad, he would have kissed her when he'd had the chance. He would have challenged the fire in her eyes, but he wasn't going there. Not tonight. The fact that she was here, in his house, showed just how unnerved she was by Nick Benedetto. She trusted Garth to help her, and he wasn't going to betray that trust.

# Chapter 5

SANDRA PARKED IN FRONT OF her duplex at three a.m. after spending most of the night with Garth, taking pictures and talking. She checked her reflection in the visor mirror. Yep, the stupid smile was still there. She couldn't remember the last time she'd had so much fun on a date.

Except it wasn't a date. Was it?

Technically, yes, it was, and she felt as if she'd escaped this Podunk town for a few hours, even if it was only make believe.

She lugged her computer and her camera into the duplex—her own place—and plunked everything down on the white acrylic table. Too wired to sleep, she booted her computer to review the photos she'd doctored, bringing yet another smile to her face. The look on Garth's face when he handed her the snowball, right before he shoved it down her back, made her laugh.

She uploaded the photos to Facebook, hid them from her timeline, and then hovered over her test picture, the one with the smiley face. She attached it to an email to Garth.

"Thought you'd like a copy of our night together. Nice smile." She sent the email off with another chuckle.

Her Facebook notifications showed Garth had posted their photo from the restaurant. Maybe that would be proof enough for Nick to leave her alone.

Garth was a good sport, she had to give him that, and he had flirted outrageously, but he'd never pressed his advantage. In fact, she'd been the one to hug him in some of their poses. He'd most definitely hugged her back but he hadn't kissed her once all night.

And this was the first time she'd thought of that? They'd come close a time or two, but realizing they hadn't kissed gave her a sinking feeling in her gut, as if she'd missed out.

Not all men were like Nick. Right? If she kissed Garth, would he insist on more?

Sandra shook her head. Garth was a good friend. If there was one thing, one person, she'd regret leaving behind when she left Edgarville, Garth would be the one.

She shut her computer off and sauntered down the short hall, bemused. She passed the bathroom before she reached into the bedroom and flipped on the light. The closet doors were a wall of mirrors. A long dresser took up the far wall, with two more mirrors centered over each end. She opened the dresser drawer where her mother said she kept sheets.

Sandra's heart pinched. Had her mother spent time in that bed?

Rumors. Mean things kids say. Except her own father had cast doubt on Sandra's parentage. When Sandra had questioned her mother later, after they knew she'd survived the accident, her mother had merely said Cal Meyer was a jealous man. She'd refused to say any more on the subject, and Sandra hadn't wanted to know. Not really.

As Sandra shook the sheets over the bed, her skin crawled, the way it might if someone was watching her. Several times she stopped to look over her shoulder, but no one was there. When she finished making the bed, she returned to the living room, checked the lock on the door and turned off the light over the table.

Without bothering to take off her clothes, Sandra stretched out on top of the turned down sheets and within minutes, she was asleep.

Sometime later, a chill woke her. Sandra rolled over to reach for the blanket, squinted into the shadowy room and sat up while she struggled to remember where she was. She checked the clock on her cell phone. Six-thirty-three. A soft glow drew her attention to one of the closet mirrors. A ray of sun poking through the drawn curtains?

The glow resembled a six-foot oblong cloud that looked suspiciously like a man. Sandra watched, fascinated as the cloud moved toward the nightstand beside her. She crawled across the bed to get away, but when she glanced at the nightstand, nothing was there. She checked the mirror once more and the cloud extended an arm to pick up a picture frame from the nightstand. Another glance at the nightstand. Still nothing.

I loved you, as best as I could.

The voice was as soft as a whisper in her ear. Her father's voice.

"Daddy?" She slid toward the apparition, her eyes darting from the mirror to the nightstand, but the cloud had disappeared. Was it a dream? "Daddy?" she called louder.

Sandra walked to the mirror, looking beyond her own reflection for someone, anyone else who might be in the room.

Tears rolled down her cheeks. "Daddy, I'm so sorry. If I hadn't been so stupid, so naïve…" She dropped to the floor, legs crossed, and hid her face in her hands.

~ ~ ~

The pounding on his front door made Garth sit straight up in bed. The sun shone through his bedroom windows. Was he late for work?

He picked up his phone to check the time. Seven thirty. But today was Saturday. He brushed a hand over his face and got out of bed.

Who the hell was pounding on his door?

He stepped into a pair of pajama pants and padded down the stairs, not prepared for the sight in front of him when he opened the front door.

"Can I come in?" Sandra asked through the screen door. Wearing the same clothes she'd left in. Her hair hadn't been brushed and her eyes were red.

"What's going on?" he asked suspiciously.

Her eyes raked over his bare chest and his morning wood turned to petrified oak, something she was bound to notice if she dropped her eyes… yep. There it was. She swallowed hard, color in her cheeks.

"Didn't you go home?" he asked, his voice rough from not being used. He cleared his throat.

"Yeah," she said. "No."

Which meant she hadn't been home. "Which is it?" he asked.

"Can I come in?"

He hesitated a moment longer, and then, sucker that he was, he opened the screen door.

"You need to put a shirt on," she said.

"If I knew someone was going to wake me from a sound sleep, I would have. Now, do you want to tell me why you're here?"

Her eyes darted to his waistband once more. Her tongue swept across her lips. Not helping things.

Garth snapped the elastic. "Want a closer look?"

She looked away, took a step back and he immediately regretted his words.

"Damn it, Garth…" She pulled a hand through her hair and stormed past him, to the kitchen, where she started a pot of coffee. In his house.

"Hey," he said.

"Can't you do something about that?" she asked, turning to face him once more and waving at the lower half of his body.

He raised his eyebrows. "I can, but it generally involves two people." Did she want an invitation to his bedroom? No, he was certain she'd turn him down. Something was wrong.

"Why are you here?" he asked more gently. "Is it Nick?"

"No, it's not Nick." She wrung her hands and drew a shaky breath. "I really need you to put a shirt on."

"And then you'll tell me?" he asked.

She nodded and turned away from him.

Garth returned to his bedroom, with a stop in the bathroom. If he'd been able to empty his bladder before he'd answered the door, things might not have reached this stage. He shook his head, knowing Sandra still would have gotten a rise out of him. She always did.

He slipped his OneRepublic concert shirt over his head and made his way to the kitchen.

Sandra sat at the table, hands shaking around a cup of coffee.

"Your sister," she said without preamble. "She told me something once that I wouldn't have expected her to know, when my grandmother died." She took a deep breath. "Does she talk to ghosts?"

Garth halted, his protective streak kicking in. "I couldn't say."

Her eyes glittered with fear. "I slept at my new place last night."

Damn it. She'd been alone. Easy prey. "Did somebody bother you?" Garth asked.

"No."

He took a step forward. "No?"

She closed her eyes and swallowed hard. "When my mom gave me the keys, she told me the duplex was haunted."

Not a surprise. Phyllis Meyer had been manipulating Sandra for years. He leaned against the counter, waiting for Sandra to continue.

"Garth, I think I saw a ghost."

Which explained why she was suddenly interested in Amy's gift, a gift they didn't tell people outside the family about—at least not directly. Amy shared the epitaphs she heard, but as far as anyone outside the family knew, those epitaphs were intuition.

"Amy doesn't talk to ghosts," he told Sandra. She heard ghosts, but she didn't talk to them. A fine distinction, but a distinction nonetheless.

"She probably hates me for telling you about her and Nick. I had my reasons. Garth, you have to know it wasn't because I was jealous."

Yeah, he knew. Tammy Calhoun had given him an earful and once he knew what to look for, he'd seen the bruises. Garth had seen Nick's handiwork firsthand. If Sandra wanted him to know the rest of the story, she would have told him years ago. "I'm pretty sure she's outgrown any lingering insecurities."

"And then when she told me my grandmother died." The catch in Sandra's voice betrayed how frightened she was. "I didn't know people would make fun of her."

Sandra trembled, sloshing coffee onto the table, and immediately went for the cloth on the sink. As she wiped the table, Garth took the cloth from her and finished cleaning the spill.

Yeah, the Crazy Amy thing had lasted a lot longer than Amy's irritation that Garth had backed Nick off, but she'd gotten over it. "You said you saw a ghost," he said. "Who?"

"My dad," she whispered. "Why? Why would he be haunting the duplex?" She settled into the chair, bowed her head and wrapped her arms around herself.

Garth rinsed the cloth in the sink. "Maybe you imagined you saw him. You didn't get much sleep. It could have been a dream. Where did you see him? Did he say anything?"

Her voice cracked, right along with his heart. "He was in the mirror."

Garth knelt beside her, put his arms around her and cradled her head to his chest. "Your first night in a new place. A trick of the light, or a flight of imagination. You were probably thinking about him." Another reason to beat the hell out of Nick Benedetto. Sandra's father had died the night Nick bragged about being caught trying to get into Sandra's pants.

He pulled away and held Sandra's face between his hands. "I'll go over there with you. We'll have a look around. What do you say?"

"I don't know." A tear slid down her cheek.

"In the meantime, you need sleep. We both need sleep. I have a second bedroom if you want to rest a while."

She put her hands on his chest and pushed him further away. "No."

"How about if we sit on the couch? Give me more of a chance to wake up. Then after I make you breakfast we'll check it out together."

"If you insist." She followed him to the living room, sat in the corner on the couch as far away from him as she could get and pulled her knees to her chest. She wrapped her arms around them in a definite "don't touch me" posture.

Garth sat in the opposite corner. He'd never seen Sandra like this, but he had a good idea where to lay the blame.

Chapter 6

SANDRA HADN'T MEANT TO FALL ASLEEP. She'd closed her eyes while she gave Garth the five or ten minutes he'd asked for, but when she heard hushed voices, she had to shake herself to wake up.

She'd probably dreamed the encounter with her father. As she crossed to the kitchen, she rehearsed an apology for pulling Garth into her drama. She should never have agreed to Amy's scheme. Sandra could fight her own battles.

She stopped when she saw who the voices belonged to, Garth and Amy. Had he called Amy as his ghost consultant? And why was Sandra surprised? She'd asked him to, after all.

Truth be told, Amy scared Sandra. More than a little. The things Amy said to Sandra when Sandra's grandmother had died were too personal to have guessed. Yes, Sandra had called her crazy that day, a kneejerk reaction. She hadn't meant for anyone to repeat it, for the nickname to take on a life of its own.

Sandra winced.

Garth rose from his chair when he saw her. "Can I get you something to eat?"

He had an empty plate at the table beside him indicating he'd already eaten. Sandra shook her head. "Don't worry about me."

Amy's eyes swept over Sandra, in the same clothes she'd been wearing yesterday. Her hair was probably a mess and she felt grungy. She needed to go home and change into clean clothes. Take a shower.

"Tell her what you told me," Garth said to Sandra, his voice deep. And raw. And so sexy it sent tremors all through her.

Sandra didn't answer. She knew how her story sounded.

"He said you thought you saw a ghost," Amy said.

Karma, meet Sandra. She huffed, not willing to sound as crazy as she felt.

"No." Amy shook her head and glared at Garth this time. "I'm not Crazy Amy anymore."

Did people still call her that, even all these years later? Sandra bowed her head and massaged her forehead. "You're not crazy. And in case I never said it before, I'm sorry. I never meant for people to make fun of you. That day, when you told me about my grandmother, you frightened me."

Amy studied her a moment. "Consider what I told you a lucky guess. Your grandmother had cancer, didn't she?" The expression on Amy's face dared Sandra to contradict her.

What Amy told her was more than a lucky guess. Before Sandra could point that out, Garth set his hands on Amy's shoulders in a protective stance. Of course he'd side with his sister. Sandra lifted her chin.

"I'm guessing she's already forgiven you," Garth said, "considering she arranged our date last night." And yet he stood ready to defend his sister.

Amy scowled. "What makes you think you saw your dad?" she asked.

"It was a dream," Sandra repeated. Except she wasn't sure. "Unless you want to go over and see for yourself if there's a ghost haunting my new place."

Amy folded her arms. "Call me oversensitive, but are you making fun of me?"

Sandra bowed her head and sighed. "No. I said I'm sorry, and I mean it. I don't understand how you know the things you do, what connection you might have to…" She bit her lip and shrugged.

"I don't see ghosts," Amy said. "And I don't talk to them."

Sandra sensed an implied, "but," but she didn't ask.

"I'm going over there with you," Garth said. "We'll have a look around and if you're not comfortable staying there, you can stay here."

"Really?" Amy said sarcastically, hands on her hips.

"Look," he told his sister. "There's a lot you don't know."

"Enlighten me."

"You're the one who suggested we pose as a couple," he reminded her.

Sandra held her hands up. "You know what," she said. "Forget it. Forget everything. This was a mistake. I'll delete the album from my Facebook account and no one will be the wiser. I can handle Nick on my own."

Garth walked to the kitchen counter and turned his laptop for her to see. "Too late. I know you didn't share the album on your wall, but people found it. You might want to read the comments."

Amy stepped in front of Sandra and looked at Garth's computer. "When did you go skiing?"

"We didn't." Sandra reached around and closed the laptop. "So now what?"

Garth grinned. "They're good, the photos."

Sandra wiggled past Amy and opened the laptop, turning it for privacy.

About time you two went public, one of the comments said.

You look good together, said another.

Dozens of "thumbs up" and "hearts" on each of the photos. Sandra looked at Garth once more. He was smiling. He'd already seen the comments and the reactions, and he was smiling. The photo session last night was the most fun she'd had in years, and the end product proved it. She and Garth *did* look good together.

Garth had his feet firmly cemented in Edgarville. Sandra had other plans. A lump settled in her throat, making her voice hoarse. "You said something about breakfast."

He pointed to the clock. "Would be lunch, now."

She checked the clock on the wall. She shouldn't be surprised she'd slept the morning away. They'd been up most of the night pretending to be in Colorado.

The photos were designed to prove she and Garth were a couple, and based on the number of people leaving comments, they'd succeeded. But they weren't a couple. Not really. What did his family think of her after all these years? After the nasty name-calling she'd incited?

"I'm sorry," she said to Amy one more time. "Once that stupid nickname got loose, I should have tried to stop it.'

Amy's expression relaxed into something close to a smile. "Ancient history."

Garth handed a cup of coffee to Sandra. "So what now?" he asked.

She looked at the Facebook photos one more time. "I hid the album from my feed so no one would see it. I wanted you to see it first, to be the one to decide." She winced when she looked at Garth again. "Are you okay with this?"

He nodded. "I told you last night I'd help you out. That hasn't changed."

What else could she say? "Thank you."

~ ~ ~

Garth set a plate of scrambled eggs in front of Sandra and watched her eat. She'd always been a force, always had a ready answer and a solution to every problem. Watching the emotions cross her face, he wanted to hug her, to reassure her everything would turn out well, but he knew she wouldn't want that.

"You want to come with us?" he asked Amy.

"No."

She wasn't still holding a grudge against Sandra, was she? "No?"

Amy huffed. "I've seen more than my fair share of ghosts. No."

Sandra's shoulders rose and her face screwed up, as if she didn't want to hear that piece of information.

"And that's what makes you uniquely qualified," he argued. "Please?"

"Even if I wanted to, and I don't, Kevin and I have wedding appointments today," Amy said.

Sandra set her fork down and waved her off. "Forget it. I'm sure it was my overactive imagination." She took a sip of coffee and pushed her plate away.

"I'm going over there with you," Garth said again.

Sandra rose to her feet. "Thanks for breakfast. Or lunch. Or whatever. And I'm sorry I woke you up this morning. I'll be fine." She shot him a look designed to emphasize her point.

Garth took her arms and met her gaze. "You call me if things don't seem right, you hear?"

In spite of her tough exterior, a shadow of indecision flitted in her eyes. She nodded and walked out.

He leaned over the countertop, stared at the burled edge while he struggled not to go after Sandra, and then turned to Amy. "Thanks for coming over. I wasn't sure what to do."

"I could call Kevin's brother-in-law," Amy said. "He's the ghost expert, not me. For the record, I don't want to be the expert."

"I know," Garth said. But Amy was tuned into a frequency the dead spoke on, a family trait she'd inherited. "Maybe you'd do me one small favor, though."

Amy eyed him suspiciously.

"Her father's buried out at Mount Hope. Maybe you'd stroll past his grave." He shrugged. "You never know what you might hear."

Amy shook a finger at him, but didn't speak.

"You do have a talent for hearing things," he said, trying to get a smile out of her.

"I still think she's going to break your heart," Amy said. She pulled open the back door, letting in the traffic noise from Center Street, and stood there a moment.

"Something wrong?" Garth asked.

Amy turned and looked at him. "Looks like someone slashed Sandra's tires."

# Chapter 7

WITH HER ARMS CROSSED, SANDRA cast a glance over her shoulder, hoping Garth wouldn't notice she was still standing in his driveway. She'd called the police, and she'd called Leo at the service station for a tow. Now if they would only hurry.

A squad car pulled up to the curb and Sandra rolled her eyes. Figured the policeman who showed up was PJ Stancy. Sandra used to babysit him. He couldn't be more than a couple of weeks out of the police academy. The whole town was going to know her business in a matter of hours. She could already hear her mother listing off the reasons Sandra wouldn't be safe on her own—or reasons her mother needed Sandra to move back home.

"Any idea who might have done this?" PJ asked.

Yeah, she knew. "I have my ideas. Not sure I could prove anything."

PJ eyed her closely. Was that something they taught him in the academy? "Probably juveniles pulling a prank." He turned his attention to the notepad in his hand. "I heard Nick Benedetto was in town. Isn't he the guy who used to come over while you were babysitting?"

As if she needed any more reminders. "Yeah."

PJ walked around her car, checking for other damage.

A hand on her shoulder startled her. Sandra spun around and looked up at Garth.

"I called for a tow," she told him. "I'll be out of your driveway soon. Sorry if I'm blocking you in."

Garth cocked his head toward her car. "Nick?"

"Probably." She sighed and forced a smile.

Garth's muscles tightened until he looked as hard as a statue. Tension radiated from him. The reflexive show of strength should have scared her, except it wasn't directed toward her.

"He's only home for a short while," she said quietly.

"He can do a lot of damage in that time."

"Not much I can do," PJ told her. "I took pictures to document the damage and I'll file the report, but hopefully this is an isolated incident."

"That's it?" Garth asked. He took a step toward PJ, hovered inside his personal space.

PJ rested a hand on his holster and returned the glare, looking up the four inches difference in height. "No evidence to go on, and she says she didn't see who did it. Like I said, I'll file the report so we have the incident documented in case anything else should happen."

When Garth took a step back, Sandra exhaled. He might not have intimidated PJ, but Garth had unsettled her.

The tow truck slowed on the street. Gears ground until the back-up signal beeped. Leo waved an arm out the window as he positioned himself behind Sandra's car.

PJ returned to his squad car, and before Leo could hop out of his truck, PJ pulled away.

"Looks like you're going to get my help moving today after all," Garth said.

She'd told him she didn't want his help. Garth wouldn't force himself on her, the way Nick had, would he? She didn't think so, but his show of strength sent an uneasy quiver through her nervous system.

Garth tilted his head. "What?"

She forced a smile. "I'm sure I can manage."

"I know you can, but I also told you I'd take a look at those mirrors to make sure there isn't something funny going on at your new place."

Leo hopped out of the truck and cleared his throat. "I'll take your car to the station. You can pick 'er up later."

Garth raised a hand. "Thanks."

Leo cleared his throat again. "Saw those pictures on Facebook. 'Bout time you two went public after all this time." He grinned. "Heard you were moving out of your mother's."

Did he think she was moving in with Garth? "Yep," she replied. "Moving into my own place."

Leo turned his head to look at her car, shot a glance at Garth's house and then looked at Sandra once more as if he thought "her own place" was a euphemism for Garth's house.

Garth slid his hand into Sandra's. "Want to go inside and wait?"

"I'll walk over to the real estate office and borrow my mother's car so I can start moving." She sent an icy glare to Leo, who shrugged his shoulders and went about his business chaining her car to the tow truck.

Garth lowered his voice. "I said I'd help."

"I don't want to drag you into my mess."

He turned to face her, squinting as he gazed into her eyes. "Too late."

Nick's return to town reminded Sandra of the bad decisions she'd made, and the consequences of her actions. If she hadn't invited Nick over that night, maybe her father would still be alive.

Garth wasn't Nick.

No, she had different reasons to be afraid of Garth. If she got involved with him, she'd never get out of Edgarville. She'd been able to avoid getting entangled so far. As long as she didn't kiss him, and God help her, she wanted that more than her next breath.

"You can move faster with my truck," he said. "I'll get my keys and be right back."

Between her ghostly dream last night and the slashed tires this morning, she was unsettled enough to accept his offer.

~ ~ ~

Nick had been a punk in high school, and judging by Sandra's flat tires, he'd never bothered to grow up, even with the assistance of the United States Army. Garth's problem was that Nick's actions inspired testosterone-based reactions.

Sandra remained suspiciously quiet, which increased Garth's desire to find Nick and lay him flat. "Talk to me."

She pivoted in the passenger seat to face him. "About what?"

He'd never asked Sandra what happened between her and Nick, never felt it was any of his business, but if Garth was going to protect her, he needed to know.

Without any evidence to prove Nick was behind Sandra's tires, the police couldn't to do anything.

"You and Nick," Garth said. The words didn't come out the way he wanted. They sounded more judgmental than he'd planned. Or jealous. Damn it! He and Sandra had never done anything but talk. Why did he feel so possessive?

"Nothing to talk about," she said.

"You could start with why you didn't file charges when he beat you up in high school."

She drew a sharp intake of breath. "Why would you say that?"

He parked the truck in front of her mother's house. "Tammy told me."

Sandra pursed her lips and glanced at the roof of the truck. "And you're just asking me about this now?"

Sandra reached for the door handle and Garth touched her arm. "Tell me about Nick?"

She took a deep breath and shot him a brave smile. "That was a long time ago. Water under the bridge."

"Apparently not, if he slashed your tires. Why are you still defending him?"

"I'm not defending him." She yanked on the door handle and jumped out of the truck. "And I've already told you, you don't have to help me move. I can manage."

"Without a car?"

She slammed the door and he got out to stand beside her.

"Let me help you," he said, taking her by the arms.

A flash of something—fear or temper?—showed in her eyes before she twisted away.

"Are you afraid of me?" Garth asked.

"I don't need you manhandling me, and I don't need your help."

"I'm not…" Garth let go of her arms and turned away.

When he faced her again, Sandra's head was bowed.

"Look," she said. "Last night was fun, but it was make-believe. Like the pictures. I don't need a bodyguard. What's more, I don't want a bodyguard. I don't need your help and I don't want your pity. That incident with Nick happened a long time ago."

"Pity?" he repeated. "Is that what you think this is? In case you haven't realized it, I care about you. You think I stop in the café when you're working because I like the coffee? I can get coffee anywhere. I stop in to see you." And if he didn't shut up right now, he was going to tell her all the rest of the things she probably didn't want to hear. Hadn't she laughed off his flirtations every time?

He wasn't backing down. Not this time. He'd made a commitment to her, and he intended to honor it. "Here's how this is going to go. We're going to take a load of boxes over to your new place, and then I'm going to walk inside. I'm going to check the mirrors for anything out of the ordinary. Not because you need a bodyguard, but because I'm worried about you. About your safety. I'm going to do it because slashing your tires is most definitely a threat. Tammy told me he'd beaten you within an inch of your life and she was worried the same thing would happen to her. Funny thing. Tammy's dead."

Her voice caught. "Do you know how Tammy died?"

He shook his head. "Not sure anyone does, other than her parents."

Sandra shuddered and took a step away from him.

He was botching this. Garth took a moment to regroup and continued. "When I'm sure you're safe, then I'll leave if you still want me to." He took a step closer. "I'm going to help you because you deserve to have someone looking out for you, but if you want to be stubborn about this, you can lock the door behind me when I leave as long as you promise me you'll call the police if anyone shows up and tries to threaten you. Do we have an understanding?"

"Yes sir." Sandra saluted him.

Smart ass. The heat in her eyes made him want to press his body to hers and kiss her senseless, throw her over his shoulder and take her home, to his bed. Was he the caveman his sister accused him of being? Garth closed his eyes and shook his head. Sandra had been sending him mixed signals for years. If she wanted to be rid of him, he'd go, but not until he knew she was safe. "Let's go."

Despite the fact that Phyllis Meyer sold real estate, she and Sandra lived in a modest brick cottage. Sandra led him through the back door, into a sunny kitchen. Oriental rugs covered the hardwood floors in the living room and dining room beyond. The matching furniture looked almost too perfect to sit on, the touches of an interior decorator, no doubt.

Sandra disappeared down the hall and reappeared with a stack of boxes. She brushed past him, but didn't say another word the entire time they loaded her things.

Half an hour later, she climbed into the cab of his truck, arms folded and stared straight ahead.

"Look, I'm sorry," he said as he started for her new address. "I'm worried about you."

"I get it. You want to know? I'll tell you. I was young and stupid and I invited him over when my parents weren't home." She paused, closed her eyes and took a deep breath. "I never considered he might want more from me beyond making out. Call me naïve."

"That's the night your dad died?"

"Yeah."

"I'd heard something about what happened." How could he tell her, thanks to Jordan's friendship with Nick, she'd been the subject of locker room talk for months.

Her voice dripped with sarcasm. "I guess that's better than Nick telling everyone I was easy."

It was worse. Nick had told the whole football team, using Jordon Greenbaum as his mouthpiece, that her father wouldn't get in the way next time. Because her father was dead.

"So he beat you up for not saying yes?" Garth asked.

"Again, I was naïve. My dad pulled Nick off me that night, and then my parents had an argument. They must have known I could hear them, so my dad took my mother for a drive. He was pretty upset, and he'd just gotten home after a long haul." She shook her head. "He should never have gotten behind the wheel."

"You don't have to tell me," Garth said.

"You asked," she pointed out, a sad smile on her face. "So when Nick said he wanted to apologize a couple days later, I agreed to meet him." She swallowed hard. "But he didn't want to apologize. He was looking for a chance to finish what he'd started. I met him at the football field and he dragged me under the bleachers. Still stupid. When I told him no, he called me a tease and started punching, and when I called for help…" She heaved a sigh. "Tammy had the objectivity I was lacking. She'd followed me and told him to leave me alone. He turned on her and told her to stay out of his business. That's when I threatened to call the police."

"Why didn't you?"

"I was afraid he'd hurt Tammy, the way he said he would. And I was embarrassed and afraid. Everything was coming apart. My dad. My mom. And my grandmother was sick—too sick to help. Tammy was the only one who knew, the one who helped me hide the bruises. My mother was so weak, I didn't want to upset her." She turned to Garth. "And then when Tammy died…do you think he killed her? Tammy?"

"I don't know what he's capable of," Garth said. The word sociopath came to mind. Amy might have been next. Could Nick have killed Tammy?

Garth stopped in front of the duplex.

Sandra grabbed his hands, held them and met his gaze. "Don't tell anyone. Please. It happened so long ago. He didn't get what he wanted from me. Tammy stopped him before he could. I'd rather forget about it."

"Nick hasn't forgotten, and it looks like he isn't giving up. Look, I didn't know you very well then, only that you were Tammy's friend. Hell, I didn't know Tammy very well other than she had a huge crush on me. I figured if you felt threatened, you would have reported the assault. It was none of my business." Garth cupped her face. "I'm making it my business this time. I won't let him hurt you, and I wish you'd consider staying with me until he leaves again."

"Garth…" she said in the same apologetic voice she used every time he tried to move past the flirting stage and into an actual date.

"I'm not asking you to move in the way you think. I have an extra bedroom." He swallowed hard. "I wouldn't force you to do anything you don't want to, not the way Nick tried to."

"I know."

Her eyes showed hesitation, and who could blame her? She was going to turn him down. Again.

"Let's get this stuff inside," he said.

Sandra led the way up the front walk of the ranch-style duplex and opened the door.

Garth carried a load of boxes and set them inside. He took in the décor, the laser prints on the wall, the brushed leather sofa. Her laptop was on the dining room table. He pointed to the hallway on his right. "The bedroom's down there? And the mirrors?"

She nodded.

Garth took long strides down the hall and glanced around. The bedroom was a hall of mirrors. No wonder Sandra had freaked out. He slid the closet doors open. First one, then the other. No wires. No visible surveillance systems that might account for manufactured images. He leaned over the dresser and glanced behind the mirrors mounted on the wall. Nothing looked out of the ordinary.

Sandra stood in the bedroom doorway. "What are you looking for?"

"A physical reason you might have seen something. Where did you see…?"

She pointed to the closet door.

"I can't find anything unusual in or around the closet."

"I told you it was probably a dream," she snapped, and retreated down the hall.

He got the message. Loud and clear. Time to go. Garth huffed and rubbed the back of his neck. The movement drew his eye to his reflection.

And something else.

# Chapter 8

HAVING GARTH IN HER BEDROOM sent a shiver of lust through Sandra. He hadn't demanded anything from her, even if he was riddled with attitude.

Garth was trying to protect her. He was still standing in her bedroom, as tempting as a chocolate brownie. What could it hurt to have a taste? One little kiss by way of thanking him for caring?

Her heart tugged. Had anyone cared about her other than her father? And she wasn't even sure who her father was.

Nick had used kissing as a prelude to other things, but Sandra didn't want those things with Nick. She shouldn't have been surprised that she wanted more than a kiss from Garth.

Sandra gathered her wits and marched down the hall, her target in sight. Garth's head swiveled between the closet mirrors and the opposite side of the room, and then he saw her coming toward him. Before she lost her nerve, she stepped up, circled her arms around him, rose to her toes and kissed him.

Garth pulled away, surprise in his eyes, and then he wove his hands into her hair and returned the kiss.

She pulled away with a gasp. All those years ago, she'd gotten the feeling Nick kissed her to distract her from the other things he tried to do to her. Garth was fully invested in her mouth, and it sent liquid heat rushing through her body. What was she supposed to do?

Sandra glanced at his waistband, at the bulge below it. The same one she'd seen straining his pajama pants this morning. Garth wasn't attacking her, rubbing against her, telling her to reach in and touch it. Not the way Nick did.

He moved toward her again and then stopped. He glanced at the mirror behind her and stepped away. Garth cupped his neck, his heated expression turned wary.

"What is it?" she asked.

He pointed and glanced from the mirror to the dresser beside the bed.

The image in the mirror was more defined now, not the nebulous outline she'd woken up to earlier. Her father stood there, a smile on his face.

The reflection walked to the nightstand, picked up a picture frame. She checked the nightstand. No picture frame. The reflection of her father opened the dresser drawer and tucked the picture inside.

And then he disappeared.

"Holy hell," Garth whispered.

"You saw him?" Sandra asked.

"Before you came in." Garth squeezed his eyes closed, his hand still wrapped behind his neck. "He was standing there, holding up a finger as if he wanted me to wait for something." His gaze locked onto Sandra. "And then you kissed me."

And he'd kissed her back. She wanted to kiss him again, but she stood her ground. Sandra struggled to control her erratic breathing. "Did you see the picture?"

"Just the frame."

Garth watched Sandra warily. Nervous laughter bubbled up inside her. *He* was afraid of *her*? More likely he was as unnerved by the ghost as she was.

Sandra crossed to the dresser and opened the drawer her father had tucked the picture frame into. Empty. "I don't understand." Her throat was thick with emotions threatening to choke her. She traced the bottom of the drawer and a sliver of wood pushed into her finger. She sucked on her finger, looking for the rough spot in the drawer and noticed an almost imperceptible slit. She reached in once more, slid a fingernail into the slit and lifted the false bottom.

~ ~ ~

Sandra gasped and pushed the drawer closed again. When she faced Garth, her eyes were wide.

"What's in the drawer?" he asked.

"Nothing."

What wasn't she telling him?

"Got a sliver," she said, holding up a finger.

Her expression said there was more.

Garth took a step toward the dresser and she put a hand to his chest to hold him back. Electricity pulsed through him and he did everything he could not to throw her onto the bed and kiss her senseless. The way she kissed…he'd be reliving that in the shower tonight, but the Bambi look in her eyes told him not to spook her by getting greedy.

Her throat undulated as her eyes swept over him like he was dessert and she was hungry, and yet she stood out of reach.

"Come home with me," he growled. Not the tone of voice he was going for.

She shook her head. Not a good sign. Then again, she'd always sent him mixed signals. Apparently today wasn't going to be any different because she kissed him again, one hand in his hair. Her other hand snaked around his waist.

After all the years of teasing, Sandra Meyer was kissing him, and he wasn't about to ask why.

One of her hands slid inside his waistband and worked its way toward the front of his pants. His knees buckled. She'd found what she was looking for. Her touch, featherlight on his tip, made him groan, and she pulled away again.

"What's wrong?" she asked, that Bambi look in her eyes again.

Was it possible she didn't know what her touch did to him? His fingers itched to touch her, but the question in her eyes stopped him.

"I like the way you touch me," he said.

"Did I…" her chest heaved and her eyes dropped to his waistband again. She backed away.

She had a nervous look on her face again, but her eyes were fixed on his erection.

Was Sandra still a virgin? He'd never seen her with anyone in all the years she'd been taking care of her mother, so it was a very real possibility, but a woman that gorgeous? She certainly talked a good game, but maybe it was only talk. She'd told him Nick beat the hell out of her for not putting out. That might explain why she was so afraid to get close.

"I won't hurt you," he said softly. "Ever."

"I know that." She took a tentative step forward. "You kiss like sin," she whispered.

"Back atcha."

"And if I touch it? Through your jeans?"

He held his hands out to invite her.

"You wouldn't want to touch me, too?"

Garth laughed. "Yeah, I want to touch you, too, but we can go at your pace."

She rested her palm against the front of his pants and he worried he might lose himself right then. Garth swallowed the groan as her hand molded to his ridge.

"Does it hurt?"

"No." His voice squeaked and he chuckled again. "It feels good." He drew another quick intake of breath as she pressed harder. "I can make you feel good, too." Damn. He felt like a high school kid all over again, experimenting, except he'd learned a few things since then. After a few brief flings during his community college days, he'd spent three years with Annabelle O'Shea, another blue-eyed blonde, discovering his way around a woman. It had taken him three years to realize Annabelle was a substitute for the woman he wanted.

The woman standing in front of him.

In spite of the flirting, Sandra kept her distance. Until now.

She pulled her hand away. "You said you'd go."

Back to mixed signals, but he was getting the impression those signals telegraphed fear more than anything else. She'd gotten too close to Nick and gotten burned.

Garth should have called the police when Tammy'd told him about Nick. His need to protect Sandra was stronger now than it had ever been, even if he had to protect her from himself. "You want me to leave?"

She nodded.

More blue balls. Garth shot another glance at the mirror. He wasn't about to make love to Sandra under the watchful eye of her ghostly father. "Come home with me," he whispered against her lips.

She responded by kissing him again, deep and dizzying. She pulled away and met his gaze. "I can't."

Even without the ghost, he knew better than to take advantage of the situation given all he'd learned about Sandra today. She was afraid to get too close, but she'd let him inside her walls. For now, he could only hope she'd trust him enough to let him stay there.

Garth walked out of her bedroom and paused by the front door. "You know where to find me if you need me."

"Yes." She stayed five paces behind.

He walked out and climbed into his truck. After she closed the door, Garth slammed a palm against his steering wheel, started the engine and drove to the monument shop.

The shop closed at noon on Saturday. He knew he'd be alone when he arrived shortly after one. He needed the solitude, without his family hovering over him asking him what was wrong. He'd never been good at hiding his feelings, and right now, he figured he looked like a thundercloud.

He unlocked the front door to the monument shop, let himself in and relocked the door behind him.

Amy kept the work orders on her desk. He flipped past Thad's folder of headstone stencils and checked his folder for the plaque orders. Among the batch of awards to be engraved for the Chamber of Commerce, he found one memorial for a cremation niche. All of them could wait until Monday, but he needed somewhere to focus his attention other than Sandra Meyer. Engraving was his preferred method of meditation. The memorial plaque wouldn't take long. It didn't bear one of Amy's renowned epitaphs, but it would provide enough time to calm his mind.

As he settled behind the engraving machine, he programmed the stencil and tugged his headphones on to turn off the outside world. He closed his eyes while the machine took over and let the comforting whine of the engraving head and hum of the vacuum vibrate through his body.

From what he knew based on his conversation with Tammy way back when, which Sandra more or less corroborated, he understood why Sandra was cautious, but if she flirted with every man she met the way she flirted with Garth, she might have invited a heap of trouble.

He'd never seen her flirt with anyone else.

Another indication she trusted him not to abuse her.

Exhibit one. She'd kissed him.

Exhibit two. She'd touched him.

The calm he sought eluded him. He was on fire for Sandra and he couldn't do anything about it. Not if he wanted to prove to her not all men were like Nick Benedetto. Garth could provide character references.

He opened his eyes and laughed, checking the progress of the engraving. One-third of the plaque was completed.

Asking an old girlfriend to provide a character reference was never a good idea. His only long-term relationship had been after community college—

Annabelle O'Shea, affectionately referred to as Saran Wrap by his brothers. When they went out in public, she had a tendency to drape herself around him, clinging tight so people knew he was with her, marking her territory.

Annabelle had accused him of being inattentive, of thinking of someone else when he was with her. He hadn't been able to argue. From the time Sandra had told him Nick had cornered Amy, Garth knew he wanted Sandra. She wasn't Nick's jealous girlfriend, like everyone believed. She wasn't trying to mark her territory, the way Annabelle did. Sandra was trying to protect the other girls when she told them to stay away from Nick. She was a better person than people gave her credit for and his admiration for her had grown over the years.

Sandra had overcome the adversity in her life. She practically ran Morning Joe, not only waiting tables, but Darrell was quick to point out what a whiz she was with his general ledger, as well.

Garth could even rationalize the stigma Sandra had attached to Amy. Sandra had said she was afraid of Amy's gift. Most people were. When someone repeated the words of a dead person, people tended to shy away. His family worked in a stereotyped industry, one where anyone associated with a cemetery or a funeral parlor was considered somber or spooky.

Garth checked the engraver once more. The short memorial was nearly done.

A sense of calm enveloped him the way it always did at the monument shop. Here he had his family.

Acceptance. Sanctuary. He grinned, thinking of Quasimodo.

The engraver finished and he switched the machine off. He tugged off his headphones, opened the protective case and pulled the plaque out. He wiped it with a cleaning cloth before he hunched and shuffled to his workbench as he repeated, "Sanctuary," out loud—and came face to face with Amy.

"Shit," he said, fumbling the plaque.

Amy broke into a fit of giggles.

"How long have you been standing there?"

"Long enough."

"You could have let me know you were here," he said, shouldering past her.

"What, and miss all the fun?" She put a finger to her chin. "Wait, let me think a minute. How many times have you told me not to interrupt you while you're working? Not to surprise you when you couldn't hear me coming?"

"Why are you here?" he asked.

"I went for a walk through the cemetery and saw your pickup out front."

He stopped, set the plaque down and faced his sister. "Am I intimidating? Scary?"

"Ho boy." She leaned against the door to the shop and folded her arms. "Didn't I tell you she'd break your heart?"

"She didn't break my heart." Much. "I've had women tell me I'm inattentive, and I've heard the 'it's not you, it's me' line a couple dozen times, but I don't think I've ever inspired fear."

Amy had that look on her face, the one that said, 'you stupid fool.' "Let me have it," he said, palms up, fingers inviting her to have her say.

"You're six-foot-four and built like a tank. Scrawny girls might be afraid you'll squish them," she teased.

"I'm not the tank. Thad is," he groused.

"All three of you are," Amy said. "My point here is that the people who know you know you're nothing more than a big teddy bear, in spite of the way you like to push people around."

"I don't push people around."

Amy laughed. "Right. So when you greet Thad or Brian, what's the first thing you do? Shake their hands?"

She had a point. "But they're my brothers."

"How many serious relationships have you had?" Amy rolled her eyes and tapped a finger to her temple. "Thick as a brick. You're no better than Nick. You really are a troglodyte."

"Now wait a minute. I never beat a woman up."

"Beat a woman up?" Amy straightened. "Nick beat Sandra up?"

Oops. Time to stop talking. He retrieved the plaque and carried it to the work table.

"Is she hurt?"

"As far as I know he hasn't gotten close to her since he's been home, other than when you saw him with her at the café."

"So he beat her up when we were in high school?"

"Let it go, Ame." It wasn't his story to tell.

"Garth?"

He shook his head. "Nope. This conversation is over."

She narrowed her eyes at him. "So when you gave Nick that black eye, when Sandra told you he kissed me in the stairwell, were you protecting me or protecting her?"

Garth's pulse kicked up and his fists closed. No one was going to hurt his little sister. "Does Kevin know about Nick? Nick hasn't tried to contact you, has he?"

Amy sighed. "No, Nick hasn't tried to contact me, and no, I didn't tell Kevin about the most embarrassing moment of my life."

Garth and his brothers hadn't tested Amy's fiancé, but Kevin was fierce in his devotion to her. Kevin had faced down Garth and Thad and Brian to prove it. "You should. Tell him."

"Nick's not interested in me," she said.

Garth hunched over the plaque and painted on a layer of Rust-Oleum.

"Want to tell me what happened with Sandra?" Amy asked gently.

He shook his head. "Nothing to tell."

"Then what's this about?" she asked.

He sat up again and looked at Amy. "I've never hurt a woman."

"She knows that." Amy lowered her eyes and toed the concrete floor, "Once Kevin pointed it out to me, I realized he was right. There's something there, Garth. Between you and Sandra." She shrugged. "Whatever you did, you should apologize."

"I didn't do anything." He looked away. He wasn't sure what had spooked Sandra. Hell, she'd kissed him first.

"Maybe that's the problem. She wanted you to do something." She grinned and shoved his shoulder playfully. "Something happened."

"Ha, ha, ha," he replied. "C'mere, squirt." He pulled her into a hug and rubbed his knuckles on the top of her head. "When did you grow up to be so smart?"

"Not until my big brothers got out of my way. You guys nearly turned me into an old maid," she replied, twisting away. "And stop doing that. I'm not a little girl anymore. Lucky for me Kevin isn't afraid of you."

"You two aren't married yet." He and his brothers had always been overprotective of her, and he was willing to concede they might have gone too far once or twice. But she'd finally found the right man.

If only Garth could make Sandra see he was the right man for her.

Chapter 9

THE MAN IN THE MIRROR wasn't a dream or imagination. Sandra sat on the bed, staring at the picture frame she'd retrieved from inside the false bottom in the dresser. The photo was one of Sandra and her parents when Sandra couldn't have been more than three years old.

Her father isn't stepping up to the plate.

But Sandra's father had been the one to say that. He'd spoken in the heat of anger and, according to her mother, he'd always been a jealous man. Why would he raise another man's child?

Who was her father if not Cal Meyer?

She checked the mirror once more, but all she saw was her own reflection and a true representation of the room around her. Sandra set the picture on the bed and picked up the second item she'd found hidden in the drawer, a journal. Every page was filled with scribbles. For half a second she wondered if they were Arabic until she remembered watching her mother take notes from a phone call. Shorthand.

Only once in all the years since her father's death had Sandra confronted her mother about what had happened the night of the accident. Her mother had been in rehab, learning to walk again.

"Cal was a good man," her mother had said, "better than I deserved. Your father loved you very much. Hold on to that."

Sandra hadn't pressed her mother for more details. Her mother was the only family she had left, and as a teenage girl, she'd chosen not to scrutinize the words for a deeper meaning. Sandra's life had changed. She'd been lucky to finish high school with the added responsibility of caring for her mother, and the money they'd set aside for college went for doctor bills.

It was time to ask more questions.

Sandra returned the photo to the drawer, inside the false bottom, but she tucked the journal into her purse. Until she was able to decipher the shorthand, she wasn't letting the book fall into anyone else's hands. While she hoped her mother had merely kept real estate notes from her time spent in the model unit, she dreaded the very real possibility the journal held the secrets of her mother's affairs.

She flung open the front door, prepared to drive into town to confront her mother, when Sandra remembered she didn't have her car. Edgarville was a small town, but she was three miles away from Center Street and her mother's office.

Sandra stared at the empty parking spot in front of the duplex. She was not going to call Garth for a ride.

She could call her mother—that was where she was headed after all—but she needed time to decide what she wanted to say. Flinging half-baked accusations wasn't going to get her the answers she needed, and that approach might send her mother into another health crisis, either real or imagined.

The walk would give her plenty of time to think. Sandra closed the door behind her, made sure it was locked and started out.

Why was her father—Cal Meyer—haunting the duplex? Sandra shook her head, well aware of how crazy she sounded. Walking was a bad idea. She'd have too much time to think about how screwed up she was. She needed someone to talk things through with, the way she used to with Tammy.

Tammy had nursed Sandra through the worst of her injuries after Nick had beaten the hell out of her, and then one day she hadn't shown up. When Sandra called to find out where she was, Tammy's mother had cried when she told Sandra Tammy was dead without any further explanation. Two weeks later, Tammy's parents had moved.

I'd hate for the same thing that happened to Tammy to happen to you.

A crawling sensation made Sandra wonder if Nick had punished Tammy for intervening, for stopping Nick before he'd killed Sandra.

She took a shaky breath and closed her eyes—a mistake because she saw the wild look in Nick's eyes that day under the bleachers, felt the fists thudding into her body, his hand around her neck. She'd been gasping for breath, her vision fading. Nick couldn't seem to stop himself. Sandra was certain she was going to die, and then through a tunnel, far away, she heard Tammy.

"She's been through enough," Tammy shrieked. "Isn't it enough her father's dead and her mother's in

the hospital? It's your fault. If you hadn't tried to attack Sandra in the first place..."

"Shut up!" Nick shouted, letting go of Sandra and rounding on Tammy.

Sandra had collapsed to the ground, gasping for air.

"Leave her alone," Tammy said.

"You shouldn't butt into other people's business," Nick said, his voice a feral growl.

"She's my best friend," Tammy said. "Maybe you don't care about her, but I do."

"You don't know what you're talking about." And then his hand was wrapped around Tammy's throat.

Sandra fished her phone from her pocket. "I'm calling the police," she rasped.

Nick pushed Tammy away and stalked off.

Sandra had been too embarrassed to call the police. She should have. If she'd reported Nick, Tammy might be alive today. Another death Sandra was responsible for, assuming Nick had exacted his revenge on Tammy. How else would he be the only one who knew how Tammy had died?

Sandra glanced over her shoulder. Walking three miles suddenly didn't seem like such a good idea. What if Nick drove by?

She'd hoped his years in the Army would teach him how to deal with the rage she'd seen that day. One look in his eyes at the café and she knew nothing had changed.

He'd invited her to go away with him, to get her out of this one-horse town. All she could think of was Nick's hand around her throat. Even if, in her wildest flights of imagination, she considered going with Nick, he could kill her and no one would ever know. People would think she'd moved away and never looked back.

Or she'd seen too many episodes of *Criminal Minds*.

The farther she walked, the more worked up she got. One thing at a time. For now, she needed answers from her mother about what happened that night, about the argument her parents didn't want Sandra to overhear.

When she turned the corner to Center Street, her cell phone rang. "What."

"Uh, Sandra?" Leo asked.

She closed her eyes, stopped walking and bent at the waist. "Yes, sorry."

"Got the new tires on. You still at Garth's?"

"No, he dropped me off..." Leo didn't need to know she was moving into the duplex. "No."

"You want me to come pick you up?"

She glanced around, getting her bearings. She was close to town. "No, I'm only a couple of blocks away. I'm going to stop in to see my mom, and then I'll be over to pick up my car. Thanks, Leo."

"Okay. Bye, then."

She disconnected the call. From where she was, she saw her mother's car in the handicapped spot where it always was, in front of the real estate office. The job had always come first, before family, before Sandra. Unless, instead of coming home, her mother went home to someone else.

Sandra took long strides to the storefront and shoved the door open.

The receptionist greeted her. "Hi, Sandra. How are you doing?"

"I'm just great," Sandra said. She headed toward her mother's desk, reached into her purse and held up the journal.

"You want to tell me what this is? Or should I go find someone else who can read shorthand?" she asked.

Her mother reached for her crutches and struggled to her feet, fear in her eyes. "How did you find that?"

"Are you going to tell me?"

"You can't let anyone else read it," her mother said. "You… you..." she blinked, massaged her chest and winced. "You…" She dropped into her chair.

"Mom?" Sandra tucked the book in her purse and knelt in front of her. "Mom?"

~ ~ ~

Garth pulled the door of the trophy shop closed behind him on his way out. Brian came out of the sandwich shop next door and nudged him.

Maybe they did have a tendency to shove each other rather than shake hands. That didn't make them threatening, did it?

Garth straightened and stuck out his hand.

Brian eyed him warily. "You going to throw me?" he asked.

"I'm trying to be more civilized."

Brian raised an eyebrow. "You'll forgive me if I'm skeptical."

Garth cupped the back of his neck with his hand instead. He was a caveman. Hell, all three of them were cavemen. No wonder none of them were married.

"And there walks the proverbial bad penny." Brian pointed the sandwich he'd bought toward the street. "Want to show *him* how civilized you are?"

Nick.

Garth hadn't used his fists to do his talking since his run-in with Nick years ago. He wasn't the caveman Amy teased him of being, but seeing Nick made him want to reconsider his peaceable stance. Had he been protecting Amy that day? Or protecting Sandra? The answer was easy enough. Between what Tammy told him and Sandra warning him Nick had his eye on Amy, he'd been protecting Amy, but not only Amy.

Amy had Kevin to protect her now. Who did Sandra have?

She had Garth, and Garth's knuckles were itching for a piece of Nick's face.

"Down boy," Brian whispered as Nick drew closer.

Garth shoved the orders from the trophy shop into Brian's hands. "Take these to the shop."

"It's Saturday," Brian said.

"Then hold them a minute."

"You don't want to do this," Brian said. "There are consequences for killing people on Center Street."

Sandra came flying out of the real estate office like she'd been shot out of a gun. She headed straight toward him and Brian as if she didn't see them, banging her shoulder against Garth as she tried to pass. Garth took hold of her and she looked up, surprised. She took a step back and then seemed to relax when she saw it was him.

"What happened?" he asked.

"Damn her! I actually thought she was having a heart attack, but no. She refused to speak to me." Sandra rested her forearms against him and tapped her forehead against his chest. Garth wrapped his arms around her and drew her close.

And that's when Nick caught up to them.

"The happy couple," Nick said. "Everything okay?"

Sandra stiffened in Garth's embrace and he held her tight.

Nick raised his eyebrows. "You look frazzled, Sandra. Is your mother okay?"

Sandra's chest rose and fell with a deep breath. She loosened her grip on Garth and turned to face Nick, but she maintained contact with Garth's body. "My mother's fine, thank you. And now, if you'll excuse us."

"If I were you, I wouldn't let the little lady out of my sight," Nick told Garth. "She seems a bit flighty."

Was that a threat?

"Don't worry. She knows I'll take care of her," Garth said, sending his own subtext.

Nick chuckled and continued on.

"Where you headed?" Garth asked Sandra.

"I need to pick up my car."

"Did you walk to town? I would have…"

"I didn't want you to," she said angrily.

Garth turned her to face him and gave a nod to the real estate office. "Do you want talk about it?"

"No, I don't want to talk about it." Her hands went to her hips.

So stubborn, so independent. What was he supposed to do? All his instincts told him to make her listen to reason, put her in his truck in spite of her objections. Instead, he took her hands in his, leaned down and kissed her cheek. "Promise to call me if you do?"

Sandra slid her arms around his waist once more and hugged him tight before she slipped away.

"Interesting," Brian said beside him, watching Sandra go.

"What?"

"She actually hugged you." Brian handed the trophy orders to Garth. "And I'm not going to the shop. Take these yourself. You're the master of engraving, after all." He unwrapped his sandwich and took a bite as he headed down the street.

Garth took a long look through the windows of the real estate office, at Phyllis Meyer, who was staring right back at him. This was one fight he couldn't help Sandra with. He'd learned early in life not to get involved in another family's drama. Whichever side you defended, the outsider was bound to lose.

Chapter 10

SANDRA'S MOTHER HAD ALWAYS BEEN distant, but refusing to talk to her? Demanding Sandra return the journal? Not going to happen.

The library would have books on shorthand. Deciphering the journal would be like cracking a secret code.

A car honked at Sandra as she crossed Center Street. After running into Garth—she let a giggle escape as she contemplated being able to knock the hulking man over—she continued to the service station.

Leo was beneath a car in one of the bays. Sandra called out to him and he told her he'd be done in a minute. The sense Nick might follow her made Sandra glance over her shoulder and duck out of sight, one hand on her cell phone.

Why was she so stubborn? Garth had shielded her from Nick and how did she repay him? By shutting down.

Sandra straightened her spine. She refused to live in fear, of Nick or anyone else. She stepped out of the shadows.

Leo wheeled the dolly from under the car, grunted as he got to his feet and grabbed a rag to wipe his hands. "Got the bill for you," he told Sandra. He retrieved an invoice from his workbench and handed it to her.

Great. Two new tires. One more bill she couldn't afford. More charges on a credit card she'd never be able to pay off. She pulled out a card and handed it to him.

Leo ran it through the system and bowed his head. "Says it's declined," he said quietly.

Of course, it was. Could this day get any worse? "Half on that one," she said, pulling out a second card, "and the other half on this one."

Leo ran the card again. "Okay, half worked." He ran the second card and set the two charge slips in front of her to sign before he handed her the car keys.

"Thank you," Sandra said.

"Gave you a discount," Leo told her.

Sandra took a deep breath and managed a smile. "Appreciate it." She stalked to her car, climbed in and drove to the library.

Her mother's journal was like a living thing inside her purse, calling out to her, daring her to discover its secrets.

Why did her mother hate her so much? Always working, never coming home. When Sandra's father died, her mother hadn't shed a tear. She'd said Cal was on the road so much, they'd grown apart. She hardly knew him by the time he died. In some twisted way, it made sense to Sandra. If only she could get their final argument out of her head.

When Sandra took on her mother's care, driving her to doctor's appointments and physical therapy and all the reconstructive surgeries, she'd done it out of duty. Not once had her mother said thank you to Sandra. What had her mother done out of duty?

Duty be damned. Sandra was done being put off by her mother. She potentially held the key to her mother's secrets in her purse, and it was long past time to unlock them.

~ ~ ~

Garth tucked the new plaque orders from the trophy store into his folder for Monday. He closed the monument shop once more and headed out. The work usually put him in a Zen state, but his run-in with Nick had destroyed any peace of mind he'd had.

Would Sandra be safe? She had the new address going in her favor. She wasn't likely to give that address to Nick. Her mother, however, was another matter.

Sandra had told him she could handle Nick, and he'd made sure she knew to call him if she ran into any trouble. With that settled, he was going to lift a few beers with his brothers and eat a great big greasy cheeseburger.

When he pulled into the parking lot at Murphy's pub, his brothers' trucks were already there.

"Look who decided to join us," Thad said, raising a beer when Garth walked in. "We're way ahead of you."

Garth shouldered his way through the Saturday night crowd and took a seat at their table.

Thad raised his hand to Patrick, the bartender. "One for my brother," he ordered.

"And a burger?" Patrick asked Garth.

"Yes, please," Garth replied.

"I'll have Delia bring it right over," Patrick said.

"Wasn't sure you'd make it," Brian said, "now that you've got a girlfriend again."

Garth scowled. "I don't."

"Sure looked like it out there on Center Street."

"And I heard about the Facebook pictures," Thad added. "Something you're keeping from us?"

"Talk to your sister," Garth grumbled. "She thought the pictures would be a good idea."

Thad leaned over the table and lowered his voice. "For the record, I agree with her. If I heard about the pictures, you can bet Nick did, too. Mission accomplished."

"I'm not so sure," Garth said.

Delia arrived at the table with a fresh round for all of them. She winked at Brian and he gave her a good, long look. She smoothed her tawny pony tail, preening under Brian's scrutiny, and looked around the table. "Nice to see you, Garth," she said.

"Delia."

"You gonna be here a while?"

Was he? He leaned back in his chair and met her gaze. Her eyes sparkled with mischief, which meant she had something in mind. Poor Brian had no idea what he'd gotten himself into. "I don't think so. Just stopped in for a bite," he told her.

Delia's smile widened. "That Sandra's a lucky woman."

What was she aiming at? Delia didn't normally flirt with him. She walked away, a deliberate sway in her hips.

"You do something to piss her off?" Garth asked Brian.

Thad's lips slanted with a half-smile.

Brian scowled into his beer.

"What'd I miss?" Garth asked Thad.

"Brian, here, asked her if she'd considered getting a respectable job," Thad replied.

"Something wrong with waiting tables?" Garth asked. He straightened his leg under the table, hooked one of the legs of Brian's chair and yanked. Brian scrambled to his feet.

"I don't like the way men look at her," Brian said, keeping hold of his chair.

"So you tell her she isn't respectable?" Garth asked.

"He's an idiot," Thad said. "And what do you mean, you're not so sure the pictures worked?"

Garth shook his head to keep up with the conversation. "Huh?"

"Nick was afraid of you once, with good reason. Wouldn't think he'd want to mess with your girl."

Garth swallowed down a sip of his beer. "I expect he's learned a few things since then. Why do you suppose he chose now to stake a claim?"

"Good question." Thad lowered his head, keeping his tone down. "I know things he might not like me to know. And I think you do, too." He met Garth's eyes.

"Like what?" Brian asked.

"You're too young to know," Thad said, not looking away from Garth.

"Too young? What exactly is your idea of too young?" Brian argued.

"Always was a little slow," Garth said tapping his temple. "And how would you know these things?"

"Used to date a nurse," Thad said. "You might remember her. She had a visit from a couple of frightened girls, right after she graduated nursing school, about the time Amy graduated high school."

Sandra and Tammy?

"What nurse?" Brian asked. "I don't remember."

Thad smiled and turned to Brian. "All in good time, little brother. All in good time."

"What aren't you telling me?"

Garth took another sip of his beer and Delia set his burger down. He took her arm and smiled up at her. "Thanks, darlin'."

Her eyes lit up. "You know, there's a light bulb out in the store room. Maybe you wouldn't mind changing it for me."

He grinned at her obvious attempt to jab Brian. "My brother Brian, here, will help you out."

She cast a sideways glance at Brian. "Thad? How about you? You Benson brothers are all pretty handy, aren't you?"

Thad raised his hands. "I'm not getting in the middle of this. Go help the girl, Brian."

Brian scowled, rose to his feet and followed her.

Thad laughed. "That boy has no idea what he's in for, does he?"

"She'll give him an education, for sure," Garth said with a grin.

Thad took a drink of his beer, set it on the table and rubbed his chin. "Not that it's any of my business, but I'm guessing you've come to an understanding with Sandra?"

Garth winced. "Not sure you'd call it an understanding." He took a bite of his burger and swiped his mouth with the napkin.

"But you mean to keep her safe, am I right?"

"Yeah."

"You do that. She's a sweet girl. Don't know what Darrell would do at the café without her."

Garth's phone buzzed in his breast pocket. He took it out and looked at the number. He shrugged and answered the call.

"Garth, it's Phyllis Meyer. Is Sandra with you?"

"How'd you get my number?" he asked.

"I did sell you your house. Still have your information on file. I'm worried about Sandra. Do you know where she is?"

He spared a glance at Thad. "No."

"She was supposed to stop over to help me tonight, but she didn't come," she said. "I know she's mad at me, but that hasn't kept her away before. I'm worried."

"Did you try calling her?" he asked.

"Yes, and she didn't answer. I know you two are friends. Would you mind checking on her for me?"

Garth had sucker written all over his face, and the whole town knew it. "I'll see if I can find her."

"You might try the duplex on Maple Street. She moved out, you know."

Yeah, he knew. He hoped Mrs. Meyer hadn't shared that information with the whole town. "I'll let you know if I find her," he said, and disconnected the call.

"What's up?" Thad asked.

Brian walked toward the table, a dazed look on his face, tucking his shirt into his jeans. Thad laughed and raised his beer. "Looks like you screwed that light bulb in good."

Garth grinned, too, before he took one more bite of his burger. "Gotta run, boys." He threw his portion of the bill on the table and gave Delia a wink as he passed her.

# Chapter 11

AN ACHE SETTLED IN SANDRA'S chest when she walked into the duplex. Part of her questioned her sanity, but Garth had seen it, too—her father in the mirror.

She wasn't afraid of the ghost. Oddly, she found the idea comforting. If only he wasn't dead. Would he talk to her? Could he talk to her?

Sandra set the library books on the kitchen table and inched down the hall toward the bedroom.

The mirrors reflected the bedroom, but she was the only person staring back. "Daddy?" she whispered, half afraid he'd answer.

The last time he'd appeared, Garth had been here. And what had Sandra done? Thrown herself at Garth. A moment away from wrapping her legs around him and pushing him to the bed. In front of her father— well, her father's ghost. She must be nuts. No self-respecting daughter would climb her boyfriend in front of her father.

Was Garth her boyfriend?

He would be, if she'd give him half a chance.

Without any sign of her father in the mirrors, she returned to the kitchen and sat at her computer for a social media break.

Mistake. Everyone, it seemed, had found the album of her pictures with Garth. She should have made it private, except that would have defeated the purpose—to discourage Nick, a plan that didn't seem to have worked.

She scrolled through the photos—good work, even if she wasn't objective. She and Garth did look good together. His arm around her, her head against his chest—the man did things to her. No wonder she'd wanted to kiss him, and memories of their kiss heated her up all over again.

She didn't have time to waste mooning over photos of a pretend date. If her mother could stay out of the hospital for a year, Sandra would be leaving Edgarville, and everyone in it, in her rearview mirror.

Sandra pulled her mother's journal from her purse, set it on the table and laid the shorthand textbook beside it. Between the two books, she opened a notepad and worked on deciphering her mother's notes. She searched YouTube and found a video to help her through the learning process.

Thirty-nine minutes later, the scribbles looked as foreign to her as when she'd started the tutorial.

"She couldn't write in longhand and make this easy on me?" Sandra called out to the ghost.

She was as crazy as Amy Benson.

Sandra rested an elbow on the table and leaned into her hand. Amy wasn't crazy, and Sandra had to stop thinking of her that way. One careless remark and a legend is born. Crazy Amy. Slutty Sandra. Cheating Phyllis. Clueless Cal.

Except Cal hadn't been clueless. If he wasn't her father, why had he raised her?

She groaned her frustration, clenched her hands in her hair and wandered to the bathroom. She splashed cold water on her face and stared into the mirror in search of her father. "Can't you help me?"

Nothing.

She returned to the kitchen and opened the textbook once more to cross reference against her mother's notes. While some of the symbols made sense, others didn't. And connecting them? What she'd managed to translate so far looked like real estate transactions, client names and their reactions to the properties. No secret diary. Then why didn't her mother want her to read it?

The doorbell interrupted her and set her heart racing. She wasn't expecting anyone. The only person who knew she was here, other than her mother, was Garth. Her mother had asked Sandra to stop over tonight, but when Sandra told her she'd want answers if she did, her mother had gone silent. No, her mother wouldn't show up, knowing what Sandra expected from her. Sandra glanced at the clock. She'd missed dinner. More likely Garth would guess that and bring her something to eat. Garth. The man with the strong arms and the warm heart.

He'd joked about her being his girlfriend for real. Did she dare?

The doorbell rang again. She owed Garth a thank you, and she had an idea for how to convey her thanks.

She checked the peephole, but couldn't see anything. When she opened the door, Nick was standing there, head bowed. He leaned with one hand on the doorframe.

Clearly, this day was about to get worse.

"What do you want?" she asked.

He pushed past her, into the duplex, and closed the door behind him.

Sandra's heart pounded. Would he kill her this time? She reached for the door to open it again. "I don't remember inviting you in."

He grabbed hold of her arm and tried to kiss her. She turned her head.

"Get out," she said.

"You're the one girl who got me," he purred. "We had something in common, you and me. My mom. Your mom. Both of them whoring around town. I know you want out of this burg, the same way I did."

"There is no you and me anymore," she said. "Not after what you did to me."

He ran a finger along her arm. "You were just nervous, but by now, you know how much fun we could have together, don't you? You owe me, Sandra. All that teasing. I've been dreaming about your sweet body since we were in high school." He tried to kiss her again and she sidestepped.

"No. I said no the night my dad threw you out because I wasn't ready. Even if there was a chance of it being a simple matter of nerves, what you did to me later reinforced my decision."

His tone grew threatening. "You owe me."

"I don't owe you anything," she said, her voice cracking. She reached for her cell phone and Nick took her by the arms.

"Do you dream about me, the way I dream about you?" he whispered in her ear. "I'm here to fulfill your fantasies, baby."

"Let go of me!"

He glanced toward the short hallway, to the bedroom beyond.

"Ironic, huh? Me nailing you in your mother's love nest." He crushed his mouth against hers. Sandra broke away, but he was stronger. He slipped one arm behind her knees and lifted her off the floor, carrying her to the bedroom.

"Let me go!" she shouted, praying the neighbors would hear and call the police.

Nick dropped her on the bed and she sprang to her feet. Sandra shoved him as hard as she could and he stumbled toward the closet mirror. Two wispy hands extended from the mirror, and a moment later, Nick disappeared.

Into the mirror.

No, she must be mistaken. Sandra ran to the mirror and pressed her palms to it, solid beneath her hands. She opened the closet door and looked inside. No Nick.

"Nick!" she yelled.

His voice was muted. "Get me out of here!"

She stepped back and saw him in the glass. To be sure, she scanned the room. No flesh and blood version of him outside of the reflection.

"Nick?" she said again, more quietly.

"Where am I?" he asked, looking around, not seeming to see her.

"I don't know," she whispered.

The front door opened and Sandra let out a yelp. She backed up, her hands over her mouth.

"Sandra?" Garth called out.

She ran to Garth and wrapped her arms around him.

"You're shaking," he said. "Is that Nick's car outside?"

She pointed to the bedroom, toward the mirror that had sucked Nick in.

Garth stormed toward the bedroom. Sandra followed, hands on his waist.

"He was here?" Garth asked, surveying the room.

"He tried to… he tried to… he… he…"

Garth faced her, rested his hands on her shoulders and met her gaze. "I've got you. Whatever he did. I've got you."

She took a deep breath to calm herself and pointed to the mirror. "He threatened to rape me, and when I pushed him away, my dad pulled him into the mirror."

~ ~ ~

If Nick had been in the room, Garth was pretty sure he'd pound him into the ground. "Into the mirror?" he repeated.

Sandra nodded, too fast. Knowing Nick had this effect on her kicked in the troglodyte gene Amy always accused Garth of having. One good fist to the top of Nick's head would drive him six feet under.

If only.

Garth extended a hand to the mirror, but Sandra stopped him.

"Don't touch it!"

All right then. She'd spooked him, too.

"We have to do something," she whispered. "We have to get him out of there. Out of here."

"Are you sure he didn't fall into the closet?" Garth asked.

"I checked. I opened the door. He's not there."

"What makes you think your dad pulled him in?"

She took a step closer, staring into his eyes, demanding his attention. "I saw two arms come out of the mirror, and then Nick stumbled backward and disappeared. How many ghosts do you think there are in one mirror? I'm not crazy."

Garth cupped her cheek. "I believe you." He didn't question what she'd seen. After all, he'd seen the ghost, too. Growing up around a cemetery forced you to acknowledge things other people might not. "But I don't know what to do about it. The police aren't likely to believe he disappeared the way you say." And he had no idea how to bring someone back from an alternate dimension, if that's what had happened. He squeezed his eyes closed and massaged the back of his neck. "First things first. Your mother's worried about you. She asked me to check on you."

Sandra's eyes lit with an idea. "My mother. Maybe she knows about this. Maybe she wrote something about the mirror in her diary."

"Diary?"

She darted to the kitchen, where three books lay open on the table. "Earlier, when we saw my dad's reflection, when we saw him open the dresser, the drawer had a false bottom. I found a diary. My mother's. Everything is in shorthand."

That might explain a couple of things. "Is that what you fought with her about?"

She nodded again, still too fast.

"How about you sit down? I can bring you a glass of water. Let's try to talk through this," he suggested.

Sandra's eyes flashed with anger. "You don't believe me."

"I can see you're upset and I'd like to sit and walk through what happened before we go any further. If Nick is trapped in the mirror, we need to find a way to get him out."

Her hands went to her hips. Not a good sign. "He *is* in there. In the mirror. With my dad. What if going through the mirror kills him? I pushed him, Garth."

"Not sure how Nick's death would be a bad thing," he said, hoping to make light of the situation. The look on Sandra's face indicated she wasn't amused. "I'm kidding."

Her voice broke. "My mother told me this place was haunted. She had to know. Why would she let me stay here?"

Garth gathered her into his arms. "We'll figure this out."

His phone buzzed in his pocket. Sandra pulled away and he checked the display. "It's your mom again."

She grabbed the phone from his hand and answered the call. "What the hell are you doing giving me the keys to a haunted house, letting me spend the night here? If you know anything about the mirrors, you have to tell me now."

Garth held out his hand, inviting her to give the phone to him.

"No," she told him, backing away. "Not until she gives me some answers. I have spent the last twelve years of my life taking care of her. Being there for her. I ask her one question and she throws me to the wolves."

She seemed to remember the phone in her hand. "What the hell, Mom? Did you tell Nick where to find me?"

Well, that didn't work so well. He'd let them hash it out. Except in the next minute, she threw his phone at the sofa. Thank heaven for cushions.

Garth retrieved his phone, checked it—Mrs. Meyer was no longer connected—and tucked it into his pocket.

"Come here," he told Sandra.

"Get out."

He shook his head. No way he was leaving her alone. She needed help, whether she wanted it or not.

"I know you, Garth Benson," she said, her voice low and threatening. "I do not need you protecting me."

He wasn't backing down. Not this time. "Well, that's too bad, because I'm going to protect you, whether you like it or not." He might regret it later, but there was no way he could leave Sandra as strung out as she was.

She wagged a finger at him. "Not going to kiss you this time. And you're not going to get me in bed."

"Don't recall asking you for either."

Her throat bobbed and her eyes filled with more tears. Her voice came out strangled. "Why not?"

Damn it all! He would never understand what she wanted from him if he lived to be a hundred. "Because that's not what you want from me right now." He approached her with caution, the way he would a skittish doe, and gathered her in once more.

Sandra pounded her fists against his chest, although her blows didn't carry much force. With a heavy sigh, she collapsed against him and he held her close.

"We'll figure this out," he said again, and kissed the top of her head.

# Chapter 12

WHEN THEY RETURNED TO THE bedroom, Sandra leaned against the tall dresser, arms wrapped around herself and shivering. She couldn't seem to get warm. Garth pulled the blanket off the bed and threw it over her shoulders while he talked to Amy using the speaker on his cell phone. Amy passed him off to her fiancé, Kevin, who in turn conferenced in Kevin's brother-in-law, who purportedly knew something about ghosts.

Garth maintained a distance from the closet mirror—from all of the mirrors.

"What do you see in the mirror now?" the tinny voice of a man with a hint of a drawl asked.

"Don't see anything other than what's in the room," Garth said.

"Mirrors can be portals to the other side. Not sure I've ever heard of anyone coming back once they've crossed over, which could be bad news for your friend, Nick."

"Not my friend," Garth muttered.

Sandra leaned closer to the phone in Garth's hand. She cleared her throat to speak, but her voice sounded strained, even to her own ears. "What are we supposed to tell people?"

"Nothing much you can tell them," the man replied. "If you say you're not sure where he's gone to, that seems like the truth to me."

"So where do we go from here?" Garth asked. "What happens if I break the mirror, beside the proverbial seven years bad luck? Would that let him loose?"

"Or trap him in forever," the man said. "In the meantime, you best steer clear. I don't know much about this ghost, this Cal Meyer, but it sounds like he has an agenda. We could make a trip up next weekend, but I'd try to keep people away from those mirrors for now."

Garth met Sandra's eye over the phone. "Will do. And thanks." He disconnected the call.

"They weren't much help," Sandra said.

He grimaced, still holding her gaze. Clearly the man had something on his mind.

"Let's hear it," she said.

"What?"

"I can see the wheels spinning."

He looked away, then turned to her. "You're not going to like it."

She shrugged.

"Come home with me. Stay with me. Until we figure this out."

Sandra shook her head.

"Then I'm going to stay with you."

A high-pitched ringing sounded, as if someone had struck a bell, followed by a juicy slurping sound. Nick appeared in the mirror, arms outstretched, and fell through, onto the floor in front of Garth.

Nick scrambled to his feet and stumbled backward, away from Garth. His eyes were wide with fear. "What the hell did you do to me, man?"

"Me?" Garth asked.

Nick backed toward the hallway, arms in front of him. "Sandra. I'm sorry. Okay? We're good. Are we good?" He glanced at Garth again. "You nearly killed me, man. I think I died for a minute there." He swallowed down hard, reached for the bedroom doorway, turned and ran. A minute later, the front door slammed shut behind him.

"And now you are definitely coming with me," Garth said. "Who knows what that whack job will do next?"

Oh, she definitely liked the protective macho man attitude more than she cared to admit. Garth wasn't menacing in his strength. Her skin tingled as she considered all the ways he could protect her. More than that, she was afraid of what Nick might do once he had time to think through everything that had happened—what *had* happened?—and she definitely didn't want to stay in this duplex any longer. But Nick had found her at Garth's once before.

Would Garth still want her when he found out she was responsible for her father's death, and maybe Tammy's, too? She didn't want to be responsible if something happened to Garth. "Look, I'm not sure I'll be any safer at your house. I can show you two shredded tires as evidence."

"My family has a hunting cabin I'm pretty sure Nick doesn't know about. We could go there."

A cabin. With Garth. *Yes, please.* As much as she wanted to, hiding out with Garth wasn't practical. She couldn't walk away from her responsibilities. "Nick's not going anywhere for a while, and I have to be at work on Monday. I can't afford to take time away."

He took her hand between both of his. "Your choice, then, but I'm not leaving you alone while that maniac is running free."

Sandra's heart cheered while her common sense told her to slow down. When she tried to speak, her voice cracked. "You said you had an extra bedroom."

"My house then."

She tore herself away from Garth. Aside from the makeup in the bathroom, Sandra hadn't done much in the way of unpacking. She retrieved the things she'd set out, zipped them into the cosmetics case and hefted her suitcase onto the bed. With a cursory glance around the room, she tucked the smaller bag inside and closed her suitcase.

The movement of a shadow caught her eye. Her father. In the mirror. Smiling at her. Instinctively, she reached for the mirror and met her father's reflection, palm to palm.

"What do you want?" Garth asked the reflection.

The reflection faded away, but her father's voice whispered in Sandra's ear. "Be safe."

She was safe with Garth.

Garth took the suitcase from her and grabbed her hand. She followed him to the kitchen where she gathered the books from the table and shoved them into her laptop bag.

Part of her wanted to stay, to sit in the bedroom and listen for any other words she might hear from her father, to apologize for being stupid the night he'd died. If she had it to do over, she wouldn't have let them leave, wouldn't have let her father drive when she knew he was exhausted from a long haul.

"Do you want to stop at the real estate office? Return the key to your mom?" Garth asked.

"Hell, no." Sandra winced. The answer came too quickly. She forced a smile. They walked out of the duplex and she locked the door behind them. "You heard the man on the phone. We're supposed to keep people out of here until we know what's going on."

Garth loaded her suitcase into her car. "I'll meet you at my house in a couple of minutes, then?"

"I guess so."

He smiled, reminding her how attractive he was, and then he did something she wasn't expecting. He leaned over and kissed her. His voice was a whisper against her lips. "Drive careful."

~ ~ ~

With both cars parked safely inside his garage, Garth led Sandra into the kitchen and handed her the second garage door opener. "You can put this in your car next time you go out."

She took the remote and laid it beside her purse without speaking a word.

He probably shouldn't have kissed her. Probably shouldn't have invited her to stay. Didn't matter. Until Nick Benedetto crawled back under his rock or was locked up, Garth was going to keep Sandra safe, whether she liked it or not.

Would she like it?

He lugged her suitcase through the living room, to the staircase. "Let me show you to your room."

The upstairs landing opened to three doors, his bedroom, the bathroom and the guest room. Was the bathroom clean? And he hadn't had a guest in a long time. He could probably write his name on the dresser in the second bedroom. "I don't get in here much to clean," he said by way of an apology.

"Don't worry about it," she said.

He set her suitcase down and went to the linen closet in the bathroom for fresh sheets.

"Let me help with that," she said when he returned to her room.

"You're my guest."

"A guest you weren't planning on. I can do my part and make the bed."

He smiled. Always so independent. "How about we do it together? An extra pair of hands makes the work easier."

With her on one side and him on the other, he shook the sheets across the bed.

"You won't be able to guard me all the time," she said. "You still have to work, too."

"But hopefully other people will be around during those times. Like Darrell, when you're at the café. Especially if he knows what's going on."

"What am I supposed to tell him?" she asked as she tucked a corner.

"Tell him Nick threatened you. I don't think that would surprise anyone."

She straightened and set her hands on her hips. "I can handle this, you know."

He raised his eyebrows. Not an hour ago, she'd been in total meltdown mode. "You said he tried to rape you."

Her throat bobbed and her nostrils flared.

"You have friends," he said more gently. "People who care about you. You don't have to weather this alone."

She sputtered. "Friends. More like acquaintances. I haven't had friends since high school. Since…" Her gaze leveled on his. "Since Tammy."

"You took on a lot of responsibility after the accident, more than any other kid your age," he said. "Whether you know it or not, you do have friends. A lot of them."

He threw the blanket over the sheets and tucked in the end. "I guess I'll let you get settled."

As he turned to go, she stopped him.

"Garth. It's not that I'm not grateful…"

"It's that you don't know how to accept help," he finished for her. Or would she think he was psychoanalyzing her? He shook his head and walked out of her room.

"I need help," she said, a step behind him. "Translating my mother's journals. I've been trying to learn this shorthand stuff. It's starting to make sense, but I could use another brain. If I read the characters off to you, do you think you could write down what I say?"

An olive branch? "If it would help." He massaged the tension in his neck. "I have a desk and a computer set up in the sunroom downstairs. That would probably be the best place to work."

"I need to freshen up. I'll be down in a minute."

Yeah, he needed a minute to freshen up, too. Or to get his head on straight. She might have crawled up his body at the duplex, but that wasn't likely to happen again, not with the concrete walls she'd built around herself. Once Nick was gone, she'd re-establish her boundaries, or leave. She had flight risk written all over her. Sandra was always talking about getting away from Edgarville.

Head. On. Straight.

He trotted down the stairs and stopped when his stomach growled. Two bites of a burger hadn't been enough dinner. "I have leftover taco fixings. Are you hungry?" he called up.

"That'd be great," she replied.

He crossed to the kitchen and opened the refrigerator, taking out lettuce, cheese and the tomatoes he'd chopped a couple of nights ago. The diced onions and cilantro came next, followed by the container with the leftover beef. He put the beef in the microwave and set the timer, then reached for the tortillas.

When he turned around, Sandra was seated at the kitchen table, opening two books, not in the sunroom like he'd suggested. Should he assume she was afraid to be alone?

"Can I get you something to drink?" he asked.

"You mean like a margarita to go with the tacos?" She flipped a hand in the air. "Olé."

At least she still had a sense of humor. "I could probably whip something up."

While he mixed the drinks, she set a notebook in front of his spot at the table.

"This is a self-service taco bar," he told her. "Make 'em how you like 'em." He lined up the ingredients.

"A little bit of everything," she said, standing beside him. "Smells delicious." She filled two shells and carried them to the table.

Garth brought the margaritas and poured them each a glass.

"My compliments to the chef. I'll have to visit this restaurant again."

Garth made himself a couple of tacos and sat beside her. "Open every night. You're always welcome." He pushed the notebook to one side and watched her take a bite of her dinner.

"I don't know what's in her journal," Sandra said, wiping her mouth. "But I trust you'll keep this between us."

"I won't say anything."

"You don't know how much that means."

Yeah, he did. "I doubt we'll be solving any mysteries tonight. Enjoy your dinner, and then we'll take a look. What do you say?"

"Sounds good. And these tacos are delicious. Who knew you could cook?"

Garth chuckled. "Hard to screw up something so simple."

Something scratched at the door, followed by a quiet mew.

Garth pushed away from the table, opened a bag of dry cat food and poured it onto a saucer. He opened the back door and crouched down. "Hey, slugger."

"Mew."

Garth extended his hand and the cat sniffed, giving him another mew of approval.

"You be careful out there," he told the cat. "I heard there's a coyote wandering around the neighborhood."

The cat circled Garth's legs to get to the saucer and ate greedily.

Garth rose and stopped when he noticed Sandra watching him. "What?"

"There are so many things I don't know about you, like you never mentioned your cat, and yet we talk almost every day at the café."

He raised his eyebrows. "Not my cat." Was she considering opening up to him?

"Right. You just feed it." She set her taco down and bowed her head. "I think you know a lot more about me."

"I doubt that." Garth wiped his hands on a napkin and returned to his seat.

"Why do you care what happens to me?" Sandra asked.

Not the question he was expecting. How honest should he be? He considered the safe answer but figured the truth would be best. "Why does the warmth of the sun make you feel good? What makes the moon and stars so fascinating? And yet some people don't even notice a clear night sky." He leaned over the table. "I notice you, Sandra. The person you are. You might try to hide from everyone, but I happen to know I'm not the only person who sees the real you. The girl who tries to shield other girls from a dangerous boyfriend, even when they question her motives. The woman who sacrificed her life to care for her mother. The smart woman who runs Morning Joe for Darrell."

"Garth…"

He shook his head. "No, you asked. And in case you decide to be embarrassed about kissing me, in case you think that was a mistake," he paused to decide if continuing down this path would be a mistake. He'd gone this far. "We joke around, tease each other, but truth is often hidden behind a joke. What I feel for you, Sandra, is no joke. I'd like to think I understand you, which means I'm not going to betray your trust in me by taking advantage of you. But if you want me," he spread his arms. "I'm all yours."

"Garth," she said again. Her pupils were dilated, and her eyes reflected the heat he knew was buried deep inside, but she didn't make a move. "You mean a lot to me," she said softly. "I'd hate to lose that."

"And you think you would?"

She turned away. "Nothing lasts forever."

All the more reason to take advantage of the time they had, but he wasn't going to point that out to her. He'd opened himself to her. The next move was hers.

Garth swallowed down the last of his margarita and poured another, then refilled her glass. "So shorthand. It looks like a foreign language. You sure you can figure this out?"

"I've already deciphered a few words here and there." She smiled, the first genuine smile he'd seen out of her since their photo session.

"Here's to cracking the code." He toasted her and they each took another drink.

# Chapter 13

NO DOUBT ABOUT IT, GARTH'S protective streak was the most attractive thing about him.

Sandra shifted the books across Garth's kitchen table. "Shorthand is phonetic. I'm going to read the characters, the forms, out loud. I think hearing them might help sound out the words, so if you could write down what I say, maybe we can put some sentences together."

"Ready."

She looked at the sparkle in his eyes, the five o'clock shadow taking over his jaw. His golden brown hair glistened with sun-kissed highlights from working outside. No, the protective streak wasn't the only thing going for Garth. He had a teddy bear quality about him, big and cuddly when he brought out his playful side, but when aroused, his virility was darn near overwhelming.

Who was she kidding? His virility was darn near overwhelming all the time, and yet he didn't impose himself on her the way…

He'd told her she could have him—that it was up to her to take what she wanted.

He raised his eyebrows. "I'm waiting."

Waiting? Oh, right. Her mother's diary. Sandra shook her head and turned her attention to the diary, comparing the scribbles to the textbook she'd checked out of the library. She took another drink of her margarita. "Ready?"

He raised his eyebrows. Right. He'd already said he was.

She smiled, grateful for the table between them. "Ish-O-D 1311 G-R-E-N S-T-R-E-T," she read.

"Ish? Garth echoed.

"The 'sh' sound. This one is easy. 'Showed 1311 Green Street.'"

"Ish?" he asked again.

She pointed to the notebook. "Are you going to help, or not?"

He saluted her and wrote what she'd said, in neat block letters.

"Nice penmanship," she said. "Ish-D make Aaron happy," she read. "Ish-D? Shed? Shod?"

"Should?" Garth suggested. "And I'm guessing she's talking about Aaron Staley, or Aaron Staley Real Estate."

"Yeah. That sounds right." She squinted at the next set of characters. "*Chay-E-P*, cheap, *S-K-A-T*." She smirked. "Nice, Mom."

"Chay?" Garth repeated.

"*F-O... defs...* that's not right. *Pretty easy. Fo defs pretty easy*?" She glanced at Garth. "Am I wasting my time?"

"Chay?" he asked again.

She giggled. "And we haven't even come across 'end' or 'ent' Wait'll we find an 'oo'." The alcohol must have kicked in. The brief forms suddenly sounded funny and she couldn't stop laughing, which made Garth laugh, and suddenly she didn't care about the diary anymore. "It's the margaritas," she said, stopping to catch her breath. She sobered. "What if there's nothing more in here than real estate notes?"

"Then your mother wouldn't have hidden it," he said, eyes still sparkling with humor. "But seriously, it'll still be there tomorrow. Whatever secrets she might have kept have been secret a long time. A few more days isn't going to make a difference."

She closed the diary and leaned over the table. "So what are you saying? Forget about my mother for an evening?"

"That's exactly what I'm saying." He winked and drained his drink.

"And what should we do instead?" she asked suggestively.

"I can think of a few things."

So could she, and with a few drinks to fortify her, she was considering picking up where she'd left off with him at the duplex. She licked her lips, remembering his broad chest when she'd woken him this morning—the impressive erection that had tented his pajama bottoms. She'd touched his erection at the duplex.

And why was her mind going that direction? Because it was Garth. Because they always exchanged verbal banter, but until yesterday at the duplex, they'd never shared anything more than words. Yes, their kiss had been pretty spectacular, and the alcohol made her brave.

"I can see those wheels spinning," he said.

"You don't have to be worried until they stop," she replied. The cocktails nudged her to share her concerns. "Garth, what happens after we sleep together?"

"We wake up refreshed?" he suggested, a silly grin on his face.

Leave it to him to tease her. "Have sex," she restated.

"Oh. That. I'd say we would both find ourselves incredibly relaxed. Want to find out?" He wagged his eyebrows at her.

Yes. She clamped her mouth shut, even though a thousand volts of electricity skittered over her skin. She had to sleep under the same roof as this man, and if she didn't stop this direction of conversation, they *would* find out. And she'd lose the best friend she had in Edgarville.

"I think the alcohol has already relaxed me," she said, her voice annoyingly breathless. "I should go to bed. Alone."

Was that disappointment in his eyes? Well, of course it was. She'd started this conversation. Certainly, he understood what was at stake. Would he feel she owed him? The way Nick did? And yet she wasn't afraid of Garth, she was more afraid of losing him.

"Things would change, don't you think?" she asked.

"Things?"

"Our relationship. Once we cross that line, everything would be different."

"I suppose it would."

She had to close her eyes. The sexy timbre of his voice amped up her already electrified skin. She blamed the alcohol. A little self-service would take care of the way he made her feel. Alone. In the guest bedroom. "Then I'll say goodnight," she said.

"You know where my room is, in case you get scared during the night," he said.

She smiled sweetly. "Nice try, big guy."

He took her arm as she passed and she fought the sensation of being trapped, afraid.

"I meant what I said," he told her. "You're safe with me, but if you want more, all you have to do is ask."

She breathed a sigh of relief. She had to clear her throat to speak. The man took her breath away. "Thank you." She blew him a kiss and headed for the staircase.

~ ~ ~

He must be masochistic. Why else had Garth invited the one woman who had always flipped his switch as easily as she flipped her beautiful blonde hair to spend the night in his house? An exercise in self-control.

He cleaned up the remnants of dinner and loaded the dishwasher.

For a moment, Sandra had considered taking that next step. He'd seen it in her eyes, and then he'd seen her back away and follow up with the question. What would happen if they had sex? Hopefully, it would be followed by more sex. Would it change their relationship? Absolutely. For one, his self-control would be out the window. If she let him in, he'd want to be all the way in, and he wasn't sure she could truly let anyone inside those walls.

Upstairs, he heard her in the bathroom. He needed sleep, too, but he'd wait until she was settled. Garth pulled a beer from the refrigerator and leaned against the counter while he popped the top.

God, she was beautiful. He took a draw from the bottle and closed his eyes, thinking of the feel of her hair in his hands. She wouldn't have kissed him if she didn't feel something for him. Certainly, she'd lower her defenses eventually, although he'd been waiting a damn long time.

When this was over, when this thing with Nick was resolved and she was safe, he'd make a stand then. That meant no more stops in the café. He swallowed another mouthful of beer.

He wanted Sandra—now more than ever, but not unless and until she wanted him, too.

With one last long draw on the bottle, he drained his beer, turned out the lights and headed upstairs. Sandra would be safely tucked into her bed by now. They'd deal with Nick tomorrow.

Out of deference to his guest—just in case—he did his bathroom routine before he doffed his clothes. Once he was in his room, he closed his door and stripped down. As he slid between the sheets, he sighed. He was in for a long night, thinking of her in the next room. So close and yet so far. He punched his pillow and rolled over, resigned, closed his eyes and waited for sleep to take over.

The floorboards creaked as they settled. A breeze pressed against the window. And then he heard something that wasn't familiar. Tentative footsteps. The door opening. Sandra?

Garth sat up and flipped on the light.

Like a deer caught in his sight, she stopped moving. One wrong move and she'd run. She placed a hand over her heart, in the center of an oversized t-shirt that barely covered her ass. Her long legs stretched on forever from the bottom of the shirt.

"You did say if I got scared…" she said, her voice breaking. She closed her eyes, shook her head, and then reached for the bottom of her shirt—and pulled it over her head.

Damn, if she wasn't the most beautiful woman he'd ever seen. He hardly noticed when the shirt fell to the floor, captivated by the view she gave him. Perfect breasts. A trim waist. A thatch of hair between those long legs. Garth threw back his sheets, inviting her into his bed.

"It's awfully bright in here," she said shyly.

"But if I turn the light out, I'll miss the view," he replied, his mouth dry.

She crossed the room and slid into bed beside him. Sandra Meyer was naked in his bed, and he didn't know what to do. For the first time in his life. Oh, he knew what he wanted to do, but was this more of her exquisite torture? And then he gasped when her hand closed around the part of him that wanted her most.

"And I thought it looked big when it was inside your pants," she joked.

He hissed when she stroked him, and in a second he had her pinned beneath him. He met her gaze, eyes locked in understanding. He nipped her lips, testing, tasting, and she smiled.

"I figured why take care of things myself when I had you in the next room," she whispered. She lifted clumsily and kissed him, the taste of tequila on her tongue.

He pulled back. As much as he wanted Sandra, he didn't want her like this. "You may have had one too many margaritas."

"No," she said. "I may have had more to drink than I'm used to, but I've never been more sure of anything in my life. If we don't do this now, I don't know if I'll ever be able to. I want this, Garth. I want you."

He had no words. With a silent prayer of thanks, he bent to her breasts, licked and gently tugged with his teeth. Her moans told him he was doing something right. He'd take care of her, all right. Garth slid a hand between her legs. She flinched.

"Are you afraid?" he asked.

"Not afraid, really." She licked her lips again. "I feel a little out of my league. Is it going to hurt?"

Sandra Meyer *was* a virgin. And she was gifting herself to Garth. If he wasn't already in love with this woman, her trust in him would have pushed him over the edge.

"I'm going to touch you," he told her. "And I want to taste you." He nipped at her lips. "If anything hurts, you tell me to stop. All right?"

"I mean after that," she said quietly. "When you…" she gasped as he stroked her.

Right. She'd mentioned self-service. "Come for me, baby," he urged, his hips moving in rhythm.

"I want… I want…" she said breathlessly. She moaned and he watched as she broke apart, crying out with her release. When her breathing normalized, she took hold of him once more. His turn to flinch.

"If I do that to you, does it feel the same?"

"If you do that to me, the party's over," he joked. He halted her ministrations and kissed her once more. "I want to be inside you."

She kissed him back and nodded.

Garth reached for his nightstand, pulled open the drawer and grabbed a foil pouch. He ripped it open and unrolled the condom in a matter of seconds. He positioned himself over her and she pushed him away.

"What's wrong?" he asked.

"Do you have to hold me down?" she asked, her eyes bright.

He rolled over so that he was beneath her. If she needed control, he'd give it to her. She lay on top of him, skin to skin. "You're in control," he said. "If it hurts, you stop." He lifted his hips so that he slipped between her legs.

Following his lead, Sandra pushed up and straddled him. Garth leaned forward and suckled on one breast while he rubbed a thumb over her other nipple.

"I want to feel you," she whispered.

He raised his hips again and nudged at her opening. "Ease down. If it hurts, stop."

She sank down on him with a gasp and a wide-eyed look.

Sweet Jesus, the feel of her hot and pulsing around him was going to send him off too soon. "You okay?" he asked, his voice strained.

"Show me what to do," she said, her voice breathy.

Garth took hold of her hips and moved, slowly at first as he watched her response. She closed her eyes and cried out.

"You okay?" he asked again.

"God yes." She found her rhythm, riding him and finding her happy place, taking him right along with her.

And then another unfamiliar sound—breaking glass.

# Chapter 14

GARTH PUT HIS HANDS ON Sandra's hips. Their eyes locked and he put a finger to his lips. He slid out from under her and stepped into his pajama bottoms. "Wait here."

His rifles were locked in the gun safe in the basement. On the off-chance a prowler was in the house, Garth could sneak downstairs and grab one, but by that time whoever had broken in would have done their damage or might even be gone.

A prowler? Or a branch broke a window.

He crept down the stairs to the main floor, still undecided about making a side trip to the basement when a woman called out to him.

"Garth, is that you? I'm so sorry about the window."

Heart pounding, he flipped on the living room light. Mrs. Meyer? She sat on the living room sofa, hunched over, her crutches on the floor.

"Why are you breaking into my house?" he asked.

"I did knock, but no one answered," she said too slowly. "And then I had an episode. Sandra is here, isn't she?"

Before he could respond, Sandra shot past him—wearing her t-shirt and a pair of shorts—and knelt in front of her mother, retrieving the crutches. "What triggered it?"

"I haven't been sleeping well," Mrs. Meyer replied. "I've been so worried about you." She straightened and looked at Garth. "I'll pay for the window."

Which still didn't answer why she was in his house. He tried not to resent the fact she'd interrupted what might be one of the most important moments in his life. Based on the arguments he'd overheard between Sandra and her mother, he suspected there was more to this incident than he knew.

"Have you been taking your medicine?" Sandra asked. "And you should be in bed instead of breaking into people's houses."

"But you wouldn't talk to me, and I had to make sure you were all right."

Hadn't he told Mrs. Meyer Sandra was all right? And Sandra had spoken to her before they left the duplex.

Sandra sent an apologetic look to Garth. "I'm fine, Mom."

"Someone told me about your tires. Why didn't you tell me?" She clutched Sandra's arm.

"I didn't want you to worry."

Mrs. Meyer lowered her voice. "And then that Nick Benedetto asked about your duplex. Didn't you want to avoid seeing him?"

"He must have seen my car there," Sandra replied. "That's why Garth insisted I stay in his guest bedroom, in case Nick came back."

"I thought as much." The smile Mrs. Meyer gave Garth didn't look quite right. "You're a good man, Garth Benson, to take care of my Sandra."

No, he didn't trust her. "Which still doesn't answer why you broke in," he said. "At this hour of the night, you might have called."

"I had to talk to you," she whispered loudly to Sandra, ignoring Garth. "They said Nick saw the ghost. He's talking crazy talk. Something about Garth pushing him into the mirror, or the ghost pulling him into the mirror. The boy is quite upset and he isn't making any sense. Is the mirror broken?"

"No," Sandra told her. She seemed to be getting the false vibe, too. She backed away and folded her arms. "This would be a good time to tell me why you rented me a haunted duplex."

"It's not true. You don't believe in that sort of thing, do you?" Mrs. Meyer grabbed hold of Sandra's hands, demanding her attention. "What did you see?"

Sandra pulled free. "I'll tell you what. Let me get dressed and I'll drive you home. Do you still have your Ambien? I'll get you settled and we'll call the doctor in the morning, let him know you had a seizure."

"Did I?"

Except Mrs. Meyer had already told them she'd had an "episode," which meant she shouldn't need them to confirm it.

Sandra shook her head. "That's what you said. Then again, you don't normally remember when you've had a seizure. And if you just had one… Mom, you can't pretend to have a seizure every time you want to get my attention."

Mrs. Meyer glanced at the back door, at the broken window. She'd reached in to turn the lock, to break in.

"Remember when I sold you this house?" she asked Garth.

"You're avoiding the issue," he said. Garth turned to Sandra. "Do you want me to follow you over?"

"I should stay with her tonight," Sandra said. "I can come back for my car in the morning when she goes to work."

"You don't have to bother," her mother said. "I can drive myself home. I needed to see if you were okay. If Garth thinks you're safer from Nick here, I won't second guess him."

"You can't drive if you've had a seizure," Garth said, challenging her to come clean. "What if you have another one?"

"I'll get dressed," Sandra said.

Mrs. Meyers remained on the sofa, head bowed.

Garth walked into the kitchen for a broom and dustpan to sweep up the glass. He had a piece of wood in the basement the right size to cover the windowpane until morning. As he passed the kitchen table, he stopped. Something was off. The notebook was there, the library book was there.

"Did you take the diary?" he asked Mrs. Meyer.

The look of panic in her eyes was enough to confirm. "What are you talking about?" she asked, her speech rapid. So much for her episode. Phyllis Meyer was a fraud.

Sandra came down the staircase in a pair of jeans and the same t-shirt she'd worn to bed. The same one she'd taken off when she'd climbed into his bed.

"Did you lose my diary?" Mrs. Meyer asked Sandra.

Sandra glanced at Garth. "Where is it?"

"She took it," he said.

"Why would you say such a thing?" Mrs. Meyer asked Garth, and then turned to Sandra once more. "You can't let anyone see my diary." She pushed against her crutches, rose to her feet and faced Garth. "That's personal property. If you took it, I'm asking you to return it."

"It was here when we went to bed," he replied. "And since you're the only one who's been in the kitchen since we went upstairs, it stands to reason you have it."

Mrs. Meyer made a good show of being insulted. "How dare you!"

Sandra stood between them. "Garth?"

"You know I don't have it," he said.

Sandra grabbed her mother's purse from the couch and looked inside. She retrieved the missing diary and held it in the air. "You didn't have a seizure, did you? You didn't come over here to check on me. You came to take your diary."

"It's my diary."

"And my father showed me where to find it."

The tremor started in Mrs. Meyer's legs, and then her eyes rolled up as it took hold of her entire body. She fell to the floor and Sandra pulled her mother's phone from the purse in her hand. Sandra pushed three numbers and then told the person on the other end, "I need an ambulance."

"What should we do?" Garth asked.

Sandra knelt beside her mother to make her comfortable. "It'll pass. They'll check her at the hospital and most likely send her home in the morning."

The paramedics arrived quickly—the fire station was on Center Street.

"Be careful what you wish for," Sandra said half to herself as they wheeled her mother away several minutes later.

"Are you sure it's real this time?" Garth asked.

"Unfortunately, my mother isn't that good of an actor."

"Do you want me to take you to the hospital?"

Sandra sighed and shook her head. "No point in sitting around there. This isn't the first time this has happened. I'm sure she'll be fine." She held up the car keys her mother had left her. "I'll drive her home in the morning. It'll take them a couple of hours to check her out."

Her eyes were bloodshot. Neither of them had gotten a decent night's sleep the night before, and it was after midnight now. "I'll probably have to pick her up in the morning," Sandra said. "I should get some sleep." Sandra hung her head and trudged up the staircase.

So much for second chances. Garth had too much pent-up energy to follow her. Instead, he measured the broken window pane, went to the basement and cut a piece of plywood to fit. He dug through his toolbox for window clips and installed the patch on the back door.

When he went upstairs, he found Sandra in his bed, fully dressed, asleep. Had he misinterpreted her "I need sleep" comment?

"Hold me?" she mumbled when he slid in beside her.

He tucked his arms around her and gathered her in.

~ ~ ~

Sandra woke with a start, the familiar sense that she had to help her mother spurring her to get out of bed, but something was holding her down.

Garth.

The night before came rushing back to her. The way she'd walked into Garth's room. The way she'd stripped in front of him. The way she'd mounted him. Mortification made her cringe. Yes, she'd wanted all that, and more, but without the alcohol to give her courage, she felt awkward, especially after her mother decided to break into Garth's home.

Her mother.

Sandra eased out from under Garth's arm. He pulled a pillow in to fill the void, but didn't seem to wake up. She tiptoed across the hall to the guest room and sat on the edge of the bed to gather her thoughts.

Garth had been so gentle with her. Sandra closed her eyes and saw images of his hard body, remembered the touch of his hands all over her. It would be so easy to slip back into bed with him, to finish what they'd started. Her womb leapt in anticipation.

And as soon as they started, her mother would be calling for a ride home from the hospital. No point in even trying to have a life. Not yet.

Sandra got dressed as quietly as she could and crept downstairs. She scribbled a note for Garth thanking him for his hospitality and squelched a laugh—hospitality, right—and telling him she'd be back for her car later. Then she let herself out as quietly as she could.

As she drove her mother's car to the hospital, church bells rang. Sunday. She was supposed to be moving into the duplex. Would she be able to? Did she want to? She shuddered at the thought Nick might be back, but she'd learned her lesson. She wouldn't open the door a second time unless she knew who was on the other side.

She had to move out. Her mother would never let her go otherwise.

For now, she had to take her mother home. One more time.

Sandra pulled into a handicapped spot in the hospital parking lot and displayed her mother's tag in the window. Her mother was probably still in the Emergency Room, but she'd check at the front desk just in case.

"Hi, Sandra," the volunteer at the desk greeted her.

And how sad was her life that the volunteers at the hospital knew her by name? "Hi, Aisha. Is my mom still in Emergency?"

"No, they moved her to a room this morning." Aisha wrote the number down on a piece of paper and handed it to Sandra.

"Thanks." Sandra took the paper. What had her mother been admitted for this time?

She stopped in the cafeteria for a cup of coffee and a muffin before she took the elevator up to her mother's room.

"You didn't have to rush over," her mother said when Sandra walked in. "I'm sure you would rather be having breakfast with Garth."

Close. She'd rather be having Garth for breakfast, but that wasn't going to happen. Not while her mother continued to meddle. "Why didn't you call when they admitted you?"

"I didn't want to disturb you."

Sandra laughed and took a seat beside her mother's bed. "You mean like breaking into Garth's house? You didn't think that might disturb me?" She set her coffee on the overbed tray, peeled back the paper on her muffin and took a bite.

"You can't let anyone read the diary," her mother said. "It isn't anyone else's business but mine."

"Then maybe you'll tell me what's in it."

"That includes you," her mother said. "It isn't any of your business, either."

Sandra took a sip of her coffee. "Why did they admit you?"

Her mother crossed her arms and turned her head.

The nurse walked in, another familiar face. Sandra's mother spent too much time in and out of hospitals.

"Good morning, Parvati," Sandra said.

"Oh, good morning! How nice to see you." She turned her attention to Sandra's mother. "I'm here to take your vitals, Phyllis."

"She won't tell me why you've admitted her," Sandra said. "And I do have medical power of attorney," she reminded her mother.

"It's nothing specific," Parvati said. "The doctor says her EKG isn't pristine, so they want to keep her for observation." She checked the chart. "She came into the Emergency Room after midnight?"

"Yes," Sandra replied.

"He wants to keep her overnight. As long as everything remains stable, he'll probably release her tomorrow morning."

Sandra finished her breakfast while Parvati did her job.

"I can take you home on my break tomorrow morning," Sandra said.

"Just leave my car in the lot. I can find my own way home. I should go to the office, anyway."

Sandra cocked an eyebrow. "Let's wait and see how you're feeling."

"You don't have to wait around here," her mother said. "I know you have other things to do today. There were still boxes in your bedroom when I looked last night."

"Now you're trying to get rid of me?" Sandra teased. "When do you expect the doctor to stop in?" she asked Parvati.

"Dr. Fuller was here early. He has a golf game today. I can page him if you'd like to speak with him."

Sandra waved the notion off. "I'm sure he'll call me if there's anything important."

Parvati smiled and patted Sandra's mother's arm. "Let me know if you need anything." She waved to Sandra. "Nice to see you."

"Sandra, that diary isn't yours," her mother said, adopting her strictest voice.

Sandra had played the meek caretaker too long. She was out of patience with her mother's machinations. "Then why did you leave it in my duplex? Hate to pull the finders-keepers card, or what's the other one?" Sandra put a finger to her chin. "Possession is nine-tenths of the law?"

"It's not yours."

She was right, but Sandra was done with the secrets. Done with being shut out. After all the years of caring for her mother, she wanted some insight into the woman. Since her mother still refused to talk, the diary was her only option.

"I forgot it was there," her mother said softly.

"Anyone could have found it."

A tear slid down her mother's cheek and Sandra almost felt guilty for not giving in. Almost. Her mother had cried when Sandra had suggested she might go to the community college. She'd cried when Sandra took the job at Morning Joe instead, even though her mother was back to work at the real estate agency part time.

Sandra folded her arms. "I'll make a deal with you. Tell me why my father said I wasn't his child and I'll give you the diary."

"I've already told you. Cal was a jealous man. Of course, you're his child."

"Did he ask for a DNA test?"

"That's really none of your business, Sandra."

Sandra chuckled. "I beg to differ. Why did you sleep in separate rooms? And while we're on the subject, why was your job more important to you than I was?"

"Oh, please! We're not going to start with that again, are we? I thought we left all that behind years ago. It isn't as if I left you alone. That woman was there to take care of you."

Sandra rose to her feet. "That woman? My grandmother? Even toward the end, when she was so sick, she paid more attention to me than you did. Did you hate her, too?"

"Stop being melodramatic. I don't hate you."

No, her mother didn't hate her. Sandra could have walked away if her mother hated her. She'd tried to earn her mother's affection by caring for her after the accident, but her mother was as distant now as she'd always been—unless she needed something from Sandra.

"I don't know anything about you," Sandra said. "I've only ever seen Phyllis Meyer, the real estate agent. I'm your daughter, and if that diary is the only thing I have that will tell me who's behind the façade, you can bet I'm going to read it."

Sandra walked out of the room, feeling like she was five years old. Why was she clinging to the diary? If the contents were as devoid of emotion as her mother, she wasn't going to learn anything, but that little book became a symbol of all the years of inattention.

She had something her mother wanted.

She was being childish. Sandra turned to apologize, but she couldn't bring herself to return to her mother's room. No. Her father had shown her where to find the diary, or rather, her father's ghost. Sandra needed to discover what he wanted her to know.

~ ~ ~

Garth sent Sandra a text offering to drive her back to his house for her car, but she hadn't replied. He told himself he was trying to help when he drove to the hospital to find her.

Phyllis Meyer's car was in the parking lot.

As he tried to find a parking spot, he saw Sandra, arms straight as she slammed through the hospital doors. She came to a stop outside and looked around before she hung her head and slouched onto one of the benches. That didn't look good. She pulled her phone from her pocket and a minute later he had a text.

If it's not too much trouble.

He steered into the horseshoe drive beside her.

She got to her feet and opened the passenger door. "That was quick."

"I was in the neighborhood."

She gave him a skeptical glance but climbed into the cab.

"Everything okay?"

"Peachy."

Didn't sound peachy. "And your mom?"

She drew a deep breath, and when she spoke, she sounded like she was reciting a practiced response. "Her test results were not pristine, so they're keeping her tonight and will release her tomorrow morning." She faced him with a weary smile. "She's fine."

Garth strummed the steering wheel, not sure what to say. Should he bring up last night or wait for her to say something? Was she having regrets?

He huffed. She had more important things to worry about.

"What?" she asked.

"Huh?"

"You huffed. If you have other things to do today, you don't have to worry about it. Once I have my car…"

"It's Sunday. I don't have anything else to do today."

She turned toward him. "Then what's wrong?"

What was wrong? He couldn't stop picturing her, sitting on his lap, her wavy blonde hair cascading down her back and her perfect breasts in his face. No, he wasn't going to tell her that. Instead, he asked, "What do you have to do today?"

"Get the rest of my boxes out of my mother's house."

Her voice was laced with venom. Good call not to tell her he wanted her naked in his bed. "You're still moving out?"

"Yes, sir."

"To the duplex on Maple Street?"

"You got a problem with that?"

Yeah, he had a problem with that. A six-foot problem with greasy black hair. He chose his words carefully. "You aren't worried you'll have more unwanted visitors?"

"I won't open the door."

"Sandra…"

She narrowed her eyes. "If you stop talking now, I'll let you help me."

He gripped the steering wheel tighter. "Then my truck will be more efficient than your car." Garth turned the corner at Greenleaf Avenue, to her mother's house.

He tried to speak when he pulled into the driveway, but Sandra stopped him. "No," she said. "No talking."

Sandra unlocked the kitchen door and returned moments later with a stack of boxes. Garth took them from her and she went back for more. They only needed three trips to the truck this time, having taken a truckload yesterday. When Sandra handed him the last box, she hesitated, glancing around her room, at the spindle bed and the rocking chair in the corner. She crossed to the closet one last time and opened the doors. She stared at a floppy bunny crumpled on the floor.

"I think you should take it," Garth said.

"Nobody asked you," she replied, her voice thick with emotion.

He set the box down. "Are you okay?"

She closed the bi-fold door and faced him with a smile, but her glistening eyes gave away her emotions. "Let's go."

Garth picked up the box and Sandra opened the closet doors once more. She grabbed the bunny and shooed Garth out.

Sandra clutched the bunny while he drove her to the duplex, a faraway look in her eyes.

"I used to have a Corduroy, the bear," he told her. "Missing button and all."

She smiled. "Do you still?"

"Didn't seem like a manly thing to have when I moved out. I left him in my old room and my mom threw him away."

"That's sad!"

"No, that's practical. I'm thirty-four years old. I don't need my teddy bear anymore."

He parked in front of the duplex and Sandra hopped out of the truck. She unlocked the door and went inside while he dropped the tailgate and grabbed the first load.

When Garth followed her inside, he found her standing in the bedroom, staring at the mirror. Her father? A chill rand down his spine as he set the boxes down.

"Sandra?"

She glanced at Garth and pointed to the mirror. The hairs on his arm stood on end, but he joined her in the bedroom.

A cross had been painted on the mirror, along with the words "and deliver us from evil." One of the bedroom windows was open. The curtains billowed in the breeze.

"You're not staying here," Garth said.

# Chapter 15

GARTH HAD TRIED TO COMFORT her, but Sandra was too jumpy. She didn't want to be near anyone. Sandra stayed in the bed in Garth's guest room all night clutching the covers like a shield.

When her phone alarm woke her for work, she dressed and snuck downstairs. Garth was waiting for her.

He handed her a cup of coffee. "I'll drive you to work."

"You have to work, too. Besides, I have to pick up my mom at the hospital."

"I can take a break, too."

She put her hands to her hips. "I can drive myself to work."

"I know you can," he snapped. "Humor me."

Sandra took a step back. Garth in a bad mood? A splash of coffee burned her shaking hands. Okay, the message on the mirror had rattled her, too.

When they arrived at Morning Joe, Garth followed her into the empty café.

"You don't have to…" she began, but he obviously didn't care what she had to say. He walked into the kitchen calling for Darrell. She was too tired to argue with him this morning. Sandra started the coffee urn and went to the office to get the drawer for her cash register.

Darrell got the short version of what happened with Nick, enough information to know to call for backup if Nick harassed Sandra while she was at work.

While she counted the money in the register, Darrell came out of the kitchen wiping his hands on a towel. He shook Garth's hand.

"You know, Sandra," Darrell said, "you've been working here long enough to take a vacation if you want to get out of Dodge for a week until this all blows over, or if you need to take time off to be with your mom."

Mr. Watson from the trophy shop stopped in for a cup of tea and a donut. Sandra rang up the sale with a smile, and when he left, she turned to Darrell.

"My mother doesn't need any help," she groused. "And neither do I." She gave Garth a significant glare.

"I understood she was in the hospital again," Darrell said.

"As a precaution. In fact, I'll need to drive her home on my break."

Garth hugged her. "I'll be by to take you. Call me if you need anything?"

"I'll be perfectly safe right here," she told him. "You don't need to make such a fuss."

"We have unfinished business," he whispered in her ear.

So that was why he was on edge. Would he demand what he felt she owed him? No, he could have come into her room last night if he meant to force her. *You're in control.*

Heart pounding, she nodded. Garth kissed her forehead and started for the door. Then stopped.

Now what?

"Hey, Darrell," Garth called. "Can you invite Micah Lynch over for a cup of coffee? I'll buy."

"Micah…The police?" Sandra followed his gaze. Nick was pacing the sidewalk on the other side of the parking lot. She ducked behind Garth, hands on his hips.

"On it," Darrell said. He stood by the counter as he made the call, and when he hung up, he came around to stand beside Sandra. "That vacation time? I think I might have to insist, for the safety of my customers."

"I can't afford…" she protested.

"Paid vacation," Darrell said. "You've earned it. Might as well take it. I'm going to call Vicki in. You got this?" he asked Garth.

"Yeah."

Darrell disappeared into the kitchen.

"And where am I supposed to go?" Sandra asked Garth. "Even if Darrell pays me, I don't have money for a hotel. There's still the financial side of things."

"The cabin's less than two hours' drive," Garth said.

"But I don't…"

"I'm going with you."

A cabin. Two hours away. Where no one would interrupt them. She tightened her grip on his waist and laid her head on his back. Her mouth practically watered at the idea of licking every inch of his body without worrying about interruptions. No Nick. No Mother.

"Why don't you go in the kitchen for a few?" Garth said.

Sandra peeked around the mountain of a man shielding her. Micah Lynch had arrived and was talking to Nick, pointing toward the café, inviting him inside.

"Yeah," Sandra said, her heart pounding. "I think Darrell might need help with the apple fritters." She passed through the swinging door to the kitchen, leaving it open a crack so she could see what happened.

Micah and Nick walked into the café, and Nick immediately raised his hands and backed away.

"Oh, no," Nick said. "That man tried to kill me once already. You can't let him hurt me, Micah."

Garth hadn't moved from his spot in the middle of the café. "Didn't touch you."

"No." Nick shook his head. "He pushed me into that mirror and I must have blacked out or something."

"What mirror is that?" Micah asked.

"The one at Sandra's place."

"And what were you doing there?" Garth asked.

Even from the kitchen, Sandra saw the fear in Nick's eyes. "I wanted to talk to Sandra."

"That's not how she tells it." Garth took a step toward them and Nick flinched.

Micah stood between them. "And why were you there, Garth?" he asked.

"Her mother asked me to check in on her. She was worried something might be wrong. Turns out she was right."

"I didn't do anything to her, I swear," Nick said.

"You said he pushed you into the mirror?" Micah asked. "I don't see any cuts. If he pushed you hard enough to knock you out, or as you say, to try to kill you, wouldn't he have broken the mirror?"

Garth smiled.

"It… it must be," Nick said. "But I don't remember. I only remember going through the mirror, and then Garth standing over me."

Sandra pushed out of the kitchen. "No, the mirror isn't broken. He went back yesterday and drew a cross on it, didn't you?" She turned to Micah. "Can I file a restraining order? Can you keep him away from me and my home?"

"Sandra!" Nick reached for her, but Micah put up a hand to hold him back.

"You want to give me your side of this mirror business, Sandra?" Micah asked.

"I answered the door. He pushed his way inside and threatened to rape me." Her breath caught. She couldn't tell Micah about her father's ghost. He'd never believe her.

"Then what happened?" Micah prompted.

"I pushed him away." She flattened her lips. "The next thing I knew Garth was there."

"I heard her scream," Garth added.

"I'm sure all the neighbors heard me scream," Sandra said. "They can tell you."

"So Garth didn't push him?" Micah asked.

Sandra shook her head. "He never touched him."

"He must have hit me," Nick said.

"But you don't know for sure?" Micah asked.

The four of them stood there, glancing between themselves.

"What's this about a cross on the mirror?" Micah asked.

"He broke in," Sandra said.

"You can't prove that," Nick said.

"How about we take a ride over there, then," Micah suggested. "Maybe I can lift some fingerprints."

"You going to believe that slut over me?" Nick asked.

Garth's hands curled into fists at his side. Sandra reached for one and shook her head. "That won't help," she said quietly.

"You go on ahead," Darrell said, standing in the kitchen doorway. "Vicki'll be here in a few minutes. I can take care of things until then." He smiled at Sandra. "And I'll see you next week?"

When had her life gotten so out of control? "I guess so," she told Darrell.

Micah led Nick out and put him in the back of the squad car. Sandra collected her purse and climbed into Garth's pickup. A few minutes later they stopped in front of her duplex. Would her father put in an appearance?

With her skin prickling and her chest tight, Sandra unlocked the door and waited for the men to pass inside.

"So where's this mirror?" Micah asked.

"In the bedroom," Nick told him, leading the way.

"And why were you in the bedroom?" Micah asked.

Nick's eyes flashed with fear once more. He wiped at his face. "We're old friends, you know." He cocked his head. "One for old time's sake."

"We aren't friends," Sandra said. "And there were never any old times."

Nick smirked. "Now, come on. Everybody knows. There's no point in keeping secrets any longer."

"The mirror?" Micah said.

Nick stopped in the bedroom doorway, then backed away.

"No broken glass," Garth pointed out.

"He tried to kill me," Nick repeated.

"You tried to rape Sandra," Garth said.

"Did you draw that cross? And what does this say? Deliver us from evil?" Micah took Nick by the arm. "My suggestion to you, Nick, is to go home and sleep it off. You smell like a brewery. But understand one thing. Whatever happened here seems to have happened without the lady's permission. I'm going to get forensics in here to dust for fingerprints, and you'd better hope they don't find yours. In the meantime, you need to stay away from Sandra. You hear?"

"Sandra, tell him he's got it wrong," Nick said.

She shook her head. "No more."

Micah wrestled Nick out the door and Garth closed it behind them. "You okay?"

She took his hands. "Punching him isn't going to help."

"You're not a slut."

She smiled. "What do you know? I did crawl into your bed."

He cupped her face. "And we were rudely interrupted."

In spite of the way her blood was racing, she stopped him. "Not going to do anything here." Not with her father looking on.

"Then we should go to the cabin. Give Nick a chance to cool off. No one will bother us there."

She glanced down the hall. "Did we imagine everything?" she asked.

"No."

She needed to know. Sandra stalked to the bedroom and stared into the mirror. "Why are you haunting the mirrors?" she whispered.

Her father's face came into focus first, followed by the rest of his body. He smiled at Sandra, crossed the room and opened the dresser. Sandra turned to look. The drawer was closed. Nobody standing beside it. In the mirror, her father held the diary. Sandra reached into her purse to check. She still had the real one. Her father opened the book to a page about a third of the way in. Sandra followed suit. In her hand, two more pages flipped by themselves. Sandra backed away, holding the book from her body.

"This page?" she asked the reflection.

Her father nodded.

"I think he's trying to help you," Garth said, his voice raising gooseflesh on Sandra's skin. She'd forgotten he was with her.

Her father looked at Garth and nodded again.

Sandra folded over the top of the page to mark it and closed the diary. "Thank you," she told the reflection.

Her father blew a kiss and disappeared.

Chapter 16

SANDRA SAT ON THE EDGE of the bed, staring at the mirror, willing her father to walk through and back into her life. Garth sat beside her and she inched away. She'd had enough of overbearing men for one day.

"Look, I don't want to tell you what to do," he started.

She chuckled. "Oh, yes you do." She crossed her arms and faced him. "Let's hear it."

"For starters, you need to file a complaint," he told her. "Against Nick."

"I intend to, but unless Micah or PJ wants to follow me around town all day every day, Nick isn't the type to be deterred."

"It makes your case for the next time he comes after you. Or, I could take him hunting," Garth said, one eyebrow raised, "and arrange for an accident."

He was probably kidding, but she didn't like the aggressive male testosterone manifesting itself. Fists or guns, both could be lethal.

Sandra rose from the bed and stared Garth down. He didn't move.

"I'm not stupid enough to go to jail for killing him," he clarified.

"I'll file the complaint," she said. "You said for starters. What else? Might as well tell me what else you think I'm too stupid to come up with on my own."

"I never said you were stupid."

She knew she sounded unreasonable but she couldn't help herself. This had been one hell of a day so far. "What else?" she asked.

"Find someone who can translate the journal for you. You could track down an old business teacher at the high school, or someone who could point you the right direction."

She shook her head. "No can do, big guy. Whatever's in the journal is private. I don't want the whole town to know my mother's business." Especially if her mother did have an affair, or affairs. "Keep going. You're on a roll."

He held out his hands. "I'm trying to help."

"What else?" she said again, rolling a hand for him to continue.

He scowled. "Darrell gave you the week off. I'm taking you to Galena."

"Can't afford a vacation," she said. "And I'll pay for your broken window."

Garth cupped the back of his head, a sure sign she was pushing him past the point of distraction. "You don't have to pay for the window, and the cabin won't cost us anything."

Sandra clenched her jaw. "I jump into your bed one time and suddenly you think we should go away together? I had too much to drink. That should never have happened." Except she'd been the one to make sure it did. She closed her eyes, praying he wouldn't call her on the lie.

"You know that's not what I'm asking for." He made half an attempt to get up and she took another step back. "All right, what's your idea?" he asked, dropping to the bed.

She swallowed. Hard. She didn't have a plan, and he damn well knew it. She was stuck in this hell hole of a town, at the mercy of a sociopath, alienating the only ally she had.

As if he'd read her mind, he said, "You need distance from Nick, and he needs time to realize terrorizing you is a bad idea. I'll give you all the space you need, I think you know that, but for now, you're stuck with me. At least for the short term."

She could do this. "He's only home for a month, on leave."

Garth shook his head. "Darrell passed along some news when we were at the café. Nick isn't going back to the Army. He was discharged."

She reached for the wall to steady herself. "That can't be right. He asked me to go with him on his next tour. Offered me my ticket out of here." And if she'd been stupid enough to say yes, he would have killed her. Nick wasn't going to Germany. "Not that I'd go anywhere with him." She stumbled toward the bed and sat. No surprise Nick had lied to her. How long before she'd found out the truth? Maybe she never would have. He might have killed her before they ever left town. Her cell phone rang and she nearly jumped out of her skin.

Eyes trained on Garth, she answered the call. He didn't move. Not a single over-developed muscle.

"Sandra, this is Dr. Fuller. I wanted to let you know I've admitted your mother."

"I know."

"Would you be able to stop by the hospital? I'd like to go over her condition with you," he continued.

Of course. Every time Sandra got anywhere near independence, something happened to prevent it. What had they found this time? "Okay," she said again, afraid to ask what her mother's condition was, but she wasn't going to get off that easily.

"Sandra, your mother's had a stroke."

She rubbed her forehead. "I'll be there as soon as I can."

She checked the mirror once more and then faced Garth. Oh yeah. They were in the middle of an argument. "Even if I wanted to, I can't leave town right now." She took a fortifying breath. Garth wasn't responsible for Sandra's problems. He didn't deserve the temper she'd thrown at him. "That was the hospital. Seems as if the wolf caught up to my mother. She's had a stroke."

Garth scooted across the bed and held her close. And she let him.

Had their argument over the journal precipitated the stroke? Was her mother afraid to be alone?

No. Her mother had broken into Garth's house. Broke. In.

Was Sandra not allowed a life of her own?

"You're wishing you'd stayed at the hospital," Garth said, more a question than a statement.

"No." None of this was new territory. Her mother had all the nurses to wait on her at the hospital. She wouldn't have wanted Sandra there, too.

Garth reached for her hand. "Sandra?"

"I know you're trying to be supportive. Everything's fine. I just don't feel like talking." Especially not to Garth. She couldn't tell him she'd reached the end of her rope. Sandra had been taking care of her mother since she was sixteen, a mother who barely acknowledged her. She couldn't live with the secrets anymore, the constant rebuffs. If she'd have had to choose which of her parents wasn't biological, she would have opted for her mother.

How was she going to care for her mother? Her mother would undoubtedly have to go to a rehabilitation center, but Sandra's new-found independence would be short-lived. Every time she tried to live her own life she was knocked down.

"I'm not going anywhere," Garth said. "I know you don't want help, but you're stuck with me until I know you're safe from Nick. And if you should decide you need someone to talk to," he tilted her face so she had no choice but to look into his eyes, "I'm here for you."

Damn him! He'd reached right in and squeezed her heart, and that was likely to hurt more than fists when she finally got her chance to leave this town for good.

~ ~ ~

When they arrived at the hospital, Garth agreed to wait for Sandra in the lobby while she went to visit her mother. He parked himself on one of two connected chairs and glared at the doors, silently daring Nick to show up.

Funny how after all the years of teasing and flirting Garth had never considered demanding anything more from Sandra. And now, when things were no longer light and fun and teasing, he couldn't stop from inserting himself into her life. It might end their friendship, might ruin his chances of any sort of future relationship, but he couldn't leave her vulnerable to another attack from Nick. If she made a fuss, Garth would hire a bodyguard for her, but he hoped she'd see reason.

The automatic doors opened and Garth narrowed his eyes, then scowled. Amy walked in, spotted him and settled in beside him on the tandem seating.

"Thought I might find you here," she said, nudging him.

"Guess you thought right."

"Loosen up. You're going to frighten away all the patients."

He lowered his arms. "How did you know I'd be here?"

"Volunteer day," she said. "I was at the extended care facility and I heard about Sandra's mom. You didn't ask for vacation time to go hunting. It isn't hunting season. And I know you well enough to recognize your Mr. Bodyguard posture."

He cocked an eyebrow. "And who suggested me for the job?"

"Yeah, yeah, yeah. So listen. Jared called me back after our group call. About the ghost in the mirror."

"And who's Jared again?"

"The ghost chaser from Louisiana. The one Kevin's sister married."

Garth rubbed the back of his neck and winced. "Okay..."

"He asked for more details about Sandra's father. All I remember is that he died in a car accident." Amy leaned forward as if asking for confirmation, but surely she knew as much about the accident as Garth did.

"Yeah," he said to get her to tell him whatever she'd come to tell him.

"So Jared says mirrors act as portals to the other side. He suggested an accident might have broken one of the car mirrors and when Sandra's father died, his soul went through. Theoretically, his spirit would see the mirror as a way to either come back or bring someone else through."

Take someone else through. And spit him back out. Garth blew out a breath. "Have you seen Nick lately?"

"No." She glanced around. "Not since you called to ask about him going through the mirror. Tell me again what happened?"

Garth leaned over his knees and lowered his voice. "Nick tried to attack Sandra. She pushed him away and she said her father reached through the mirror and pulled him in."

"You think he's dead?"

Garth shook his head. "Shortly after we got done talking to Jared, Nick came back through."

Amy grabbed hold of Garth's hands. "What happened? Did he say?"

"He wasn't sure. He thought I'd tried to kill him, said he was pretty sure he was dead for a minute." Garth sat up and took another deep breath. "He seemed a tad confused about the entire experience. Micah Lynch figured he was trying to avoid assault charges and threatened him with stalking if Nick didn't leave Sandra alone."

"I want to talk to him," Amy said. "To Nick."

"No."

"If he went through to the other side…"

"No," Garth repeated. "Amy, I told you before there were things you didn't know. Out of respect for Sandra's privacy, I chose not to tell you or anyone else, but you need to know Nick is dangerous. She didn't tell me he kissed you that day because she was jealous. She told me because she was afraid he'd hurt you. The way he hurt her. Amy, Nick beat Sandra up, and there's half a chance he killed Tammy Calhoun for preventing him from finishing the job."

Amy backed away and put a hand over her mouth.

"You need to stay away from him," Garth repeated. "Nick Benedetto is dangerous."

"I get it," she whispered.

"And I'd appreciate if you keep what I told you in confidence. It isn't my story to tell, and I'm sure she has her reasons for not wanting anyone to know, but I'll be damned if I let him hurt you, too."

Sandra rounded the corner, coming toward him. Amy rose from her seat, met Sandra halfway and gave her a hug.

"I'm sorry about your mom," Amy said. "I was at the rehab center when they called to reserve a room for her."

Sandra didn't look up. "Thank you," she replied. Dark circles shadowed her eyes. More bad news?

Amy turned to Garth. "I'd better get going. I'll talk to you later."

Garth rose to his feet and Amy hugged him, too, before she left.

Sandra took Garth's hand and led him to the seats. "They took her into surgery," Sandra said. "Brain surgery. They have to control the bleeding. She was already sedated when I got there. With all her other health conditions…" she drew a deep breath. "Depending on how she does, they'll be sending her to in-patient rehab in a couple of days and we'll see how she progresses from there."

"She's a fighter. She's been through so much."

"The odds are against her this time." Sandra shook her head. "I can't do this anymore."

He took her hands in his. "One day at a time."

Sandra folded her arms and looked at a television monitor in the waiting room. Whatever was going on inside her head, she clearly wanted to work through it by herself. She'd had to finish high school while running her mother to doctor's appointments and rehab. She'd had to forego college, instead working in a café. Did she want to get married? Have children of her own? Sandra hadn't been given a choice in life. She'd assumed the role of caregiver before she had a chance to take on a life of her own. Was that why she was so desperate to leave Edgarville?

"I'll help you," he said.

She closed her eyes, took another deep breath and nodded slowly.

Done talking, apparently. He'd be there when she was ready.

They watched television. Sandra paced. He poured them both a cup of coffee. As he considered going to the cafeteria to bring her dinner, the doctor came to the waiting room, a smile on his face.

"The surgery went well," the doctor told her. "She's in recovery and we will be moving her to her room shortly. Let's go into a conference room and I can give you more details about what you might expect."

Garth rose beside Sandra and she put a hand to his chest. She shook her head. "I'll be back in a minute."

Okay. She didn't want him there, and he had no right to insist. Garth resumed his seat.

Five minutes later, she returned. Garth stood again, waiting to see what she'd tell him.

Sandra rubbed her bloodshot eyes and sniffed. "He said a couple of days in the hospital, then to rehab. The outlook isn't rosy and there's a good chance she'll spend the rest of her life in a professional nursing facility." She stood straight, her chin held high. Her posture indicated she didn't want a hug, as badly as he wanted to give her one. She was stubborn and obviously determined to deal with this on her own, the way she always had.

She shouldn't have to.

"So what do you want to do?" he asked.

"I'm going to her room to let her know I'm here, assure her she's still alive." Sandra swallowed hard. "And then I want you to take me home."

Pushing him away? Or asking to stay with him? "Home to my place or home to your place?"

She cracked a smile. "You mean I have a choice?"

And then he did hug her, as much because he needed to as because he thought she needed one. "You always have a choice, as long as I get to go with you."

Chapter 17

ONCE SANDRA'S MOTHER WAS SETTLED for the evening, Garth took Sandra back to his house. Dark clouds hung heavy in the western sky. Sandra leaned forward in her lawn chair and peeked around the awning that hung over Garth's back porch, assessing how long it would be before the rain started and she'd have to go inside. Outside, she didn't feel quite so much like a captive.

Garth wasn't holding her captive, but she wasn't in her own place. By herself. For the first time.

A rumble told her the storm was getting closer. A low growl drew her attention to the cat, hiding in the bushes near the bottom step.

Sandra walked down the steps. "Hey, Cat. You'll want to go somewhere you won't get wet." She extended a hand to pet it and the cat hissed at her, followed with another low growl. "Fine. Have it your way."

The cat crouched low.

A fat raindrop splashed on the sidewalk. Sandra looked around for somewhere the cat could take shelter. The awning over the porch would provide some cover, but not for long with the breeze redirecting the rain. A second raindrop fell.

"Seriously, Cat."

It growled again, as if she was responsible for the raindrop that landed on its back.

Sandra glanced at the closed garage.

"You're going to get wet," Garth called from the back door.

"So's the cat," she replied.

Garth made kissy noises with his lips, but the cat remained in its standoff position with Sandra.

"What'd you do to piss him off?" Garth asked.

"Told him he was going to get wet," she replied.

He chuckled. "Don't take it personally. He's probably feral. Either that or his owners don't take good care of him. He tends to be distrustful."

"Not with you," she pointed out.

"I feed him. That's the only time I get to touch him. Kind of like with you."

She wanted to laugh. He wasn't far off.

The skies opened up, soaking both Sandra and the cat in a torrential downpour.

"My mother used to say something about not having enough sense to come in out of the rain," Garth said.

"I can't leave him out here. Cats don't like to get wet." She bent down and reached for the cat. It swatted her, a claw drawing blood.

"You can't help him if he doesn't want to be helped. Come inside. He's not going to find shelter as long as he thinks you're going to grab him."

Sandra sucked on her sliced finger and ran up the steps, into the house. She stopped on the doormat, her hair dripping.

"Stay there a minute. I'll get you a towel. You're soaked."

"Thanks, Captain Obvious."

Garth grinned at her and disappeared.

Sandra glanced out the door. The cat was also soaked, and still crouching beneath the bushes. "I just wanted to help you," she whispered. The words echoed inside her head. Wasn't that what Garth was trying to do? To help her? And she was being as stubborn as the cat, feeling trapped and threatened when all Garth had ever done was treat her kindly.

He's not Nick.

As she toed off her shoes, Garth reappeared, holding a towel. Sandra thanked him and patted herself down. "I guess I'd better change into dry clothes now that I won't leave a drip trail through your house," she said.

She inched past him and up the stairs, closing the guest room door behind her. As she peeled off layers of wet clothes, she considered not getting dressed. Going downstairs and finishing what they'd started. They'd already slept together, after all—well, technically. Until her mother had broken in.

He'd felt so good inside her, and his hands—his hands were magical.

If anything hurts, you tell me to stop. And she knew he would have, unlike Nick, who ignored her pleas. Garth didn't try to frighten her, didn't force himself on her.

Walking downstairs naked wasn't the same as walking naked into his bedroom. For one, he was wearing more clothes. And in the second place, he was more intimidating standing up. No, she wasn't ready to try that technique again, although if he kissed her again, the way he did last night, she was pretty sure she'd melt in his arms and let him do whatever he wanted.

Was she as stubborn as that stupid cat? Refusing to let people help her to her own detriment?

A knock on the front door startled her out of her reverie. When she heard the door open, any thoughts about walking downstairs naked disappeared. She slipped into a clean pair of jeans and a sweater, toweled off her hair and left the towel in the bathroom on her way downstairs.

Micah Lynch stood in the foyer, fidgeting with the policeman's cap in his hand.

"Sandra," he said, giving her a nod.

"Officer Lynch," she replied, getting a half-smile from him at her formality.

"Figured I might find you here after what happened yesterday."

Garth invited him into the living room. The two exchanged a meaningful glance that set Sandra on guard again.

"Okay," she said. "So what happened? Why are you looking for me?"

"Someone broke into your duplex," he said.

"I know."

"Again."

Damn, damn, damn, damn. So much for independence. "Isn't that just a piece of cherry pie," she muttered.

Micah's brow creased. "Excuse me?"

"Something my grandmother used to say." She sighed. "I don't think I had anything valuable enough to steal. Any idea why?"

Micah exchanged another glance with Garth.

Sandra set her hands on her hips. "What is going on between you two? If you keep making eyes at each other, I'm going to think I'm interrupting something private. You did say someone broke into *my* duplex?"

"This time they saw him," Garth told her. "It was Nick."

He'd come after her. Again. Like she'd taken a knee to the gut, she couldn't breathe. And then a punch to her face, to her kidneys, and another fist to her gut. Sandra covered her head, ducking under the imaginary blows. Hands took her shoulders and she twisted away, striking out and hitting a rock-hard chest. Garth.

Sandra took a step back and swallowed down the fear. "Why?" she asked Micah.

"We got a B and E call from one of your neighbors. When PJ got there, he said he heard breaking glass. The door was open and he called for back-up, but before the back-up arrived, Nick came running out." Micah frowned. "He got away. We checked with his mother, but she hasn't seen him today."

Sandra shuddered. "And the breaking glass?"

"The mirror on the closet door." Micah glanced between them. "We have an outstanding warrant to charge him with breaking and entering when he shows up, but there's still the issue of your personal safety."

She inched closer to Garth, leaning into his strength, and he rested his hand on her shoulder.

"PJ mentioned you had a problem with your tires," Micah went on. "The assumption is it could have been Nick?"

"That's a fair assumption," she said.

"Pretty sure now that you and Garth have gone public, everyone's going to know where to find you, including Nick."

"She's safe with me." Garth's deep voice reverberated all through her.

Micah nodded his approval.

Something had changed in Garth after Nick's first visit to her duplex, which was both comforting and terrifying.

Sandra stepped out of his embrace and wrapped her arms around herself.

"I was telling Micah what I'd heard, that Nick was discharged," Garth told her.

"From a legal standpoint, there aren't many avenues we can pursue regarding your personal safety, not yet, but we'll do everything we can," Micah said.

Nick had broken into her home. She wasn't sure she'd ever feel truly safe again.

~ ~ ~

Sandra sat on Garth's sofa with her head bowed, her hands woven into her damp hair. He didn't know whether to comfort her or keep his distance. One thing he knew for sure, if he wanted to touch her, he should give her advance warning. Since Nick arrived on the scene, any unexpected contact seemed to terrify her. She'd shown a glimmer of her old self with Micah, but once he'd told her why he came, she'd recoiled.

"What can I do?" Garth asked after Micah left.

"Nothing," she said sullenly.

He deserved that for being heavy handed and insisting on protecting her, but surely she realized... "You can see why I wanted you to stay here, with me, can't you?" he asked. "If you'd have been at your place…"

She raised her head and locked eyes with him. "Yes. I get it. Thank you for sheltering me. I'm grateful."

"You don't sound so grateful."

"I'm sorry. What do you expect? You said Tammy told you how Nick beat me to a pulp as his way of expressing his condolences after my dad died. Where were you then? I had no one to protect me. No one to take care of my cuts and bruises. No one except Tammy. My grandmother was days away from giving up her fight with cancer, and my mother was in the hospital. She never knew. Just Tammy." Tears welled in her eyes.

"I'll protect you," he said quietly.

"I survived then, and I'll survive now," she told him.

A scratch at his back door told him the cat was there. Garth glanced at the window. The rain had stopped. He crossed to the kitchen and poured a saucer of kibble for the cat, opened the door and set the saucer on the porch.

The cat shook himself, licked his fur, and gazed at Garth as if it was Garth's fault he was wet. "Sorry, pal. Sometimes you have to learn to trust the people who take care of you." Which made him wonder what he'd done to betray Sandra's trust in him.

He closed the door again, set his hands behind him on the counter and leaned back, watching Sandra.

"I heard that," she whispered.

"Heard what?"

She rose to her feet and walked toward him. "When it started raining, I got to thinking how stupid the cat was for refusing help, and maybe I'm not so different." She stopped five feet away from him. "I do trust you. It's just that since Nick got back to town, all the old memories, all the fear and the hurt. They're as potent as Nick's fists. And then my mom's stroke. Like I can't catch a break. I can't get away. From Nick. From my mom. From Edgarville."

Was he part of her prison? "From me?" Garth asked.

She hung her head. "I know I've been psycho, and I'm sure you're having trouble keeping up. I am, too. You're probably the best friend I've had since Tammy…" She paused and took a deep breath before she continued. "Died." She took another cleansing breath. "I don't want to lose you."

And yet he felt like she was disappearing, a little at a time, right in front of him. "I don't want to lose you, either."

"Do you think he killed her? Tammy?"

"I'd say it's a possibility."

"I don't want him to hurt you."

Garth smiled and flexed his biceps. "I might be able to defend myself better than Tammy could."

Sandra's eyes flashed and she licked her lips. "Is it normal? The way I feel?"

His gaze dropped to her sweater. Headlights. *Right there with you.* "Tell me how you feel."

She took a hesitant step toward him, her eyes on the arm he'd flexed, and wrapped her hand around it, squeezing gently. He didn't move. Didn't breathe.

"Have you ever hit a woman?"

"No. And I never would."

She met his gaze, fire in her eyes. "I believe you."

Still, he didn't move, afraid to spook her. "You were asking me if something was normal?" The headlights were on full beam, her eyes warm and inviting. His body responded, straining to offer her whatever comfort she needed.

"The way I feel when I'm with you," she said. Her mouth tilted with a half-smile. "The way you make me feel when we're kidding around at the café, like I'm a lava cake and you melt the gooey middle."

He grinned. "Are you flirting with me?"

She took hold of his other arm for balance, rose on her toes and nipped his lips. "I think we've graduated beyond flirting." She nipped at his lips again. "I need to know. The way I want you? Is that normal? Or is this an oddball reaction to everything else that's going on?"

He placed a hand behind her head and slanted his lips over hers. "If I was melting your middle before all this happened, I'd have to go with normal." He deepened the kiss, struggling to keep up with her changing moods. "For the record, I want you, too. I get that this is all scary for you thanks to a certain asshole who shall remain unnamed." Another kiss and then he leaned his forehead to hers. "We can take this at your pace, as fast or as slow as you want."

"I want," she said, her voice thick with passion. "As fast or as slow as you want to go." She kissed him back, eyes wide. "I trust you, Garth."

He bent to carry her up to his bed, but she stepped away. What had he done this time?

Sandra shook her head and reached for his belt. "I don't want you to carry me." She glanced at the counter. "Can we do it here?" She slid his zipper down and reached inside.

"We can do it anywhere you want." He stole another kiss. "On the counter. On the table. On the sofa. On the floor."

"All of the above."

He chuckled. "Then I'd better grab a supply of condoms so we can get started."

Chapter 18

THEY'D MADE THEIR WAY FROM the kitchen, through the living room and up the stairs. As Garth lay sleeping beside her, Sandra wanted him again. This couldn't be normal.

Everywhere Garth had touched her, kissed her, sizzled to feel him again, begged for the way he made her combust.

Sandra needed time to regroup, to manage her addiction to this man. She slipped out of bed and tugged his t-shirt over her head, pausing to inhale his musk. Probably not a good idea unless she wanted to crawl back into bed with him. She traded his shirt for one of her own and padded down the stairs.

The journal would distract her. She had yet to decipher what her mother had written, what her father had presented to her.

Would her father disappear now that the mirror was broken? Maybe his spirit had lingered to show Sandra the journal. A sense of loss descended on her once again, losing her father for the second time. She drew a deep breath—and smelled Garth, even in her own shirt. And no wonder. They'd been pressed against each other all night.

She glanced at the clock. Two a.m. The journal could wait until morning. She needed more of the man sleeping upstairs, normal or not. More of his closeness. More of his tenderness. Her pulse quickened. He'd loved her slow and easy, and he'd loved her hard and fast. He'd laughed while she traced every sinew of his body, memorizing him with her touch, and he'd done the same to her, lighting up the volcano inside her every time.

She'd been right to tell Nick no. Oh, she'd liked kissing Nick back in the day, but he never lit her up the way Garth did, never tempted her to throw caution to the wind and climb him the way she had Garth. No, there'd always been something unapproachable about Nick, like a snake ready to strike.

She shuddered and glanced at the ceiling. No use trying to fight it. She wanted Garth inside her again, wanted him so close nothing could fit between them, needed to be connected. Sandra flipped off the kitchen light and tiptoed toward the staircase.

Her phone rang and Sandra stubbed her toe in an effort to retrieve it before it woke Garth. "Hello?" she whispered loudly.

"I saw you."

Nick. Sandra's heart missed a beat.

"What?"

"Tonight. With Garth. I didn't believe it. But then I saw you."

She glanced around the room, at the wall of windows at the front of the house, and ducked into the foyer. "What are you talking about?"

"I always knew you had a gorgeous body."

She swallowed hard. How many other people had seen them through the windows?

"You were supposed to fuck me. That night. When your dad came home."

She crouched into a corner. "I distinctly remember telling you no that night."

"But you invited me over, and you kissed me the way a woman wants to be kissed when she wants more."

"Where are you?" She asked scanning the room around her.

"I'll be watching," he said, his voice quiet. "And when you're alone, we'll both get what we want. You'd like that, wouldn't you?"

"No."

"Don't lie to me."

A step creaked on the staircase and Sandra jumped to her feet, her back to the opposite wall. Garth loomed in the shadows. "Who is it?"

She handed the phone to him and the call ended. And then she saw the shotgun Garth was carrying. She flattened against the wall. "What are you going to do with that?"

"I normally keep the guns locked up, but lately I've kept one under the bed in case of emergencies. What did he say to you?"

Sandra put a hand to her chest to slow her racing heart. "He was watching us. He said he'd be watching until he could get me alone."

Garth raised the gun and stepped into the living room, pivoting as he walked toward the front windows. Across the street, a car pulled away from the curb. Garth lowered the gun and returned to where Sandra was still plastered to the wall. He took her hand and tugged her toward the stairs.

"We're leaving," he said.

"Where?"

He paused, looked at her, and laid the gun down. He pulled her into an embrace and stroked her hair. "I'm getting you out of Edgarville. At least temporarily."

"But my mother…"

"Is getting round the clock care, and if you want to continue to be her caretaker, you need to protect yourself."

No, she didn't want to be her mother's caretaker, but she didn't have a choice, at least not in her mind.

Nick was out there. Watching. Waiting.

"I'm going to call Micah and ask him to watch the house so we can get some sleep," he said. "And then we'll leave first thing in the morning."

If nothing else, a couple of days away would give her the time she needed to decipher her mother's diary.

~ ~ ~

Garth took Sandra to the police station before they left town. Even with the complaint against him, Nick wasn't likely to be deterred. Hopefully Nick would cool off while they were out of town.

As they left the flat landscape of Illinois behind in favor of the hills of the Mississippi River valley, Garth cast a glance at Sandra beside him in the truck. She'd spent the past hour poring through her mother's diary, cross checking against the textbook. The only conversation they'd had was when she'd tried to sound out the characters she wasn't sure of to get to the words.

In another half hour, they'd be at the cabin. Garth reached for the radio, then stopped himself. Sandra might not be able to concentrate with background noise. He gazed across the scenic farmland, at the sprouting crops in the fields.

The silence was making him antsy. If he'd been driving alone, at least he'd have had music to listen to. "You making any headway?" he asked.

"I think so. I haven't read what I've got so far, not all put together." She sighed and closed the books in her lap. "Not to mention I'm having trouble concentrating. What do you think happened to Nick when he went through the mirror? That was weird, don't you think?"

"To say the least," he muttered.

"But you saw the way he came back through, right?"

"Yeah, I saw."

She turned in her seat to face him. "Why did my father pull Nick into the mirror? How did he pull Nick into the mirror?"

"That's fairly obvious. He was trying to protect you. As to how, I have no idea."

Her voice quieted. "Can I tell you something I've never told anyone?"

"Of course." Both hands on the wheel, he braced himself for whatever came next.

"And you won't tell anyone?"

He smiled. "You wouldn't tell me if you thought I would."

"I don't think Cal Meyer was my real dad."

Garth shot her a look. Her eyes glistened and her throat undulated. "What makes you say that?" he asked.

"The night of the accident, the night he died, he and my mother were having an argument. He said something—something about my real dad not stepping up to the plate."

"I'm pretty sure your dad's world revolved around you—Cal Meyer's, that is. I know he traveled a lot, but my dad always used to talk about how your dad doted on his little girl. You. Couldn't talk about anything else." He smiled. "Must be something to do with daddies and daughters. I can't imagine he'd do that if he wasn't your real dad." When he cast another glance Sandra's way, a tear rolled down her cheek. "Hey, I didn't mean to upset you."

She shook her head. "No. He was a good dad." She huffed. "My mother, on the other hand, wasn't interested in raising a daughter."

Garth reached across and held her hand. "If Cal wasn't your father, I have to wonder why they didn't get divorced. It takes a special person to raise another man's child."

Sandra smiled. "You would."

Would he? "Haven't run into that situation. Not sure what I'd do."

Sandra pulled her hand free and turned toward the window. "Didn't know there was anything other than flat land in Illinois. The hill country here is pretty."

Back to safer topics, then. "Galena is located in the Driftless Zone, an area that wasn't covered by glaciers during the ice age. Glaciers scraped away the land, leveling and filling valleys. Since this part of Illinois missed that, we still have the hills."

"Aren't you the wealth of information," she teased.

He shrugged. "You asked."

They continued awhile in silence, until he'd crossed into the city limits. "Almost there." Garth drove onto Stagecoach Trail, along the tree-lined road. He steered into the driveway and shut off the engine. "This is it."

Sandra leaned forward to look out the window. "I was picturing something more rustic. You call this a cabin?"

"In deference to my mother, she insisted on running water and a kitchen. Come on. I'll show you around." He hopped out of the truck and grabbed their suitcases from the back.

Sandra wasn't wrong. The house was more than a cabin, but set in the woods the way it was, well, that's what they called it.

He led her onto the veranda, set the suitcases down and unlocked the door. "After you."

Sandra walked in and immediately looked toward the vaulted ceilings. Skylights lit the living room. She passed the partial wall that divided the circular kitchen from the living area and set her purse on the island.

"Not a big kitchen," he said, "but it works."

She continued through the kitchen, to the dining area, and stopped in front of the French doors that overlooked the hilly backyard. "This is beautiful!"

So was she, but if he told her that, she'd laugh at him. Instead, he walked behind her, slid his arms around her waist and rested his head on her shoulder. "Want to see the bedroom?" he whispered in her ear, giving it a nibble before he kissed her cheek.

She turned in his arms, a teasing smile on her face. "Is there only one?"

"No. There are three. And two bathrooms."

She trailed a finger down his chest. "I don't suppose we need more than one of each, at least until we get 'this' out of our systems." She nipped at his lips.

"Out of our systems?" he repeated.

"Well, yeah. You know, this craving we have for each other. I'd guess that at some point it becomes too much of a good thing and turns into a chore."

He raised an eyebrow. "A chore? How do you figure that?" As far as he knew, she hadn't dated anyone other than Nick Benedetto. The thought of her with *any* other guy tugged an uncomfortable piece of his brain, the part that said he wanted to kick somebody's ass.

"Oh, come on," she said. "Everything gets boring after a while, don't you think?"

Was he missing something?

"I'd say it's more like a favorite meal. A glass of wine after dinner. When it's good, you always have a taste for it." He leaned down and kissed her, long and deep. The dazed look on her face when he was done made him feel better. "You let me know if I start to bore you."

Before he could pull away, she reached for his head and drew him in for another kiss. Invitation accepted. He lifted her off the floor and both her legs circled his waist. He carried her down the hallway, to the master bedroom at the end, and dropped her on the bed.

"I'll be right back," he said, heading for the door to retrieve his suitcase.

"Where are you going?" she asked.

"This is a hunting cabin. As far as I know, no one keeps condoms in the nightstand out here."

"Not a cabin," she called after him.

She wasn't bored with him. Not yet.

When he returned to the bedroom, she stood beside the window, looking out across the yard. Did she really think he'd get bored with her?

"Yesterday, you asked if it was normal, the way you wanted me," he said.

She turned at the window, her head cocked to one side. "It is a little unnerving, the way you make me feel."

"Then why do you think it'll get old? Stale? Boring?"

Sandra shrugged. "Doesn't it?"

"I can't imagine not wanting you," he said.

"But that isn't the same as being in love with me, is it?" A look of panic crossed her face, as if she'd said something she didn't mean to. A nervous laugh followed. Her way of taking her words back.

He did love her. Had loved her for years. Something told him she wouldn't believe him. He'd have to tread lightly. "Love isn't about the things you say, it's in the things you do. Words don't mean anything without actions to back them up. If you can't tell how I feel about you from the way I treat you, telling you won't make much of a difference. Nick probably told you he loved you once. How'd that work out for you?"

Her expression darkened.

He couldn't have stopped before he took that last jab? Too late.

Sandra brushed past him and slammed the book tote on the coffee table in the living room.

"I shouldn't have said that," he said, following her.

"I guess if I want answers about my mother, I should get to work on her diary."

And he'd probably have to make sure Amy's bedroom was made up for company. Sandra might want a separate bedroom after all.

Chapter 19

SANDRA STARED AT THE SQUIGGLES and arcs on the pages of her mother's diary and hugged herself to ease her frustration. With the help of the textbook, she'd been able to figure out portions of what her mother had written, but it might as well be hieroglyphics.

Outside she heard the thump and crack of Garth splitting logs. She'd hazarded a glance to see what the noise was earlier, after he'd gone out. He'd been chopping wood steadily for the past half hour.

Half an hour ago she'd still been angry. She wasn't angry anymore.

Sandra knew she was being ridiculous, and yet she couldn't help herself. She wanted to blame Amy for the change in her relationship with Garth, but she knew it wasn't Amy's fault.

"Curiosity killed the cat," she muttered. Curiosity over what she'd been missing out on all these years, the mysteries between men and women. After Nick had tried to force her, she'd been afraid to find out for herself, and now she couldn't stop wanting Garth.

What made her think it wouldn't continue to be fun?

Separate bedrooms. That's what. Sandra couldn't remember her parents being affectionate with one another. She'd assumed that's what happened after time.

The idea of losing Garth's affection sat like a rock in her chest. He was the best friend she had in Edgarville, one of the few things that made being trapped there palatable, and she was alienating him. Her fault for taking advantage of him, climbing into his bed. He had every right to be upset with her.

She closed the books and laid them on the table, determined to make things right. She should apologize.

As she turned toward the French doors, she caught sight of herself in a gilt-edged mirror that hung over the fireplace. Not a pretty picture. The mirror showed her a woman who'd made Amy's life miserable in high school, even if she hadn't meant to, and Sandra had crossed a line with Garth, too. He wouldn't have to wait for an apology, the way Amy had.

Sandra hesitated at the glass door, watching Garth heft the ax. Sweat circles had formed in his armpits, his t-shirt clinging to his torso. Another spot of sweat collected in the middle of his chest. He paused and pulled his collar up to wipe the lower half of his face, lifting his shirt enough to show the dimples at the bottom of his back above his low-slung jeans. He glanced up, to where she stood at the door, as if he could feel her watching. Sandra considering ducking into the shadows, but she wasn't a coward. She took a deep breath, opened the door and walked onto the wood deck and down the five steps to the yard where he was working.

"I'm sorry," she told him. There. She'd done it. Why didn't she feel better?

Garth set the ax beside the stump and folded his arms.

"Things are different between us and I don't know how to act," she continued.

"Do you have to act?" he asked.

Okay, he was still mad. But his answer raised her hackles again. "No. But you've changed."

"We've changed," he said. "It's called evolution. Our relationship has evolved. Some people might say it's because we've taken it to the next level, although personally, I hate comparing relationships to video games."

"I'm not good at relationships."

He took a step toward her, his muscles rippling with tension. Damn. The man had muscles on top of muscles, and they were all pumped up. The now familiar sensation of wanting coursed through her, oozing through her like hot fudge.

"I don't play games," he said, his voice deep and rumbly. He stopped, out of reach, and spread his stance.

"You think I'm playing games?" she asked.

"I suppose that was the point from the start, wasn't it? We were both playing along to keep Nick away, but this is about more than Nick."

Defense mechanisms kicked in. She was going to say more stupid stuff, engage in another argument. And that's when the realization hit her. She wasn't afraid to engage Garth. Arguing with him didn't come with physical consequences. He allowed her an opinion, a voice, without fear of retribution.

Emboldened, she continued. "I'm off balance. This is uncharted territory for me. The way you make me feel…"

"That should tell you something," he argued, pointing at her. "The wanting? The way you feel? You say it's uncharted territory. You haven't felt this way before. That's because this is something special."

"Have you felt this way before?"

He hesitated. There was her answer. "Now you know why I expect this'll get old," she said. "This thing between us. If it didn't, you would have stayed with whoever 'she' was."

Garth took a step closer and leaned toward her. "You think I'm going to stop wanting you?" He placed her hand on the fly of his jeans, letting her feel how much he wanted her. "Relationships are about more than the wanting, and I thought you and I had more, but you're making me wonder. I haven't changed, Sandra."

She pulled her hand away. "You're saying I have?"

He hesitated again. Another affirmative response by her reckoning. That rock in her chest grew heavier.

"You have a lot going on," he said. "I get that, and I've offered to help you any way I can, but I have some pride, too." He stepped inside her personal space, his breath hot on her cheek. "Sex is easy. It's the rest that's hard. I want more from you than your body, Sandra, but if that's more than you can give me, walk away."

Her heart thudded against her rib cage. "Too far to walk back home," she joked.

Garth cracked a smile and turned away. "I'm going inside to clean up, and then I'll make dinner."

~ ~ ~

Garth stood under the shower head, washing off wood chips and dirt. This was only the first night. His visions of a romantic interlude tucked away in their cabin in the woods were replaced with thinking up ways to keep his hands off Sandra. Whatever was going on inside her head, the sex was complicating things.

He bowed his head under the stream to wash his hair and was startled when hands circled his waist from behind, followed by soft breasts pressing into his back. The hands dropped lower and took hold of his growing erection.

He was fighting a losing battle, but they were here, and as long as she was willing to share a small part of herself, he'd take what she could give him. By the time they went home, she'd see what they had was worth fighting for.

"Please?" she whispered against his back. "You said you'd help. Help me, Garth."

He turned, wiped the water from his eyes and leaned down to kiss her. "You don't play fair." His voice vibrated against the skin of her neck while he slid one hand between her legs. He circled a slippery thumb across her nipples and she moaned her appreciation.

"Neither do you," she said between gasps. "The way you make me feel isn't fair."

"You want to feel?" he asked, pressing her against the shower wall. He used the water to stroke her sweet spot while he held her up. "Come for me," he urged.

Her release came quickly. She dug her nails into his back and moaned. "I need you inside me."

Garth turned her and slid past her cheeks, into her core. She cried out once more and he growled in response. No, this wasn't like anything he'd felt before. They fit together like they'd been made for each other. When they were like this, he had no doubts.

"What you do to me," he said in a low growl. "I don't know if I can hold back."

"Don't," she said, between sighs of pleasure. "I'm not afraid. I want all of you."

She met him stroke for stroke as he buried himself deep inside of her, crying out as her muscles tightened around him once more. God, she felt so good. And then he was on the edge, ready to join her.

He wasn't wearing a condom.

Garth groaned and pulled out as the first wave of his climax took him. A second later, Sandra was on her knees in front of him, taking him in her mouth, draining him.

When the tremors stopped, he pulled her to her feet and kissed her.

"This is never going to get old with you," he told her.

That didn't mean it wouldn't end, but he had the rest of the week before he'd have to let her go.

Chapter 20

THE MOON SHONE THROUGH THE skylight in the family room, bright enough to act as a lantern. Sandra stared at the words she'd written, at her attempts to translate her mother's diary. She'd found the patterns, started to understand the forms, but she still doubted what she'd transcribed.

> Cal stopped at the model to let me know he was home, and I was so happy to see him I locked the door and took him to bed. He seemed happy enough with my welcome, until I gave him the news.
>
> He accused me of cheating. Asked how many men I'd slept with in that same bed while I was working. And then he had the gall to ask if the baby was his. The idiot doesn't seem to understand that I don't care how long he's gone, as long as he comes home at the end of the run.
>
> I don't know how to be a mother. What am I going to do if he disowns this child? It isn't as if I planned to get pregnant.

Sandra must have translated one of the words wrong, gotten one of the phrases wrong.

Her head ached from the effort. She shuddered as a chill passed through her. She missed Garth's closeness, his warmth, but he deserved to sleep. She'd already put him through enough of her emotional rollercoaster ride—what must he think of her?

This is never going to get old.

For her part, she agreed, but would it? For him? Eventually he'd get tired of her insecurities, her personal psychoses and inappropriate coping mechanisms. Like he said, there was more to a relationship than sex.

I thought we already had more.

Like the way her day brightened when he walked into the café. The way she looked forward to talking with him, flirting with him, laughing with him. They did have more until she tried to sabotage it.

I haven't changed.

She read the words on her tablet once more.

Why does he always look for the worst in me? Doesn't he know how much I love him? No one can ever be to me what he is.

Was Sandra like her father? Always looking for the lead underbelly instead of the silver lining?

If she'd translated the diary correctly, her mother craved her father's touch the way Sandra craved Garth's. Thinking about her parents having sex gave her the willies, but the diary explained a lot of things.

Her mother had always said her father was a jealous man. Was he battling the same demons Sandra battled now? Loving her mother so much he was willing to stay, even when he believed she'd cheated on him? Conceived another man's child? And her mother. The diary plainly talked about how much she loved Cal. She'd put up with his insecurities and stayed with him. Or was that because she wanted him to take care of the baby?

Sandra's very existence had caused the wedge between her parents. Her mother didn't want to get pregnant and her father didn't believe Sandra was his.

She loves you.

As soft as a breeze, she heard her father's words in her ear.

Sandra rose from the couch and glanced around the dark room. A cloudy shadow appeared in the gilt mirror over the fireplace. "Daddy?" She wiped at the tears that stained her cheeks.

The pages of the diary turned, but there was no wind.

Sandra sighed, daunted by the task of deciphering more of the journal. She might be learning the foreign language, but it taxed her brain at a time when she had too many other things to think about. Nick. Her mother's stroke.

Garth.

Speaking of which, he called to her from the bedroom. "Sandra?" A moment later he padded into the family room. "You couldn't sleep?" He glanced at the mirror and pulled Sandra into a protective embrace.

The ghost in the mirror nodded and then it was gone.

"Are you okay?" Garth asked.

"Apparently your cabin is haunted, too. I don't understand any of this."

"If what Kevin's brother-in-law says is true, if mirrors are portals to the other side, I'm not sure it matters where the mirror is—not if we're seeing your father here, too."

"Or he had to move on when Nick broke the other mirror." She smirked. "Seven years bad luck for Nick." Sandra picked up the diary. "I got through the page he showed us in Edgarville. Apparently there's more." She stuck a pen in the crease.

Garth smoothed her hair. "You want to talk about it?"

"If I read this right, Cal Meyer was my father, and what my mother told me was the truth. Seems he did have a problem with jealousy."

"That's good, right?"

"Yes, but…" Sandra wished she could talk to her father's ghost instead of waiting for him to show up, turning pages in the diary and whispering in her ear. "My mother didn't want to be pregnant. She hadn't planned on me coming along."

Garth studied her, his arms still around her. "Come back to bed."

"I didn't want to disturb your sleep." She shrugged. "I guess I'm restless."

Garth smiled. "I know a way to help with that."

Sandra chuckled. "Nope, it's not getting old yet." She rocked onto her toes and gave Garth a quick kiss. "My mother loved my father. And he loved her. Which makes me wonder why they were so distant while I was growing up."

"A question for your mother?" He tugged her toward the couch and sat beside her. "We're not going back to bed, are we?"

"I guess I have a lot on my mind." She leaned into him, giving him a nudge. "Although you are pretty good at erasing every coherent thought."

"Sounds like you need those thoughts right now. Time to think?"

"Yeah."

"Then I'll hold you while you think. Would that be okay? Just don't get mad at me if I fall asleep." He yawned to emphasize his point and Sandra laughed again.

He rested his head on her shoulder and closed his eyes. Sandra leaned into him, gazing across the dark room for several minutes. She pictured her life, sitting beside Garth, in his arms, covered by his body, laughing with him over dinner at the kitchen table. Their future together. She couldn't picture herself with anyone else. Ever.

"I love you, Garth."

He didn't answer. Sandra turned to look at him and his eyes were closed, his mouth half open, sound asleep.

Probably better he didn't hear. She wasn't sure she could be the person he wanted her to be.

Chapter 21

GARTH HADN'T CHECKED THE CLOCK when Sandra led him back to bed, but considering he'd found her in the living room shortly after midnight, he knew it had been late. Or early, depending on perspective.

He woke up alone, and the sun was shining. The smell of bacon told him Sandra was likely in the kitchen. Garth threw his legs over the side of the bed, slipped his shorts on and wandered down the hall.

"How long you been up?" he asked when he found Sandra scrambling eggs.

She jerked and gasped. "I didn't hear you coming."

He circled his arms around her waist and nuzzled her neck. "Smells good."

"I was going to bring you breakfast in bed. I hope you don't mind me taking over your kitchen. Figured it was my turn to cook." She turned off the burner and divided the eggs onto two plates. "Since you're here, why don't you carry these to the table? I'll bring the bacon and the coffee."

Garth picked up the plates and set them on the table beside the French doors, pausing to glance at the green hills and emerging tulips. It was going to be a beautiful day.

"Did you manage to get some sleep?" he asked when Sandra joined him.

"Some. I'm not looking forward to the prospect of decoding more of that journal. My mother might have been right. It's private. I feel like I'm intruding on her life." Then she smiled. "It is nice to have answers to some of my questions, though."

Garth sat and took a sip of his coffee. "We have all week, and you could use a break. How about if we walk around town today? Have you ever been to Galena?"

She shook her head.

"I think you'll like it. Lots of shops, things to see. We could even do a wine tasting, if you'd like. The diary will still be here when we get back." He plucked a piece of bacon off the plate and took a bite. "Thanks for making breakfast, by the way."

"It's the least I could do after all you've done for me." She looked at him across the top of her coffee cup. "I'm not used to people taking care of me. My dad used to try, but he was gone so much…" She set her cup down. "Did we really see him last night? Or was that my imagination?"

Garth hesitated, wondering if he should lie. Sandra had said she was spooked when Amy recited Sandra's grandmother's epitaph, but that was a lifetime ago. "I saw him."

She leaned over the table. "Do you suppose he can pop up in any mirror, then?" Her cheeks pinked, and he guessed she might be thinking about the mirror in the bedroom.

"I don't know how it works, but I suppose that's possible."

"We're covering some of the mirrors." She sat back and picked up her fork.

Garth laughed. "No argument from me."

"It's comforting to know he's watching over me." She raised her eyebrows. "Some of the time. But why now? After all these years?"

"Is this the first time you've been inside the duplex? Your mother did say it was haunted."

"She showed it to me when I signed the lease, but don't you think she would have told me it was haunted then? That my dad was the one doing the haunting? And if he was in the mirror here, couldn't he have popped up in another mirror before now?" She took a bite of her eggs.

"I don't have the answers, and I wouldn't even begin to guess at your mother's motivations."

Sandra snickered and took a sip of coffee. "You and me both."

Her brow furrowed, but she didn't say anything more. Something was still bothering her. He'd learned the hard way asking might well tweak her into another argument. She seemed to be opening up more, relaxing around him. He could wait until she was ready to tell him whatever it was.

~ ~ ~

Sandra struggled not to hop into the shower with Garth again after breakfast. If he could exercise self-control, so could she. Watching him dress was like putting clothes over Michelangelo's David. The man's physique was nothing short of magnificent. She'd felt the heat from his gaze a time or two—and slowed down to make sure he got the full benefit of what he was watching—and yet he maintained his distance.

He was being a gentleman—she was sure of it—and probably trying not to spook her, but the time for restraint had passed. At least she thought so. He'd seen every inch of her body, and she'd told him she wasn't afraid of his passion. Was he humoring her? Letting her have her way with him but not invested enough to initiate?

They hadn't spoken a word since they'd finished washing the breakfast dishes together, and as he pocketed the keys to his pickup, he asked if she was ready. One word.

Sandra answered him with a nod and they headed to town.

She was overanalyzing, and she knew it. Garth had been patient with her, kind to her, and when they were naked, she had no question he was interested in her. Why did she feel he was holding back?

They drove over a steel arch bridge with a sign telling them the Galena River flowed beneath it. The river carved a path through hills on either side. Garth turned to the right, down an incline toward flood gates that stood open on either side of the road. A banner strung between the gates welcomed visitors to Galena.

To her left, the landscape rose sharply. She could see entire buildings loom tall on the next street over. To her right, the hills dropped gently to the river's edge and a footbridge crossed to the other side.

Garth drove into a parking lot inside the flood gates. "You up for a walk?" he asked.

She smiled, enchanted by the historic feel of the buildings that stood shoulder to shoulder ahead of them. "Yeah."

"I figure we can make our way up the other side of Main Street and then stop at the winery on our way back." The first building beside the parking lot sported a sign depicting a bunch of grapes interwoven with the name of the winery. A second sign posted wine-tasting hours.

"Sounds good." Sandra turned her face toward the sun, soaking in the warmth as they crossed the street. "What a beautiful day."

"I thought you might like to get out for a while."

She slipped her arm through his. "And you thought right." The only vacation time she'd taken since the accident had been spent taking her mother to the hospital or the doctor or to rehab. Being somewhere other than Edgarville—anywhere other than Edgarville—was invigorating. For the first time in a long time, Sandra was free of the burdens that tied her down, even if only temporarily. No hurrying to do her own chores before she did her mother's. No café to open. No wondering if everyone she knew judged her for what happened that night so long ago. She shivered.

A stab of guilt reminded her she should be with her mother, but Garth was right. Her mother had round the clock care. If the doctor thought Sandra should be there, he'd call.

"Chilly?" Garth asked.

She beamed at him. "No, just the opposite. I was enjoying the sunshine and thinking how nice it is not to have to worry about anything."

He slowed in front of the first store. "Want to go in? I've seen it all before, so this is your vacation. Let me know which stores you want to go inside."

She glanced at the window, an olive oil shop. They bragged dozens of varieties. Beside the entrance, a second door advertised a tea and spice shop. "Let's go in that one," she said, pointing.

The minute she stepped inside, she stopped to inhale. Cinnamon. Nutmeg. Other pungent aromas vied for attention. Wooden baskets with hinged covers were labeled with various spices and teas.

"Can I help you?" a woman asked.

The scents made her think of chai tea, and she pictured relaxing on the deck of Garth's 'cabin' with a cup. "Do you have chai tea?"

"No, we don't, but I can mix a blend for you." She put a finger to her chin. "Let's see. Cinnamon, and anise… I think I have a recipe somewhere."

Ten minutes later, they walked out with her purchase. Sandra turned to Garth. "I didn't even ask you. Do you like tea?"

"I've never tried chai before. Do you have enough to share?"

"Yes, I do," she said brightly.

The next shop held shoes, and the one past that had clothes in the window. They passed a chocolatier and a bakery, and when Sandra found the bulk candy store, she tugged Garth inside. "I love salt water taffy. Look at all the different flavors." Kid, meet candy shop. She was in heaven. She bought a pound of taffy.

They walked three blocks, past novelty shops and t-shirt shops, a pub, more clothes shops and custom furniture shops. By the time they started down the other side of the street, which held more of the same, it was lunchtime. Garth guided her into one of the pubs and they sat down to order.

"How long has your family had the house here?" Sandra asked, setting her purchases on an empty chair at their table.

"I think my dad bought the place after his father died. He wanted somewhere we could all be together as a family."

Sandra's heart tugged. She'd missed out on so many things. "So while you boys go out and shoot defenseless animals, the womenfolk come into town and spend all your hard-earned money?"

"Pretty much."

He ordered a beer. Sandra stuck with a soft drink.

"I'm jealous," she said when the server had taken their orders.

"No need to be. You could always join us. Judging by your purchases today, looks like you could keep up with the ladies just fine."

The server set their drinks in front of them and Sandra played with the condensation on the outside of her glass. "I'm not sure I'd be welcome."

He swatted the air. "You still worried about Amy? She said she forgave you. She's not one to hold a grudge."

"What must your mother think of me?"

"Hey." He reached across the table for her hands. "What's going on? I thought we were having fun."

"We are." She pulled free, raised her glass and toasted. "To fun."

He tapped his glass to hers and took a drink, but he didn't take his eyes off her. "So what's bothering you?"

"I told you. I'm jealous. I was practically raised by my grandmother with my dad traveling and my mom always at the real estate office. You grew up with the Waltons.”

Garth laughed, drawing the attention of the other lunch patrons. “You ever see Seven Brides for Seven Brothers? We’re probably more like that. Messy and uncivilized sometimes.” He leaned forward again. “You going to make me sleep in a tree on our wedding night?”

“You like musicals?” she asked. “Seven Brides for Seven Brothers isn’t exactly mainstream.”

“My mom always watched them. Osmosis, you know.” He sang a chorus of “Sobbin’ Women” and Sandra put a hand over her heart.

“*And* you can sing? All these hidden talents. Be still my heart. Who would have thought such a big lunk could be cultured, too?” she joked. “At the rate we’re going, you’ll be begging to sleep in that tree.”

His eyes flashed with heat. Oh. That was new. They’d made similar jokes in the café, but he’d never looked at her that way in public before, so sexy she wanted to skip lunch and go back to the cabin.

“Still not getting old,” he said quietly, his voice all rumbly.

Flirting with him melted the chocolate inside her proverbial lava cake.

Garth straightened. “But I do need sustenance if you intend to keep having your wicked way with me.”

“Oh, I do,” she said without thinking. “But what about you? Why am I always the one jumping you?” She leaned back and ran her hands along her body. “How do I bypass your steely self-control?”

“Don’t tempt me.”

"I thought I already had." She held the glass to her throat and let the condensation cool her a moment before she took another sip.

"Hot?" he asked, watching her like a lion watches a gazelle. "I could lick that sweat off your throat if you'd like."

She wagged a finger at him. "Uh-uh-uh. Then I'd be hotter."

"I like you hot."

The server appeared and set baskets with hamburgers and fries in front of them. "Can I get you anything else?" he asked.

A room, Sandra thought. "No, we're fine."

"The check, when you get a chance," Garth said. "We're kind of in a hurry."

Chapter 22

THEY'D SKIPPED THE WINE TASTING in favor of returning to the Benson's so-called hunting cabin, and after more sheet tangling, Sandra sat on the deck, drinking her chai tea and watching a deer nibble plants at the tree line.

Funny how quickly the repartee returned with Garth, but now they had a new dimension. It was more fun than casual flirting.

Wedding night? All part of the joke, right? Part of the Seven Brides reference, except suddenly she had visions of white dresses and flowers and a chapel on the hill.

Sandra shook her head. *It was a joke*. A casual comment. A movie reference. She was Garth's project, something to do with his protective streak.

She closed her eyes to push the images away. Garth wanted to stay right where he was, in Edgarville, and she was looking for her ticket out.

Galena was away. It might be a good compromise. She loved it here. The rolling hills. The kitschy shops. The peace and quiet. The landscape reminded her of her trip to Breckenridge with Andrea's family. Okay, the hills weren't mountains, but the same sense of peace, of being somewhere else, cloaked her. Would Garth go to Breckenridge with her for real? They could ski all day, make love all night.

Still not getting old. But would it? She couldn't imagine it would, at least not for her.

She was daydreaming again.

The French door opened and Garth stepped outside.

"Getting chilly," he said. "I could set up the fire pit."

She rose from her chair. "I'll come inside. I should see if I can make headway with my mother's diary."

"You sure? It's a nice night. We could stare at the stars, watch the moon move across the sky. Do unspeakable things to each other under a blanket." He wagged his eyebrows and Sandra laughed.

"Didn't we just do that?" She asked. "Might be too much of a good thing."

"Not yet." He took her cup from her hands and sipped her tea. "This is good. Didn't you say you'd make me a cup?"

"You said you didn't want any."

"That's because I wanted you instead." He intertwined his fingers with hers and lifted her to her feet, pulling her closer for a kiss.

He held one hand, setting his other on her waist, then swayed under the moon to a tuneless song. "Dance with me?" he asked.

Sandra lay her head on his shoulder, breathing in the essence of Garth. He made it easy to forget everything else when she was in his arms, in his bed. "This is so nice," she whispered.

"Yes, it is." He turned her face so she looked at him. "And I'm dead serious when I tell you the reason

I don't initiate is because if I did, you'd never leave my bed."

She laughed. "I see how that might be a problem. Oh wait. No, I don't." And yet she was perfectly content as they were, dancing in the moonlight.

"What were you thinking? Before I came out," he asked.

No, she couldn't tell him she'd been fantasizing about a happily ever after with him, planning her future as Mrs. Garth Benson. Sandra didn't want to spoil the perfection of what they'd found with insecurities and fears. "Nothing."

"Do you want to go into Dubuque tomorrow? Do a riverboat cruise?"

Any day spent with Garth sounded like pure heaven right about now. Instead, she said, "Sounds like fun." Too soon, the fantasy would come to a crashing end and they'd have to go back to reality.

"Then how about you come inside. Or we could go back into town. We might have missed the official wine tasting, but they do have testers at the bar you can try if you want to pick up a bottle."

Sandra laughed. "I think I spent every penny of my discretionary money today. I'm safer staying away from town until next payday." She arched her back in a stretch. "Besides, it would seem my father wants me to read more of my mother's diary."

Garth opened the door for her and followed her into the kitchen.

"Then let me make you something to eat. After that, I'll light a fire in the fireplace and I can read while you work. How does that sound?"

Like a slice of heaven, and a little unsettling. "I'm not used to being the one waited on," she told him.

"You're on vacation. As long as you're my guest, I plan to do everything to make your week as comfortable and relaxing as possible."

"You don't have to take care of me," she told him yet again. "I appreciate you getting me out of town and away from the drama, but it's still going to be there when we get back. I don't need anybody…"

Garth's smile vanished. "Stop."

"Garth…"

"No." He set her mug in the sink and stroked her arm. "Yes, I'm trying to protect you from a very real threat, but if you think that's the only reason we're here, think again. I selfishly wanted you all to myself for a couple of days." He shook his head. "And that didn't sound right, either. I'm not always good with words, don't always say the right thing." He cupped her face in his big bear paw of a hand. "I don't want to lose you, and I'm afraid Nick might hurt you, or worse. If you walk away from me, that's one thing, but if someone takes you from me against your will, that's something altogether different."

Sandra's heart ached at the tenderness in his voice. She didn't want to lose Garth, either, but she didn't know how to accept help, much less the emotions he stirred inside her.

"And now the light is gone from your eyes again. I'd hoped you'd stopped being afraid." He dropped his hand from her face. "You aren't afraid of me, are you?"

She scoffed. "No." More like she was afraid of herself when she was with him. He touched parts of her soul no one had reached before. All these years, she'd been able to pretend it was nothing, a game, the way she and Garth teased each other. The teasing had grown into something much bigger, something she could no longer ignore. Something she wasn't ready to face with everything else going on.

"Did you mention food?" she asked, giving him a silly grin to change the subject.

Garth leaned over and kissed her—softly, gently, and with so much care she thought she might cry.

"I'll call you when it's ready."

~ ~ ~

The bookshelves at the cabin were lined with old favorites, books Garth's parents had read and passed along to their children. Most of the books were worth a second look, and the Ken Follett novel Garth selected was one he'd read before and enjoyed.

Except he was distracted. After every chapter, he paused to glance at Sandra. She sat hunched over the coffee table, her head pivoting between the textbook and her mother's diary while she transcribed into a separate notebook. Her computer stood ready for additional reference. From her intensity, he gathered she must be making progress, unlike her first attempts that had her huffing and sighing in frustration.

She paused, a faraway look in her eyes, until she realized he'd been watching her.

"What?" she asked.

He shook his head. "Giving my eyes a rest. You are awful easy on the eyes, you know."

Her lips quirked as if to avoid a smile. "What are you reading, anyway? When you're not giving your eyes a rest, that is."

He turned the cover so she could read it.

"Mm-hmm. Another in your long list of attributes? He sings, he reads, he likes musicals. Sometimes I feel like I don't know you at all."

The problem was she knew him too well, so he couldn't finesse her with hidden charms. When she'd called him a big lunk, she'd described him perfectly. He didn't have a subtle bone in his body and his habit of speaking plainly didn't always win him friends. But he had a rapport with Sandra. "No great mystery here," he replied. "Anything you didn't know before you surely know now, right down to my…" he wagged his eyebrows to add innuendo, "collar size."

She laughed.

"How's the detective work going? Learning anything new?" he asked.

She picked up the notebook and drew a deep breath. "I finished the entry I was working on. To tell you the truth, I haven't been paying attention to what it says so much as trying to translate it."

She scanned what she'd written, and while she stared at the page, a tear fell to the notebook.

Garth set his book down and knelt beside her. "What is it?"

Sandra handed her notebook to him. Words were scribbled, some crossed out, some with question marks beside them. The passage covered most of the page and began with notes about Phyllis Meyer's clients and how she hoped to sell a high-priced luxury estate, then wandered into toasting the sale with Cal and how she wished he spent less time on the road and more time at home.

He's so good with Sandra, so ??
(smitten?) with ~~faood hood~~ (fatherhood?),
even if he doesn't ~~bring~~ believe she's his.
He doesn't understand how every time he
~~cms~~ comes home it's like Christmas for
me, a chance to ~~redeskoov~~ rediscover my
favorite ~~PR~~ present. Him. How could he
believe ~~Im~~ I'd want anyone else? He
moved out of our bedroom, into one of his
own, and ~~et~~ yet every time he comes
home, he still stops at the ~~duples~~ duplex
when I'm on-site. Makes me feel more like
his ~~mstres~~ mistress than his wife – good
and bad. Maybe there he can pretend I'm
still his wife ~~anot~~ (and not?) a poor ~~asmpl~~
(example?) of a ~~me-ith~~ mother.

I feel so ~~enadeket~~ (inadequate?) when it
comes to Sandra. I don't know how to be a
mother, and I feel as if everything I do is
the wrong thing. She'd be better off if he
~~oo-s~~ was the one at home with her and I
was the one traveling to earn my living.
Maybe one day she'll know how ~~ve~~ very
much she means to me, but as with her
father, I can't do anything right.

Garth checked the date at the top and did the
math. Sandra was a year younger than Amy. Thirteen
years ago would mean she'd have been 15, plus or
minus, when her mother wrote the entry. Tough age
for both parents and teenagers.

He set the notebook on the end table beside
Sandra, took her in his arms and whispered into her

hair. "Whenever my mother gets frustrated and thinks she's doing the wrong thing by us kids, she says 'I'm doing the best I can.' That's all we can ask from our parents. From what I've seen, it's a tough job."

"She didn't know how to be a mom," Sandra said. She sniffled, and her voice hitched. "But she does love me."

"Of course she loves you."

Sandra shook her head. "She's always buried herself in her job. I suppose because she was good at it and her job made her feel she'd done something right. Her sense of affirmation."

Garth pulled away and brushed a tear from Sandra's face with the pad of his thumb. "So are these happy tears or sad tears?"

"Sad. Don't get me wrong, it's good to know she loves me, but all these years. She should have said something. Instead, whenever things got heated between us, or when she might have told me she was proud of me, or she loved me, she ran off to work. Her escape hatch."

"Maybe she was afraid you didn't love her."

Sandra held out her arms. "I've been taking care of her for the past twelve years. Out of obligation?" She squeezed her eyes shut. "Don't answer that."

Her expression told him there was something she wasn't telling him. He wasn't going to let her back away from the truth, not when she'd shared this much. "I'm going to say yes, out of obligation, but also because you love her. But there's something else."

"It's my fault. The accident. My fault my father died, my fault my mother will never be the same."

Garth shook his head. "How can you believe that?"

"He shouldn't have gone out. He was always exhausted when he got home from a long haul, but they argued. About me. And they never argued in front of me, so they left. He was angry and he was tired…"

"They could have argued in the backyard. They could have walked down the block. You didn't put the keys in his hand." Garth put a finger to her chin and tipped her face to meet his gaze. "As I remember it, your dad wasn't at fault."

"That doesn't matter. What matters is they were in the car in the first place."

"Not your fault." Garth stroked her hair. "It isn't true."

Her phone buzzed on the coffee table. Sandra drew a shaky breath and picked it up.

"Hello? Yes, this is Sandra." She bowed her head and frowned. "I understand. I'll be there." She disconnected the call and stared at the phone a minute. She met Garth's gaze once more with a sad smile. "That was the hospital. They're moving my mother to the rehab center tomorrow. I have to go home."

She glanced at the mirror over the fireplace and damn if her father wasn't there again, watching. Cal blew her a kiss, smiled and evaporated.

Every muscle in Garth's body tensed. Friendly ghost or not, it was unnerving to see a dead man looking at you. He reined in his uneasiness and hugged Sandra once more.

"Proves my point," he said. "If your father blamed you for his accident, he wouldn't be blowing you kisses."

Chapter 23

SANDRA'S MOOD FLATTENED THE CLOSER they got to home, like she was returning to prison.

"I'm sorry about my mother," she said.

"What?" Garth asked, shooting her a glance.

"For breaking into your house, for cutting our vacation short."

"Don't be silly."

"If I hadn't been there in the first place…"

Garth reached for her hand and pulled it to his lips. "Who would have predicted your mother would break into my house? Not your fault. And for the record, you'll still be staying with me until I can be sure you're safe."

Except Nick already knew she was staying with Garth. Sleeping with Garth.

He's going to pay for taking what's mine.

Nick's words made her shudder. She couldn't bring danger to Garth's doorstep.

"I know that look," Garth said. "And before you say you can take care of yourself, don't forget what that psycho tried to do to you at your new home."

As if she could forget. "So what am I supposed to do? Be afraid all the time? I don't want to drag you into this any more than I already have."

"I'm already all the way in," he said.

Then she had to get him out. Protect him. "I won't be responsible for you getting hurt while you're playing knight in shining armor. I don't want to be a damsel in distress, so stop treating me like one."

"I've never treated you like a damsel in distress," he argued.

"Oh, no? Then why are you assuming my care until I'm 'safe?'"

His fingers tightened on the steering wheel and the muscles in his jaw pulsed as if he was clenching his teeth.

His cell phone vibrated in the cup holder.

Garth checked the Bluetooth display. Thad. He pressed the button on his steering wheel to answer the call. "Yeah?"

"Thought you'd want to know," Thad told him. "Nick Benedetto cornered Amy. He's looking for Sandra and spouting all kinds of nonsense."

Garth glanced at Sandra.

"Is Amy okay?" Sandra asked.

"Yeah. Between Kevin and Brian and me, he figured the odds were against him. I'm not sure he's giving up quite yet. You guys should be safe at the cabin."

Garth cupped his neck. "About that. We're on our way back. They're releasing Sandra's mother from the hospital today."

"Hmm. That does complicate things," Thad said. "Sandra?"

"Yeah?"

"We got your back."

Her nose tingled and she sniffed at the emotions warring inside. She'd never felt so sheltered before. She didn't know how to respond.

"What's Nick saying?" Garth asked his brother.

"Something about how he almost died. He figures the two of you did some sort of hocus pocus on him. He talked about casting spells or conjuring demons, or I don't even know what all. He asked Amy to cast a spell to protect him since she's got that connection to the other side. She nearly clocked him right then and there."

Garth laughed. "That's my little sister."

"Yeah, but then he decided she must have taught the dark arts to Sandra now that they're friends. The guy's gone off the deep end. Oh, but I saved the best for last."

"And what's that?" Garth asked.

"Apparently his mother has a black eye and a broken arm. She says she ran into a door, but one of the neighbors said he heard Nick arguing with her. Insulting her. Blaming her for ruining his life and keeping him from the one woman he ever loved."

"Nick never loved anyone. He's a sociopath." Garth growled. "And why didn't the neighbor call the cops? There's an open arrest warrant for him."

"They did, but by the time the police got there, he was gone again," Thad said. "Bottom line, he's dangerous. Sorry, Sandra, but like I said, we got your back."

Garth reached for Sandra's hand. "He speaks for all of us."

"Why?" she whispered.

"Cuz Nick Benedetto's an asshole," Thad replied.

Garth laughed. "Mind your manners. Keep me posted. We'll be there in about an hour."

"Will do. Oh, and since you're headed to town, Old Man Watson asked you to stop by the trophy shop. Said he had something he needed to talk to you about."

"I'm on vacation."

Thad chuckled. "Didn't sound like he wanted to discuss engraving, but I expect it'll keep."

Garth's expression became guarded. "I'll check in with him," he told Thad, and disconnected. "You okay?" he asked Sandra.

No. She wanted to go anywhere but Edgarville, where everyone would be talking about her, watching her. With her mother's latest setback, Sandra would never have a life of her own, never be able to leave Edgarville.

Garth shot her a glance "Wasn't I telling you that you have more friends than you think?"

"He's your brother," Sandra replied, "and he thinks we're dating. He's not protecting me, he's backing up your interests."

"Not going to tell you why I don't believe that's true, but so long as you know he's there for you, that's what's important right now."

"No one's ever done that before," she said meekly. "I'm not sure what to say. What to do."

Garth faced her in the car. "No one?"

She shook her head.

"But your dad… your mom…"

She shook her head again. "My dad tried. The night he died, he pointed out to my mother how no one else was stepping up to the plate before they left to continue their argument out of earshot. Garth, people who try to help me have a tendency to get hurt."

Garth pulled to the side of the road and shifted into park. He turned toward Sandra and took her in his arms. Reflexively, she returned the hug. He felt good. Safe. Sandra drew a deep breath, inhaling the scent of him. Her heart ached when she considered this might be temporary.

She pulled away.

Garth watched her, too closely. "I won't let Nick hurt you. And you heard Thad. He's there for you, too."

If she needed protection from Nick, she apparently had two Benson brothers for the price of one, and they could be pretty intimidating. Could they keep her safe, or would they get hurt in the process? With luck, she wouldn't need them. "One day at a time."

"And you'll stay with me until we get this whole Nick situation ironed out?"

The fluttering in her belly won out. More nights in Garth's bed trumped common sense. "Okay."

Sandra had the unwelcome thought this was how her mother felt when her father came home after a week driving his truck across the country. Desire? Obsession?

Or was this what love felt like?

~ ~ ~

Mr. Watson's hand had grown less steady with age and since Garth was in charge of the etching at the cemetery, it was a natural progression to subcontract for the engraving at the trophy shop. Mr. Watson had offered Garth a partnership, and for the past five years, Garth had drawn a good income from his share of the business.

Was Mr. Watson calling it quits?

Garth turned to Sandra. "Does it bother you that I work in the cemetery?"

Sandra laughed. "Where did that come from?"

He shrugged. "There are people who view it as a creepy profession."

"Headstones? You guys don't do the burials, do you? Don't you engrave the plaques I see around town?" She smiled and patted his leg. "No, I never thought of your job as creepy, if that's what you're asking. Your sister, on the other hand," She looked away and her smile faded. "I never meant to hurt her, never meant for people to make fun of her." Sandra rolled her eyes. "And now I'm the crazy one." She rested her hand on his leg once more. "She's not crazy. That's not what I meant."

"You need to find a better way to express your misgivings. I saw your father's spirit, too, you know, and I don't think it's crazy. Bizarre, yes. Unsettling, definitely."

Her voice softened. "Have you seen ghosts before?"

He shook his head. "No."

"Why now?" she said, half to herself. "And why is he following me?"

"Apparently he wanted you to find the journal, to know the truth. He opened it to the pages he wanted you to read. You think you'll translate the rest of her journal?"

Sandra closed her eyes and leaned against the headrest. "I don't know. I still feel guilty about invading her privacy. Kind of."

He exited the highway, and as they neared town, Sandra stiffened beside him. Garth took her hand once more. "It's going to be okay."

"If anything happens to you because of me," she whispered.

"It wouldn't be your fault." He glanced at her. "I'm here because I want to be, not because you asked me to be. Nothing's going to happen to me, and I want to make sure the same holds true for you."

Too soon, they arrived at the hospital. When he'd parked, Sandra didn't get out of his truck immediately. She stared at the entrance as if it was the gate to hell, and yet he knew she was anxious to check on her mother.

Garth jumped out of the truck, walked around and opened her door. He extended a hand and she pressed her lips into a forced smile.

"I should have stayed with her," she said.

"After what Nick said to you? No. You're smarter to stay out of his way," he said. "Besides, you stayed with her after the accident. You are not remiss."

Sandra took his hand, stepping down from the truck. "You don't have to go in with me."

"Maybe you didn't notice the part where I told you you're stuck with me. At least for the short term."

"I want to talk to her alone."

Garth led her to the entrance. "I'll wait outside the room."

"Garth…" As the automatic doors whooshed open, she pulled her hand out of his. Sandra turned to him, rose on her toes and pressed a kiss to his lips. "Thank you."

He nodded, but the strain had returned, the creases in her forehead, the lines at the corners of her eyes. For a couple of days, he'd made those lines disappear. At the cabin, she'd glowed like a well-satisfied woman, and he felt a stab of pride that he'd been able to put a smile on her face during a difficult time. Garth had to trust they'd get through the latest trial together, and Sandra would revert to the laughing, teasing woman he knew.

They rode the elevator to Mrs. Meyer's room and outside the door, Sandra hesitated. She looped one arm through Garth's and held on with her other hand.

"I've got you," he said, and led her in.

The nurse taking her mother's blood pressure looked up and smiled. "She's doing well, today, but we've decided to keep her an extra day as a precaution. Your mother had a rough night last night."

Sandra let go of Garth and approached the bed. "Mama?"

Her mother reached up with her left hand. The right side of her face drooped. She tried to speak, but it came out as a groan. Sandra took her mother's hand and sat on the side of the bed.

"I'm here now," Sandra said.

Again her mother groaned, one eye finding Garth. Her other eye didn't track. Not a good sign. Mrs. Meyer pulled her hand free and pointed to Garth.

"I'll take care of her," he told Mrs. Meyer.

She closed her eyes and relaxed.

Sandra looked at Garth. His cue to leave.

"I'll wait in the lounge across the hall," he told Sandra.

Against his better judgment, Garth left the two of them alone and found a seat in the lounge. All through the years, he'd seen Sandra give the world a brave face at the coffee shop. He liked to believe he'd helped Sandra forget about her responsibilities on the tough days, teasing her out of a funk. She rarely let on that she was depressed or overburdened. How much of a life had she had, working at the café and taking care of her mother? No wonder she talked about moving to Paris, or Rome, away from her responsibilities. Coping mechanism? Garth knew how much moving out of her mother's house meant to Sandra. From what Sandra had learned from the diary, he'd bet she'd want to stay close. She wouldn't leave her mother.

With time to waste, he took out his phone and called Mr. Watson.

"Garth, I thought you might stop in," Mr. Watson said.

"I just got back to town. Thad said you were looking for me."

"I'd like to talk to you when you have time. Eloise wants to know if you'd stop over for dinner tonight."

Garth glanced at the room across the hall. "I'm kind of tied up this week. Still technically on vacation. What's going on?"

"I figured it's time to hang up my shingle. My wife has been diagnosed with cancer, and I'd like to spend my days with her instead of lumbering around this old shop. I thought you might like to buy my half, unless you want to cash out."

"I'm sorry to hear about your wife," Garth said. Watson's was the only trophy-slash-sign shop in town, the reason it had been such a profitable investment for Garth. Mrs. Watson had always handled the business side of things. "Any suggestions for a good bookkeeper?"

Mr. Watson chuckled. "I hear you been seeing that Meyer girl. She's got a good head on her shoulders, you know. Sounds like it would be a good fit, not that I'm trying to steal her away from Darrell and the café. He says she's been running things over there for him like clockwork."

"Tell you what, I'll swing by first chance I get and we'll figure out what to do," Garth said.

"You do that. And Garth, that Sandra Meyer? She's a sweet girl. I'm glad you two finally got together."

Garth raised his eyebrows. "I'll be in touch." He disconnected the call and trained his attention on Mrs. Meyer's room. Sandra did the books for Darrell at the café. Would she want to be his bookkeeper at the trophy store? He knew how much she loved working for Darrell. Would she do both?

What would his father say when Garth told him he'd be taking over the trophy shop? Garth chortled. That was easy. His father would slap him on the back and congratulate him.

And then he remembered what Sandra had said in the car. No one had ever had her back. No one had encouraged her, and yet she'd thrived. She was respected around town, whether she knew it or not.

Mr. Watson's praise supported that. Garth wanted to make sure she knew it.

~ ~ ~

Sandra had seen her mother through various health struggles through the years, but nothing like this.

The guilt from leaving when her mother was in the hospital lay heavy on Sandra's shoulders. Instead of running off and having a "vacation" with Garth, she should have stayed. Her mother needed her, and Nick be damned.

How would they be able to afford a nursing home? The doctors had said her mother had a long road to recovery, and that road wasn't well-paved with her mother's other physical limitations.

"I know it's difficult for you to speak," Sandra said slowly when the nurse left the room. She took her mother's good hand. "Blink to say yes, if you understand me. If you want me to repeat myself, squeeze my hand."

Her mother blinked.

"Did you know my father was the one haunting the duplex?"

"Nnnnnnnn," her mother moaned.

"No?"

Her mother blinked.

Tears welled in Sandra's eyes. "He showed me where to find your diary." Her throat clogged with emotion. "He showed me what pages to read."

"Nnnnnn," her mother tried again.

Sandra smiled. "Too late. I already did. You should have told me. All of it."

Again her mother tried to speak, and again the words wouldn't come. The beeping of her heart monitor came faster.

"It's okay," Sandra soothed. "You aren't supposed to get excited, but I wanted you to know it's okay. You told me he was jealous, and I didn't understand if it was justified or not." A tear slid down her face. "You know how people will talk, and there was that thing he said the night… the night…" Sandra shuddered.

Her mother blinked. *I understand.*

Sandra nodded. "I read how you were afraid to be a mom. Afraid to screw up. Didn't know what you were doing." She squeezed her mother's hand. "I wish I'd known sooner."

Her mother looked away, a tear sliding down her cheek.

"I don't know why I'm seeing Daddy now, after all this time." Sandra bowed her head. "But I want you to know I won't leave you. We'll see this through. Like all the other times."

"Gahhhhhh."

Sandra scowled, frustrated she couldn't understand what her mother wanted to say. "When you get better, will you help me decipher the rest of your diary? It's time we got to know each other better."

Chapter 24

AS SHE WALKED OUT OF her mother's hospital room, Sandra stopped short. She'd forgotten Garth was waiting for her in the lounge. Her own personal bodyguard, a blessing and a curse.

She needed time to herself, time to think through things. Time to figure out where she was going to find the money for a nursing home.

"You ready for dinner?" Garth asked, meeting her at the elevators.

She was ready to run screaming down the hall. That, or bury her head in Garth's chest and forget about everything else except the way he made her feel. She ignored both options, smiled and simply answered, "yes."

"How'd it go?" he asked. "Did they tell you when they'll release her?"

Sandra wrapped her arms around her head. Too many questions. Too many decisions. Information overload.

"Hey," he said, stepping in front of her. "It's okay. I'm here for you."

Which meant more to her than he'd ever know, and yet she didn't know what to do with that information. No one had ever "been there for her." How was she supposed to act? What was she supposed to do?

Nick had been a threat before, and he was making it clear he was a threat now. Sandra couldn't handle any more people being hurt on her behalf.

The elevator doors opened and they stepped inside. Garth watched her too closely, as if he thought she'd explode. She just might. The doors closed and Garth took her in his arms. He felt so good, so safe, and yet she was so overwrought she couldn't hug him back.

So many things to think about.

Mrs. Benedetto has a black eye.

The elevator doors opened on the ground floor and Sandra hesitated. Would Nick be out there? Waiting for her?

She took a deep breath and stepped off the elevator, determined to return to a semblance of normalcy. She was back in her prison, back in a town she'd never escape. As much as she hated it, Edgarville was familiar. She knew her way around. Only one thing had changed. Garth.

He insisted on taking care of her, but if she let him, she'd lose her own identity, lose control of her life. No man wanted to take care of someone else's mother. Sandra was no longer a mystery to him, unobtainable. How long before he grew tired of her? She couldn't depend on him to stick around. She had too much baggage to carry.

They walked out to his truck and when she crawled inside, she closed her eyes, determined to take back her life.

"I don't think I have anything in the fridge. I cleaned it out figuring we'd be gone all week," Garth said as he drove out of the hospital parking lot. "We could order a pizza."

"That's fine," she said, staring out the window.

Tomorrow, after they transferred her mother to the rehab facility, Sandra would go to the Social Security office and apply for disability benefits for her mother. She'd been turned down before because her mother insisted on returning to work—and made too much money to qualify. Her mother had returned to work to pay the hospital bills. It was a vicious cycle, but this time, her mother wouldn't be able to go about her business. Once, Sandra had suggested they sell the house to pay the bills, but her mother had pooh-poohed her, telling her it was all under control.

After the stroke, it might be months before her mother would be able to tell Sandra how she managed to keep things under control. Sandra would have to improvise.

"You're a million miles away," Garth said.

If only. "They said the doctor would probably sign off on her release by two o'clock tomorrow. They're moving her to a nursing home, maybe permanently. I don't know how I'm going to pay for a nursing home." She hadn't meant to tell him, but apparently her filters for what to say and what to keep to herself were turned off.

He didn't respond immediately, and what did she expect him to say? Did she think he knew about buried treasure in the cemetery and she could go help herself? Better to apologize for opening her mouth. "I shouldn't have said anything."

"No, I might have an idea for you, but I'm not sure how you'd feel about it."

"Right now? I'm desperate."

He turned the corner and, two minutes later, he parked beside her car inside his garage.

Garth handed her the house keys. "I'll get the suitcases and meet you inside."

Sandra walked up the back steps and stopped when she heard a low growl from the bushes. The cat. She leaned over the railing to locate it.

"Didn't anybody feed you while he was gone?" she asked the cat.

It stepped out of the bushes, walked up the steps and wound around Sandra's legs. It *must* be starving if it was being nice to her.

"I'll bring you some munchies," she told it while she unlocked the door.

Garth kept the saucer he used beside the bag of food on the counter inside the door. Sandra poured out a handful of food. Garth brought the suitcases in and Sandra passed him in the doorway, taking the saucer to the porch. When she set it down, the cat purred and ate as if it was starving to death. Sandra stroked the matted fur along its back, reminded once again the cat was a stray, but even strays had to trust people sometimes.

She could trust Garth.

"So you said you had an idea," she said when she walked inside.

Garth disconnected his cell phone. "Pizza will be here shortly."

She rolled her hands to get him to talk. If he knew a way to pay for healthcare that she didn't, she wanted to know.

"Mr. Watson suggested it," Garth began.

"Old Mr. Watson from the trophy store?"

Garth nodded. "He's retiring. That's why he wanted to talk to me."

Right. Because Garth picked up extra work there in addition to the engravings he did at the cemetery. "Is that going to put a strain on you financially?" she asked.

"Actually, it will probably improve my financial outlook. You see, I'm partners with Mr. Watson. He's selling the rest of the business to me. Mrs. Watson has cancer and he wants to take the time off to spend with her. Since she's his bookkeeper, he suggested you might like to take over for her, but I didn't want to take you away from Darrell and the café. If you kept the two jobs…"

Her ears rang and her vision clouded. Whatever Garth said after that was enveloped in the fog inside her head. "You're taking over the trophy shop?" she repeated.

"Yes."

She blinked to restore her vision, her chest heavy, but she was aware Garth had stopped talking. His brows were drawn together. He looked confused. Hell, she was confused, too. What had made her think…?

"Sandra?"

She laughed and dropped into a chair beside the kitchen table. "I don't know why I thought things would be different. I had no reason to. I know how tied you are to Edgarville. You've always said you were. I just thought…" she had trouble catching her breath. With a hand to her chest she continued. "After what's happened between us, after our trip to Galena…" And why had she imagined they might escape together? Garth didn't want to escape. She was suffocating in this town and Garth was assuring his future here. "My head must be made of straw." When had he crept into her plans to get away from this town? "Haven't I been telling you I don't want your help? And this is why."

"I'm not following."

She was near to hysteria, and she didn't care. "I don't want to stay here, in Edgarville. You know that. I want to get as far away as I can and leave all the bad memories behind. Memories like what happened with Nick the night of the accident. The way he punished me after my father threw him out. Losing my father. Nursing my mother." A nervous laugh escaped. "Not that I can go anywhere anyhow. I'll never be able to leave with my mother the way she is. Why not take two jobs? It isn't as if I have any kind of a life anyway. I'll never be able to leave."

Garth rested his hands on her arms and she shook them off, taking a step backward. "I should never have agreed to let you help me, never allowed myself to get carried away. I'm going home. By myself."

He shook his head. "Not while Nick is still slinking around."

The mention of Nick's name sent a chill down her spine. No, she wouldn't let Nick find her alone. "Fine," she said, her voice low. "But I'm sleeping in the other bedroom." Even as she said it, her heart tore in half. That wasn't what she wanted, not even close. She wanted Garth to wrap his arms around her and tell her everything was going to be all right, even if she knew better. She wanted to lose herself in the way he made her feel, forget about the world for a while in his embrace, but that would be giving into the fantasy world she'd created when she wasn't paying attention. She was used to dealing with cold, hard reality. Time to get her head out of the clouds.

"If that's what you want."

She was one of Garth's strays, but she wasn't a helpless cat. She was a strong woman, and she'd been taking care of things all of her adult life. Nothing had changed.

As much as she hoped it might, nothing had changed.

~ ~ ~

Garth heard Sandra tiptoeing around at five a.m. He followed her downstairs but she'd already slipped out the door. He found a note on the kitchen table—*Went to work.*

Darrell would be there. She wouldn't be alone. He'd call Micah and make sure the police kept an eye on her, as well.

He didn't know what else to do.

She'd talked about moving out of Edgarville for as long as he'd known her, but she'd never leave her mother. After all these years of caring for Phyllis, she wouldn't abandon her now, so why was she so upset he was taking over the trophy store? The store accounted for a big chunk of his income, and it gave him something other than the family business to fall back on, the family business that would go to Thad when their father retired.

Was it Garth's fault Sandra had created a fantasy life he knew nothing about? A life that took them God knows where? Their families were in Edgarville. Their lives.

Garth had a fantasy, too. One where Sandra stayed in Edgarville, with him. She'd come to life again when they'd gone to Galena, away from the everyday problems and responsibilities. Even with a ghost accompanying them, she'd been more relaxed and carefree than he could remember seeing her since this whole debacle started. Every mile they'd traveled closer to home, he'd seen the muscles tighten, the tension return.

He couldn't hold her back.

Maybe it was his fault. He was the one who kept telling her he'd be there for her, he'd protect her. What was she supposed to think?

She wasn't the only one who was confused.

Garth stormed up the stairs and went back to bed. He closed his eyes, punched his pillow which refused to cradle his head properly, and tossed and turned for half an hour before he gave up. Might as well shower and go to the monument shop. He'd have to tell his dad about the Watsons and let him know he'd be working out of the trophy shop instead of the monument shop before long.

His mother was at her desk when he showed up for work a few minutes after eight.

"I wasn't expecting to see you," she said. "Everything okay at the cabin?"

"Everything's fine," he said.

She pushed away from the desk and rose to stop him before he could disappear into the shop behind the showroom. "And Sandra?" she asked.

"Her mother will be moved to a rehab facility today."

"I'm sure that's for the best."

The front door opened and Amy walked in. She stopped when she saw him. Garth greeted her and pushed through the door into the workshop. With any luck, there would be a stone to mount.

Amy followed him and closed the door behind her. She didn't say anything, but waited for him to acknowledge her.

"What?" he said.

She handed him the cup in her hand, one from Morning Joe. "Thought you might like some coffee."

"You didn't know I'd be here. That's yours."

"But I think you need it more than I do."

She pushed the coffee forward again and he took it from her. "Thanks."

Amy leaned against the wall and crossed one foot over the other.

"What?" he asked again.

"You broke Sandra."

He chuffed. "She was already broken."

"Yeah, but we figured if anybody could fix her, it'd be you."

Garth took a drink of the coffee. "She needs more help than I'm qualified to give her."

"And you?"

He glared at her. "What about me?"

"I don't remember the last time I saw you so surly. Want to talk about it?"

Garth set his coffee cup down, not about to discuss his love life with his little sister. "You're the one who started this, remember? All for show to keep Nick off her back. Speaking of which, what'd he do to you while I was gone? Do I have to break his neck?"

"Nick's an entirely different subject," she told him, crossing her arms. "And I didn't start anything, I merely gave the two of you a reason to stop circling each other and get on with it."

"Nick is the subject. He's in the middle of all of this. Thad said he gave you a hard time." He shook a finger at her. "I told you what he did to Sandra. He's unstable."

"And you don't think my other troglodyte brothers stepped up in your absence?"

Garth drew a breath. Thad and Brian, and now Amy's fiancé Kevin, would protect Amy. "Sandra doesn't have anybody," he said quietly.

"She has you," Amy reminded him.

"She doesn't want me."

"You sure about that?"

Garth turned away. "She doesn't know how to accept help."

Amy laid a hand on his arm. "Seems like she has an awful lot going on right now. I heard her mother's in bad shape. Give her time."

"I get that." He faced Amy. "Tell me what Nick said to you. How unhinged is he?"

"He said the two of you did something to him, but he isn't sure what. He rambled on about magic and demons and stepping one foot into hell. He went back and forth about how you must have knocked him out, and then how Sandra must be a witch and cast a spell on him, which he equated to me teaching her the dark arts." She chuffed. "Unhinged? He's certifiable."

"Which means Sandra is definitely in danger." And what was he supposed to do about it? Wait until Nick made his move?

Garth yanked open the shop door.

"Where are you going?" Amy called after him.

Garth stopped, turned, and held out his arms. "I have to do something." He wasn't sure what, but even if it meant pissing Sandra off further, he couldn't stand by and wait for Nick to hurt her again.

Chapter 25

THE WHOLE TOWN HAD STOPPED into the café this morning, or at least it seemed that way to Sandra. In spite of Darrell telling her she should go home and enjoy the rest of her vacation, he didn't argue when Vicki wasn't able to keep up with the increase in traffic. The downside was everyone wanted to stop and chat, to ask about Sandra's mother, to ask about her relationship with Garth. As if her personal life was suddenly a matter of public record.

It wasn't.

Sandra needed routine. Normalcy. The café had come to represent that in her life. How could Garth think she'd even consider walking out on Darrell? Oh, wait. He'd told her she could add one more job to her already overburdened life.

By midmorning, the breakfast crowd thinned. Sandra left Vicki to man the register and took a cloth to the dining room to clean tables. Work. Something to do with herself other than think about her mother. Or Garth. Or Nick. Or her unpaid credit cards.

A tap on her shoulder startled her. Sandra straightened and turned to face…

Mrs. Benedetto.

Sandra's eyes grew wide, but she tried to control her reaction to the bruise under Mrs. Benedetto's eye and the cast on her arm. *And they were blaming Nick for this?*

"Sandra." Mrs. Benedetto's gravelly voice masked her emotions. "Can't you tell Nicky you're sorry? Make up with him? We all know this thing with you and Garth is only to make Nick jealous."

Did she believe that? Sandra couldn't stop her mouth from gaping. Manners be damned, she was going to point out how wrong Mrs. Benedetto was.

"Did he do this to you?" Sandra asked.

"He was angry. I tried to calm him. He didn't mean it."

Sandra urged Nick's mother to a chair at the table she'd been cleaning. "He has no impulse control. Whether he meant it or not, it is never okay to hurt another human being, especially when they are trying to help you. You can't defend him." She swallowed the memories of Nick's fists pummeling her. "He told me he was sorry for trying to hurt me once, and I believed him. He asked me to meet him so he could make it up to me, and you know what he did? He beat me to within an inch of my life. Without the intervention of a friend, he very likely would have killed me." She opened a palm. "Look what he's done to you. He needs help, Mrs. Benedetto, and the Army didn't work."

"No, you're wrong about Nick…" but her words held no conviction.

"If you haven't already done so, you should file charges against him."

"But he's my son. I couldn't do that."

Sandra rested her hand on Mrs. Benedetto's good arm. "He needs help. I should have filed charges all those years ago, but I didn't. My father had just died, my mother was in and out of the hospital and rehab. I was alone and I didn't know any better."

"You're lying. Nicky would never hurt you. He loves you. He told me so. I never saw any bruises on you."

Sandra straightened. "I was embarrassed and ashamed. The only person who knew how badly Nick had beaten me was my best friend."

Mrs. Benedetto pursed her lips. "That Calhoun girl."

A shiver ran down Sandra's spine. "What do you know about Tammy Calhoun?"

"Only that she came over threatening my Nicky. I think she wanted him all to herself. She wasn't a good friend to you, trying to steal your boyfriend."

Another of Mrs. Benedetto's delusions? Tammy had hated Nick. "What makes you think she wanted him to be her boyfriend?"

Mrs. Benedetto shrugged. Now she was playing coy? "Boys will be boys, I suppose."

"What are you talking about?"

"He said he'd do the same to her that he did to you if he ever found her under the bleachers alone." She tsked. "Not that I'm condoning the kinds of things teenagers do under the bleachers. I did hope he'd limit his adventures."

Sandra quaked. She pushed away from the table and rose to her feet. "And did he find her under the bleachers?"

Again Mrs. Benedetto shrugged. "How would I know? I only know that when I asked him about her, he said she wouldn't be bothering him again. I guess he was right. I haven't seen her since."

Sandra measured her words. "You do know Tammy Calhoun died, don't you?"

Mrs. Benedetto rose to her feet, clutching her purse tightly to her chest. "What are you implying?"

"Did he kill her?"

With a huff, Mrs. Benedetto lifted her chin and walked out of the café, leaving Sandra chilled to the bone.

The last of the breakfast customers walked out with Mrs. Benedetto and Sandra moved to the next table to wipe it down. She closed her eyes, concentrating on the smooth, easy strokes to calm herself.

She walked behind the counter, inventoried the supplies and swept the floor. After she restocked, she'd go to the office and update the order inventory and balance the ledger. Avoid the customers for a while. She went to the walk-in cooler to refill the creamers in the holding bin behind the counter and smiled as she passed Darrell.

"How you holding up?" he asked, and then pointed a finger at her. "And you should still be on vacation."

"Are you complaining again?"

He wrapped a brotherly arm across her shoulders. "Never. Just looking out for you."

She gave him a smile. "I'm fine."

He undid his apron and hung it on a hook on the prep table. "I'm going to run the deposit over to the bank. Be right back."

"'Kay," Sandra replied.

She carried individual cartons of milk and juice to the cooler behind the counter and checked the coffee pot.

Vicki stood outside the front door, taking a smoke break and waved when she saw Sandra behind the counter. She opened the door and leaned in. "Hey, I'm out of smokes. I'm going to run down to the drugstore and buy a pack while there's a break in the action."

Sandra waved to her and went to the storeroom for boxes of salt and ketchup to prep for lunch.

~ ~ ~

The trees over the sidewalk had leafed out while Garth hadn't been paying attention. A cool breeze brought gooseflesh to the bare skin beneath his rolled up sleeves, although in the direct sunlight, he'd been too warm.

Along the four blocks to the café, Garth practiced what he'd say to Sandra when he saw her. Scolding her for running off on her own wasn't a smart tack. Expressing his concern had already yielded zero results. He figured playing it casual was his best move. He was going to the café for his usual cup of coffee, but instead of ordering a to-go cup, he'd park himself at a table and make himself at home, whether she liked it or not. Hopefully, she wouldn't mind. Much.

He shook his head. She'd mind, even if she didn't say anything.

A car honked behind him and Garth turned to look. Micah Lynch, in his squad car. He pulled up beside Garth, stopped and Micah punched the gear shift noisily into park before he got out of the car and leaned over the roof.

"Where you headed?"

"To the café for a cup of coffee."

"Where's Sandra?" Micah asked.

"At the café."

"At least Darrell should be there."

Which Garth translated to mean Micah agreed Sandra shouldn't be alone. "What's up?"

"I ran into Mrs. Benedetto a couple of minutes ago. She asked if she could file charges against Sandra for refusing to cooperate with her."

Garth cast a nervous glance up the block. Was Nick's mother helping Nick terrorize Sandra?

"She also asked me about Tammy Calhoun," Micah said, lowering his voice. "How she died, where they found her."

Garth took a step toward the car. "Because…?"

Micah shrugged. "I don't know, but she was rattled when I told her where we found Tammy's body. Set my spidey senses on alert. I asked her where Nick was. Her answer? How should I know? She knows I have a warrant with his name on it. She told me I should stop picking on him, that he couldn't have been the one who'd broken into Sandra's place."

That wasn't a good sign. "Gotta get to the café," Garth said.

"I'll give you a ride."

Two more blocks, but suddenly Garth was in a hurry.

"Darrell's there," Micah said again when Garth slipped into the passenger seat of the squad car. "And Vicki. Got my coffee from her this morning. I'm sure Sandra's fine."

Nick wasn't the type to be deterred if he had something in mind.

Micah stopped in front of the café and Garth jumped out. His skin tingled with the sense something was wrong. The blinds on the door were drawn and the sign was turned to closed.

"I'm going around back," he called to Micah, who was on his radio, watching over the top of the car again.

Before Garth reached the corner of the building, Darrell walked toward him on the sidewalk. "Closed?" Garth asked.

"No, taking the deposit to the bank. The girls should be inside…" Darrell stopped when he saw the drawn blinds, the closed sign. "That's not right."

And then Vicki walked out of the drug store. She glanced from Garth to Darrell. "What's up?"

"I thought you were with Sandra," Darrell said.

"Stepped out to buy a pack of smokes. I was only gone a minute." And then she saw the sign. "Why's the café closed?"

Garth darted to the back door. She was in there alone. Scratch that. He'd bet his share of the trophy store Nick was in there with her.

Chapter 26

THE DINING ROOM SEEMED DARKER when Sandra came out to refill the salt shakers on the tables. The blinds on the door were closed.

"Vicki?"

"Try again."

Sandra gasped and took a step backward, but Nick blocked the way she'd come. Instead of the come-hither look he used to brag he'd perfected, his eyes showed more white than brown. He had several days' growth of beard covering his chin, and strangest of all, he was wearing blue jeans and a tee beneath a flannel shirt. She'd seen him in Army fatigues, but outside of that, his uniform tended toward black jeans, white t-shirts and black leather jackets like the old James Dean poster in his high school locker.

Sandra kept a table between them, well-acquainted with what could happen if she got too close.

"Whatever you did to me, you need to undo it," he said, his voice low and menacing.

"I didn't do anything to you."

He placed his hands on the table and feinted to one side. Sandra reacted the opposite direction and he grinned. He changed direction, and she followed suit.

"Never woulda believed you and Garth were really a couple if I hadn't seen it with my own eyes."

He stood tall. "You blew your chance. Not taking you back now."

Her heart pounded. "Am I supposed to be sorry about that?"

He feinted toward her again and again she reacted.

"Funny thing, they trained me to kill in the Army. They didn't realize I already knew how."

Sandra shuddered.

"If I apologize for running your father off the road, will you undo what you did?"

A burst of spots dotted Sandra's vision. "You did what?"

"Oh, you didn't know that? Forget I mentioned it. Maybe you put the spell on me for killing Tammy, but that was on her. She's the one who brought the gun. Didn't take much to get it away from her, and when I put it back in her hand, they figured she'd offed herself."

Sandra's legs turned to jelly. Her worst fears confirmed. But what was he talking about? Spell?

"I should have figured it out when Crazy Amy offered to help you. Did she make you a witch, too?"

He darted around the corner of the table and Sandra mirrored his move.

"So what gave me away?" she asked, hoping he'd give her something more, something she could use to stall him until Darrell and Vicki got back.

"I have to admit, I wasn't sure what happened at first. And then when your meathead boyfriend showed up, I thought he'd clocked me and I'd imagined being sucked into that place." A flash of fear showed in his eyes. "Like being underwater, except I could breathe."

He brushed at his arms and took a step back. "People clawing at me." He shouted then. "What did you do to me?"

When he'd gone through the mirror? Sandra channeled what courage she had left. "When a woman tells you no, you need to stop."

Nick narrowed his eyes. "Yeah, your father said the same thing, but you didn't want me to stop then, either. You were trying to save face."

"No," she said firmly. "I didn't want you then and I don't want you now." She raised her arms in her best guess at what a witch might do in these circumstances. Nick was uncertain, unhinged, and her only chance at escaping whatever he had decided to do to her was to prey on his fears.

He backed off. "We could have had fun together." He shook his head. "Now I have no choice but to kill you." He shook his wrist and a knife slid into his hand. "Kill the witch, cancel the spell."

"It doesn't work that way." But her lungs wouldn't give her enough air. Her voice didn't carry any strength.

Sandra made a move toward the storeroom, toward the back door. Nick countered. He'd get there first. He angled toward her, daring Sandra to try and get past him. Behind him, the swinging door to the kitchen opened slowly.

Garth put a finger to his lips as he crept behind Nick.

"You got nowhere to run, Sandra. Time for you to pay for what you did to me," Nick said.

"I didn't do anything to you," she said, her confidence growing. If Garth was there, he probably wasn't alone. By now Darrell and Vicki should be back. Had they called the police? "If you leave now, you can get away before the police get here," she told him. "But if you kill me, they'll put you in jail."

"I'll be gone before they ever know I was here." He raised the knife and advanced toward her.

Garth twisted Nick's hand behind his back and the knife fell to the floor. Sandra winced at the sound of flesh hitting flesh, Garth's fist connecting with Nick's jaw. Nick picked up a chair and brought it down over Garth's shoulder. Sandra went to one knee when the crunch of bones reverberated through her. She pushed to her feet and ran toward the front door to unlock it, but Nick was there first. He swiped at the blood running from his nose before he pinned her arms behind her back.

Garth rose to his feet slowly, holding his left shoulder. "Let her go," he said through clenched teeth. His face was twisted into a mask of pain.

Sandra struggled a moment before she realized Nick was trembling. He was afraid?

"So what," Nick whispered in her ear, nudging her hair with his broken nose. "You're one of them now? Raising the dead to do your dirty work? I'm not going to let you kill me, witch. Send your father back to his grave." He tightened his hold on her arms. "Now!" he shouted.

Her father. Nick had seen him, too. "Is he haunting you?" she asked. "When you look in the mirror, is he looking back at you?" She shook free and turned to face Nick. His skin had gone pale, his eyes wide with fear. Funny what a guilty conscience would do to a person. "What about Tammy? Is she haunting you, too?"

Nick crouched and retrieved his knife, brandishing it while Sandra took refuge beside Garth.

"It's your fault," Nick said again. "Once you're dead they'll leave me alone."

She shook her head. "No. It's nothing I've done. They've come for you."

Nick jabbed the knife toward them and Garth pushed Sandra behind him. Garth winced as he tried to raise his left arm, then took a wild swing with his right hand and connected with the side of Nick's head. Nick's arm circled blindly and the knife stuck in Garth's left arm. Garth growled and landed another punch. And another. And another.

Sandra cried out and crawled under a table, each thud reminding her of the blows Nick had dealt her.

The front door crashed open. Dark blue pants. Micah Lynch's voice. "Police."

A tree trunk in blue denim dropping to the floor. Garth. Micah's pants beside him.

Another voice yelled, "Call an ambulance!"

"I told you not to go vigilante on me," Micah said.

Darrell, knelt beside the table, holding out a hand to Sandra. "She's bleeding." His voice sounded far away, like he was in a tunnel.

Nick had nuzzled her ear with his bloody nose. "Not my blood," she said. And then she closed her eyes and the world went away.

~ ~ ~

Garth watched helplessly as a policeman eased Sandra into a chair, her back to him.

"Is she okay?" Garth asked while the paramedic put his arm in a sling.

"Probably in shock," he replied. "But otherwise she seems to be in good shape."

Garth winced and grunted as the paramedic jostled him.

"Why can't I move my arm? Is it broken?"

"It's dislocated," the paramedic told him.

"What about this thing in my arm? Take it out," Garth growled, staring down the knife.

"Not until you get to the hospital, big guy. We don't want to cause additional damage." The paramedic stopped and checked Garth's eyes. "You hanging in there?"

"Other than feeling as if a slab of granite fell on me, yeah."

"We'll give you something for the pain."

Garth cast another glance at Sandra. She was cradling her head with her hands, elbows on the table. "You sure she's okay?" he asked again.

She turned her head to look at him, streaks of blood dark in her blonde hair, and nodded. The gesture wasn't much, but it was enough. Her voice was soft and he had to strain to hear her. "I'm so sorry, Garth."

He reached out with his right hand—more pain. His hand was wrapped in gauze. When had they done that? A second paramedic set the cot beside Garth and the two paramedics raised him enough to get the cot beneath him. A fresh spear of pain shot through his dislocated shoulder. Garth clenched as they wheeled him outside.

"Ready for those painkillers anytime," he said.

"Got you covered," the paramedic told him.

Garth opened his eyes. They'd attached an IV when he wasn't paying attention. Or had he passed out? Didn't matter. A haze settled around him, reducing the pain to a throb and a sting.

He tried to speak, but his speech was slurred. "You sure Sandra's okay?"

Micah opened the ambulance door. "Just a little shaken up. Lucky for her you don't follow instructions very well."

"Shouldn't have let her go to work," Garth mumbled, struggling to hold onto consciousness.

Micah laughed. "You think you could have stopped her?"

Garth smiled. He was well acquainted with her stubbornness and determination. "Not likely."

The paramedics lifted the gurney into the ambulance and hopped in beside him.

"I'm sure she'll be by to see you shortly," Micah said. He closed the doors and followed it up with two taps.

"Can't you guys pop my shoulder back into place?" Garth asked.

"The doctors would rather you wait until you get to the hospital. It's a short ride." The paramedic hovering over him checked the IV bag. "It sounds from your speech like the meds are doing the job. Are you still in pain?"

Garth scowled. "Is my shoulder still dislocated? Do I still have a knife sticking out of my arm?"

The second paramedic laughed. "Fair point."

"We'll be at the hospital in a minute," paramedic one told him. "You probably won't even have to stay once they fix you up. With a little luck, a quick pop, a few stitches and you'll be good as new."

Good as new. "Hah." At least Sandra would be safe now. "And if I'm not lucky?"

"Depends on if there's a break or other damage. There's a chance you'd need surgery."

"What about Nick?" he asked his captors.

The two exchanged a look. "My guess is he's likely to be in the hospital a while," paramedic one said.

"Remind me not to get on your bad side," paramedic two added.

Garth turned his head. He hadn't used his fists in a long time, not since the last time he'd hit Nick. He wasn't proud of what he'd done, but he'd do it again to save Sandra.

Chapter 27

SANDRA WALKED INTO THE EMERGENCY room and stopped short. What if they didn't let her see Garth?

Did she want to see Garth?

The sounds continued to echo in her ears, the thud of fists, the cracking of bones—as fresh today as they'd been all those years ago. She flinched with the impact each sound made and turned to walk out. She couldn't do this.

She ran straight into Amy.

Amy took her by the arms. "Sandra, are you okay? What happened?"

When Sandra didn't respond, Amy pulled her into a hug.

Sandra stepped out of Amy's embrace and cleared her throat. "I'm pretty sure I heard them say they'd be able to send Garth home after they fixed him up."

Amy pulled her over to a chair in the waiting room. "The hospital called to tell us he was here, and then Kevin called to tell me the newspaper had a lead on a knife fight at the café." She shuddered. "The nurse told me I had to wait before I could see Garth. How bad is he hurt?"

Again, Sandra flinched. Garth had gone into full-on protector mode, but the memory of flying fists, the thuds as those fists connected…

Amy rested her hand on Sandra's arm. "You're scaring me."

"Nick pulled a knife. Garth hit him and knocked it loose and then Nick hit him with a chair. Nick got the knife back. He kept hitting…" Her breath froze. She took hold of Amy's arms and stared at her. "He just kept hitting."

"Garth?" Amy gathered Sandra into her arms again. "He would never hurt you. Ever. Garth stepped in to protect you. You know that, right?"

"I know," Sandra said softly.

"Garth told me what Nick did to you, why you told him Nick cornered me in the stairwell in high school," Amy said. "I didn't know about his violent streak back then. Garth told me you were trying to protect me."

"It's the truth. You have to believe me."

Amy pulled away. "And then when I told you your grandmother died, you called me Crazy Amy. I thought you did it because you were jealous. I should have known I'd scared you with the epitaph, but kids are so clueless when they're in high school."

"I'm so sorry. I didn't know it would get so out of hand."

A nurse approached. "Miss Benson? I can take you to your brother now."

Amy stood and took Sandra's hand. "Want to come with me? I know you're worried, too."

Sandra wrapped her arms around herself. "I don't know if I can." She shot a quick glance at the nurse and lowered her voice. "He just kept hitting…"

"Can I have a minute?" Amy asked the nurse.

"Let me know when you're ready."

The nurse walked away and Amy sat beside Sandra once more.

"Are you afraid of Garth?" Amy asked.

"I've never seen him like that. The look on his face, like Nick that day…"

"Listen. My brothers are all rough and tumble. They shove each other around all the time. Heck, I shove them around, too, but none of them would ever lay a finger on a woman. Ever. I've watched them spar my whole life, and I've watched them hover over me like avenging angels." She shrugged. "Or troglodytes."

Sandra laughed at the characterization.

"My point is Garth would never do the same thing to you that Nick did. If he beat the hell of out Nick today, it was in defense of you, and I'm pretty sure Nick should have been able to defend himself." She rolled her eyes. "My brothers, the defenders of the defenseless. Not that you're defenseless, but there is that guy/girl thing, and muscle mass, and all of that."

A cell phone rang and both Sandra and Amy checked their purses.

"It's me," Sandra said before she answered the call. "Hello?"

"Hi, Sandra. This is Parvati at the hospital. We're getting ready to transport your mom. The Medicar should be here in a few minutes."

"Thanks. I'm here now. I'll stop up and see you."

Sandra disconnected and slipped the phone into her purse.

"So you want to go give him hell with me?" Amy asked.

Sandra laughed again. "Not right now. They're going to transport my mom. I should make sure she's settled at the rehab facility. I'll catch up with Garth when he gets home."

"How's your mom doing?"

"She's got a long road ahead of her. The doctors aren't optimistic."

"If you need anything…"

Tears streamed down Sandra's cheek. And why hadn't she liked Amy in high school? Oh yeah. Amy had everything Sandra didn't, including a scary extra sense. "Why are you being so nice to me?" Sandra choked out.

"Because my brother loves you, and because we all make stupid mistakes when we're frightened."

Sandra hugged Amy this time. "Thank you."

~ ~ ~

Sandra needed a shower. She'd been able to brush Nick's blood out of her hair, but she still felt dirty. And she needed a change of clothes. But she couldn't bring herself to leave her mother's side.

Learning what she had from the diary, Sandra understood so much more. She wasn't the only dysfunctional member of her family. Was that why her father had appeared in the mirror? He wanted to bring Sandra and her mother closer?

The room at the rehab facility was only slightly more homey than a regular hospital room. Her mother's vitals had been checked, her belongings had been stored, she'd been made comfortable. The only thing left was to begin her therapy, which was scheduled to start later this afternoon. The last of the rehab nurses left the room, leaving Sandra alone with her mother.

Her mother clasped Sandra's hand.

"Not a bad place," Sandra said. "And the people seem nice."

Her mother squeezed her hand, leaned forward and tried to speak. "Llllll…" she fell against her pillows with a sigh, half of her mouth turned down into a frown.

"They'll help you to learn to speak again," Sandra reassured her.

Her mother touched her heart and opened her palm toward Sandra.

"I think she's trying to say I love you," a nurse said behind her.

Yeah. Sandra got that. For the first time that she could remember. She swallowed down the lump in her throat and brushed at the tears stinging her eyes. "I love you, too," she whispered.

Her mother blinked. *I understand.*

"Would you like to take her for a walk? Get a look at the rest of the facility?" the nurse asked.

"Walk?" Sandra repeated.

"In her wheelchair," the nurse clarified. "There's a lovely waterfall in the atrium. The patients like that."

"'Ome," her mother said, pointing a shaky finger at Sandra.

"I'll go home," Sandra replied. "After I take you for a walk. I won't be back again until tomorrow, so you might as well take advantage of me while you can." She smiled, no longer crushed under the burden of caring for her mother. They had a lot of catching up to do.

The nurse helped position her mother in the wheelchair and tied a strap around her to hold her in place. "You can follow the signs to the atrium," she said.

"I'm not sure how we're going to manage," Sandra said as she pushed, "but we'll find a way. We always do."

Her mother reached over her shoulder to pat Sandra's hand.

Sandra wasn't sure what she should say, so she rambled on with what was in her head. "I'll move my stuff back home and let the real estate office know they can rent out the duplex again. Or try. Or not. Do you think Daddy will move on? I have to wonder if he wasn't trying to bring us closer together. If I'd known…" she stopped and sighed. "But you and I never talked much other than everyday stuff."

She followed the signs into a hexagonal room. Four of the walls were lined with windows overlooking a garden. The fifth wall was painted with a mural. The sixth wall was lined with mirrors to give the illusion the whole room looked outside. A waterfall trickled in the center of the room. "And this must be the atrium." Sandra wheeled her mother beside the waterfall, which was designed with rocks and crags. Pennies lined the pool at the bottom.

Her mother raised a hand and pointed to the mirrored wall with a shaky finger.

"No, you don't want to look at yourself. Not now."

Her mother shook her hand, insistently pointing to the mirror.

Sandra huffed and pushed her toward the wall. "You're going to get better. Remember that." She stopped when her father appeared, sending shivers across her skin like a nest of spiders. He smiled and blew a kiss. Sandra returned the smile. He directed his gaze to her mother and held out a hand. In the mirror, Sandra watched her mother extend her hand and rise from the chair.

"Mom…" Sandra turned to her mother, slumped in her chair, the functional half of her face turned up in a smile. Sandra checked the mirror once more. Her mother stepped into her father's embrace, and they both turned to Sandra and waved.

"Mom?"

"How are you ladies getting along?" The nurse who'd helped put her mother in the chair ran into the atrium and knelt in front of the wheelchair. "Phyllis?" She checked for a pulse and immediately pulled her phone from her hip. "Code blue in the atrium."

Sandra stood back as a team rushed into the atrium and tried to revive her mother, but they were too late. Her mother had already gone.

Her mother was finally whole again, at peace.

Chapter 28

SANDRA HAD HARDLY SPOKEN TO Garth since the day of the incident, the same day her mother had died, but she'd stayed at his house for the next three days—in the guest room—insistent on nursing him. He'd tried to tease her into his bed, to comfort her, but she was careful to keep her distance. Garth sensed an air of anticipation around her while she planned the funeral, as if she was biding her time. Without her mother to hold her back, she was free to move away, the way she'd always talked about. Would she go?

The whole town turned out for Phyllis Meyer's funeral. He shrugged inside his good suit and tugged at the collar. The sling supporting his shoulder fought back and the fit of his coat was no better than it had been a second ago.

Sandra greeted well-wishers beside the cremation niche after the graveside ceremony. Garth hung back, staying close in case she looked like she'd crumble, but Sandra maintained a brave face.

Amy approached Sandra and the two of them walked a few steps, heads together. Sandra looked up and met his watchful gaze. She put a hand over her mouth, said something more to Amy and gave Amy a hug before Amy shot him a look and walked away. What was that about?

Garth moved from his spot and approached Sandra. "I'll have the plaque for her tomorrow," he said. "How are you holding up?"

"She's at peace," she replied. "She went with my father. Somehow I don't think we'll be seeing him in any more mirrors."

"But I asked about you."

Sandra glanced around, at the people dispersing. She cupped Garth's elbow and led him toward the bench beside the niches. "You seem to be doing pretty well. Healing."

"Sandra…"

She held up a hand. "I know. You asked about me." She clasped her hands in her lap and stared at them while she fidgeted. "I'm going away, Garth. I need time to sort through everything. Now that Nick's in jail, I don't have to look over my shoulder anymore. You don't have to keep protecting me."

"And if I want to keep protecting you?"

She shook her head. "I let you push me around when I was in trouble, but I have to find my own way now. Everything's changed. Everything's different. I'm not sure what I should do. I need to find my way again."

"You should stay with me." He gave her a sheepish smile. "It isn't getting old yet."

She chuckled. "I've already told you, I'm not sleeping with you while you're hurt."

"You might recall I didn't need two arms our first night together."

She looked away. "Yeah, but sleeping with you only complicates things."

Then she really was leaving. "Well, I did tell you to kick me to the curb when this was all over, but I was hoping you wouldn't. I thought you might decide you liked being with me."

"I do." Her eyes glistened. "This isn't about us. This is about me." She took his hands and brought them to her lips. "I have to go. I made a promise to myself, and I never break my promises. Especially to myself."

Damn. His eyes were watering. "You promise to call me if you need me?"

She smiled again. "I promise."

"And you just said you never break your promises."

"It's time to pack my things. I have to go."

"Where?"

She looked up, found Amy's retreating form on the footpath out of the cemetery. "I'd rather not say."

"So this is goodbye?"

She nodded and a tear shook loose. "If you could give me a few minutes before you go home, I'd appreciate it."

He wanted to shout 'no,' to tell her not to go, but he couldn't hold her back.

"Don't look so glum, chum," she joked, wiping at her eyes. "It isn't like you're in love with me or anything."

"Don't be so sure."

"So, what? Are you going to tell me you love me now?"

He raised an eyebrow. He didn't need to tell her. She knew.

Her cheeks pinked and she looked away.

"I'm sorry, I guess I'm frustrated that you're leaving," he said. "Thanks for taking care of me these last couple of days."

"It was the least I could do after you nearly got killed saving my life."

Then she took care of him out of obligation, not love. Garth rose to his feet. He bowed his head, struggling for the right words, but Amy was right. He was a caveman. He had no words. And why was his vision still so damn blurry? He wiped at his eyes to clear them. "Be happy." He turned and walked to the monument shop.

~ ~ ~

Sandra had the luxury of time now. Who knew her mother had tucked a small fortune into a trust fund? Between that and the life insurance, Sandra had been able to pay all the bills and had enough left over to go college and get the degree she'd foregone after the accident. She could travel to Paris or Italy or Hawaii, the way she'd always dreamed. She could find a job once she figured out where she wanted to settle.

First stop, her vacation rental. She'd booked a cute little house closer to Chicago and the airport for a week until she decided where to go next.

Sandra stuffed the few things she'd moved to Garth's house into her suitcase, blubbering all the while. She was finally getting out of Edgarville, so why was she so upset?

Time to suck it up. Her life was waiting for her, right outside that back door. Sandra threw it open, pausing a moment to touch the piece of wood covering the missing windowpane, the window her mother had broken. Was that only a few days ago? It seemed a lifetime.

"Meow."

The cat slinked out from under the bushes, looking skinnier than it had the last time she'd seen it. "I can see your ribs," she told the cat.

"Meow." It shot its tail up in the air and marched up the stairs.

"I suppose you're hungry."

The cat wove around her ankles, purring.

Sandra set down her suitcase, reached inside for the saucer and took out a handful of food, but she didn't set the saucer on the back porch.

"He said you're a stray," she told the cat. "I've been in your shoes, kitty, and it's kinda nice letting someone take care of you sometimes."

"Meow."

"That settles it." She set the saucer on the counter, picked up her suitcase and loaded it in her car. Sandra went back for the cat food and picked up the cat. "You're coming with me."

Chapter 29

AS THE THIRD WEEK DREW to a close, Sandra called the owner one more time asking to extend the agreement on her vacation rental. This time, he said no. She'd have to leave by Thursday so the other people who'd reserved the house could come in.

Three weeks, going into four, and she hadn't booked any flights.

Sandra had spent her time reading and walking through the neighborhood. Everyone was in such a hurry. When she greeted people, they gave her suspicious looks and kept going. Not like in Edgarville.

The cat jumped into her lap, his once matted fur now shiny and healthy. Sandra stroked his back and scratched his ears.

"It's your fault, you know," she said. "How am I supposed to go jetting around the world with a cat in tow? Yes, I know I could carry you with me, but that would scare you all over again and you've only just started to trust me." Her hand rested on his back, sympathizing with the cat, and yet she hadn't given it a name, hadn't wanted to "own" it. Somehow, the idea of giving it a name meant stealing its individuality. "I should have left you with Garth. He would have taken care of you. Taken you in."

Garth would have taken care of her, too.

The cat closed his eyes, a contented rumbling vibrating against Sandra's legs.

"He's only an hour away. I could still take you back. Then I could fly anywhere I wanted to, like Paris." Except she didn't have a passport. "I could go to Colorado." More thoughts of Garth, of their faux skiing trip, crowded in. They'd had so much fun. She'd be expecting to see him around every corner if she went to Breckenridge, even if their trip had been make believe. "Not Colorado, then," she said softly.

The cat jumped down and wandered into the kitchen to empty its food bowl.

She had to go somewhere.

Do you want to do a riverboat cruise in Dubuque?

She and Garth hadn't gotten the opportunity to take that cruise, and suddenly it seemed like the most important thing she had to do. Galena was filled with inns. She could drop the cat off in Edgarville, and after the cruise, she'd book a flight to anywhere.

Alone.

To where?

She shook her head. Sandra couldn't leave the cat outside Garth's door, not without telling Garth. Not after she'd nursed it back to health. It didn't deserve to be homeless again.

She didn't deserve to be homeless again.

She had a home. In Edgarville.

Sandra retrieved her computer from the coffee table.

"Dubuque," she said. "I'm going to take that riverboat cruise."

She found an inn that offered a package deal, two nights and tickets on the Mississippi River paddleboat. And there was a marine museum on the pier. Before she changed her mind, she booked it.

"My chance to see the world, and I'm going to Iowa," she told the cat sarcastically.

Her email chimed with the confirmation. Sandra switched programs and found another email. From Amy.

An invitation to the wedding. "Less than a week to go. I know Garth would love to see you, if you can make it."

One more way her life had flipped on its axis. Sandra would never have guessed her parents actually loved each other. She'd never imagined her mother could truly love her. And she would never have predicted that ten years out of high school, Amy Benson would be her best friend.

Sandra needed a friendly voice. She picked up her phone and called Amy.

"I'm so glad you called! Tell me about your travels." Amy's voice was the first genuine human contact she'd had in three weeks, and it brought tears to Sandra's eyes.

"That's boring," Sandra said. "Tell me how things are going for the wedding. Are you ready? You must be so excited."

Amy proceeded to tell her about the glitch in the florist's order, that due to a monsoon in wherever they got the flowers from, they didn't have enough and they had to substitute with another flower Amy clearly considered inferior. She talked about the cupcake tower and fretted that she'd gained weight and her dress wouldn't fit. It all sounded so normal, and so much more of a fuss than Sandra would go through for her wedding. A justice of the peace, a couple of friends, say your "I dos" and be done with it.

"Sandra?"

Amy's voice brought her back to the conversation.

"I'm sorry, I guess I was daydreaming, imagining it all."

"You don't have to imagine it."

"I can't come home. Not yet. I'm sorry."

"Where are you staying?"

Sandra glanced out the window. If she told Amy she was only an hour away, would Amy tell Garth? And then he'd think he had to come rescue her… "I'm actually travelling today. I have reservations for the weekend."

"I won't tell him," Amy said, reading Sandra's mind. "Aren't you tired of staying in a hotel?"

"I haven't been staying in a hotel." But she was going to an inn, and that would be essentially the same thing. "At least not until tonight."

"My offer still stands. If you need a place, you can stay at the cabin in Galena. My family only goes one weekend a month during the summer. It's our busy time at work, and with the wedding coming up, nobody's going anywhere for a while. It isn't likely anyone will go before hunting season opens in the fall. Then again, you said you don't have to watch your finances quite so closely anymore. You can go anywhere you want."

Yeah, but if she didn't watch her finances, she'd blow through her entire trust fund and be back where she started.

The cabin would give Sandra a base until she figured out what she wanted to do next. "And you won't tell Garth?" she asked. "You won't send him out to save me?"

Amy laughed. "No. Not this time. But I wish you'd call him. Talk to him."

A voice deep down inside said the same thing. "Not yet," Sandra replied. She wrote down what Amy told her, directions to the house and where to find the spare key, wished Amy happiness on her wedding and hung up.

At least she had somewhere to go that wasn't Edgarville, somewhere she could plan her next adventure.

"C'mon, Cat. We're going for a ride."

~ ~ ~

The first thing the innkeeper asked was when Sandra's husband would be joining her. When Sandra informed her there was no husband, the woman unapologetically prattled on, talking as if they'd known each other forever—the way people would in Edgarville. The innkeeper didn't mention animals weren't allowed until Sandra brought the cat inside. At least they'd refunded her deposit.

Good thing she had the Benson's cabin to fall back on.

"I don't suppose I was thinking when I decided to drag you along," Sandra told the cat when she set him down inside the familiar living room. "But I'd do it again."

She glanced at the surroundings, at the gilt mirror over the fireplace. Her father hadn't put in an appearance since he'd walked her mother home. Sandra figured that's what he'd been waiting for, why he'd come back.

They were both at peace.

New ghosts haunted the cabin now. Everywhere Sandra looked, she saw Garth. Reading in the chair. Cooking in the kitchen. Teasing her while they ate beside the French doors. Swinging an ax in the backyard.

Driving a spike through her heart.

"I can't do it," she whispered. "I need help."

She woke up her phone and searched for references on local counselors.

# Chapter 30

"ANOTHER ROUND," THAD TOLD DELIA when she stopped by to check on their table.

"Don't waste your money on me," Garth said, holding up a hand. "I'm at my limit."

"This is the first time you've been out in almost a month," Brian said. "You can't quit on us that easy."

"And I wouldn't be here now if it wasn't for this idiot who wants to marry our sister," Garth replied.

At the other end of the table, Kevin's friends from the newspaper laughed raucously at a joke Garth and his brothers missed. He'd had enough fun for one night. Garth raised his mug to toast. "To Kevin and Amy. May the two of you live happily ever after."

A chorus of male voices called out, "Hear, hear."

He drained his beer, thumped the mug on the table and mumbled, "Somebody has to."

"The night is young," Kevin called down the table. "Bring on the dancing girls."

"I don't think Amy would approve," Garth said.

Brian pulled Delia into his lap. "Hey, you got a friend for Garth? He needs cheering up. I'm tired of watching him mope around."

Delia giggled and swatted at Brian. "I wouldn't do that to my friends. They want to have fun, not play substitute for a heartbroken man." She gave him a quick kiss and jumped off his lap.

"I'm not that bad," Garth argued. "Quit making it sound worse than it is."

Thad raised his eyebrows. "Really? You want to go there?"

Garth pushed away from the table and rose to his feet. "I'm going home."

"Hang on, now. You can't leave us yet. The fun's only starting." Brian pulled out his cell phone and opened an app. "And what is this? Garth Benson on my dating app?"

Delia leaned over and swatted Brian again. "And why do you have a dating app on your phone?"

He ducked and showed her his phone. "It isn't for me. It's for my sorry excuse for a brother. Check it out. Three women in this bar swiped right for you." He turned the phone for Garth to see.

Asshole. Garth shot a glance at Delia and withheld the epithet. "I thought this was a bachelor party for Kevin. Why are you trolling for dates?"

"Because you seem to be in a rut," Thad chimed in.

"And what about you?" Garth asked, facing down his older brother. "When's the last time you enjoyed the company of a woman?"

"Yeah, but that's par for the course for me," Thad replied. "I've gotten used to being on my own. A woman would cramp my style."

"He probably hasn't had a boner since the stone ages," Brian joked. "Thad wouldn't know what to do with it."

Thad reached across the table and cuffed the side of Brian's head. "Is that how you talk in front of a lady?"

"Thank you, Thad," Delia said. She raised a hand to the group. "Another round everybody?"

Kevin's friends all raised their glasses.

She turned on one heel and left the table.

"Seriously, Garth. You're making me depressed," Brian said.

"Boo hoo for you." Garth walked to the other end of the table and clapped Kevin on the shoulder. "Hey, I hate to bail on you…"

"But you're going back into seclusion," Kevin finished. He rose to his feet. "Hey, I'm glad you came out, but you're going to miss those dancing girls."

Garth chuckled. "You keep on dreaming." Before he could escape, a brunette approached the table, wearing a crop top under an open sweater looking thing. He wasn't sure exactly what it was, but from Garth's vantage point, he figured she probably should keep it closed. The crop top wasn't doing her any favors by showing off her middle, and the top side showed more of her boobs than it covered. That might be nice in private, but in a bar, he had to wonder what she was peddling.

"Hi," she said sheepishly, eyes on Garth. She surveyed the table quickly. "I right-swiped you."

She had courage to approach a table full of half-drunk men. He had to give her points for that. Or subtract them…

"Sorry to waste your time," Garth told her. "The profile was my brother, playing a prank."

"That's okay, but it doesn't have to be a prank if you don't want it to be. My name's Sissy."

Brian nudged Thad and giggled. "And here I thought Garth was the sissy."

Thad rocked back in his chair and laughed.

Garth shoved Thad and forced a smile for the brunette. "Nice to meet you, Sissy, and I am sorry, but I'm truly not interested in a date."

"That's okay. We can still have fun. You wouldn't have to take me out or anything."

Brian covered his mouth and laughed.

Thad hooked a foot under Brian's chair and unsuccessfully tried to unseat him.

"Maybe my brother, here, wouldn't mind spending time with you," Garth said. "After all, he's the one who set up the profile, so he's probably a closer match to you than I am."

Brian's eyes widened and he jumped to his feet to avoid another attempt at losing his chair. "Delia'd kill me."

Garth grabbed Brian's phone from the table, studied it a moment, and swiped left. "My apologies."

Sissy shrugged and walked away.

Phone in hand, Garth went through the screens to delete the profile Brian had created. "Nice try, numbnuts. I don't need any help from you geniuses."

"Then maybe you'll buy me a drink," another woman said behind him.

Garth turned to face her. Another brunette, tall with a little extra padding to hold onto. If he wasn't so screwed up, he might have obliged her.

She held out a hand to shake and smiled. "Jackie."

"Nice to meet you, Jackie, but I'm not looking for company."

She took a step back and the smile slipped from her face.

"Whatever my brothers put you up to, you don't have to."

She looked over the table. "These are your brothers? All of them?"

"Not all of them. We're toasting our soon to be brother-in-law," Garth told her. "At least that's what I was told. Then again, considering Kevin isn't much of a drinker, I'm not sure why we're here."

"Sorry to intrude. I was under the impression… I swiped right…" Jackie pursed her lips. "You don't look like you're celebrating, you look forlorn. Thought you might like someone to talk to."

Yeah, he was forlorn, and that was the best way to scare her off. Tell her why. "Going through a bad breakup." Wouldn't hurt to overdramatize. "I just can't get over her."

Jackie stared at his arm, touched it, wrapped her hand around his biceps. "Sensitive. I like that. Maybe I can help you move forward."

Not going the way he planned. "I deleted the profile my brother set up," he told her. "I'm not looking for help, or a drink, or anything else." He forced a smile. "Thanks anyway." He had to get out of here before the third right-swiper found him.

Garth turned to say his goodnights and found his brothers laughing into their beers. Kevin raised his mug to toast him. Garth flipped them off and walked out of Murphy's. Alone. He'd had enough socializing for one night.

He walked half a block and turned the corner. Amy was sitting on a bench on the sidewalk.

"You leaving already?" she asked.

"And what are you doing here?" he asked suspiciously.

She rose from the bench and hugged him.

He rubbed his knuckles on the top of her head. "You waiting for your fiancé or are you trying to cheer me up, too?"

She grinned. "I told them it wouldn't work. I'm in favor of you giving Sandra a call."

Garth rubbed his neck again. "I don't feel comfortable doing that. She's the one who walked away."

Amy rolled her eyes. "Give her a break! After what that poor woman's been through?"

He chuckled. "Listen to you, defending the woman who coined Crazy Amy."

She punched his shoulder. "Actually, it was the other kids. As I remember, the only thing she said was, 'You're crazy, Amy.' How was she to know the mean girls would run with it?"

He threw an arm across his sister's shoulders and walked toward home. "You're a good person, Amy."

"Which is why you should listen to me when I tell you to call Sandra."

Garth stopped and withdrew his arm. "Not you, too. Please?"

"Ask her how she's doing. Doesn't hurt to let her know you care."

She was wrong. The pellet in his heart still hurt like hell. "Yeah, it does. If she wants to talk to me, she's got my number."

"But you would? Talk to her, I mean."

He cocked his head, eyeing Amy suspiciously. "Don't screw with this, Amy."

"You've been in love with Sandra Meyer since the first time you laid eyes on her."

"And what if you're wrong? If I was in love with her, why did I spend three years of my life with Annabelle?"

Amy's laugh echoed down the empty street. "That's a good one. And I should probably tell you I know why Annabelle broke up with you. She wasn't afraid to tell everyone she knew how you wouldn't own up to being in love with someone else and you were just using her."

He gazed into the distance, feeling like a heel all over again. Everyone knew he was in love with Sandra, including Annabelle. Everyone except Garth, himself. "I *am* a big dumb ox who couldn't admit the truth to himself."

"But you know the truth now." Amy rested a hand on his arm. "Never pegged you for a quitter."

Now Amy was making him mad. "I didn't quit. She did."

"So if she called you, say tomorrow, you wouldn't hang up on her?"

He brushed a hand across his face. His nose tingled and something seemed to be caught in his eye. "I don't know what I'd do." He met Amy's insistent stare. "She made herself pretty clear when she left. She doesn't want any part of Edgarville, including me, so there's no point to this conversation. Now if you're done harassing me, you should probably go back and wait for your fiancé. Unless that was all a ruse, too."

"He texted me that he wasn't leaving until you guys brought in the dancing girls," she said, resisting another smile.

"Then he's going to be waiting a long time. That poor man is going to be sorely disappointed." He pulled Amy in for another hug. "Go home, squirt, and stop trying to fix things. I'm fine."

She pulled away, holding tight to his arms. "Remember when you told me there were things I didn't know?"

He narrowed his eyes. What was she getting at?

"Well, there are things *you* don't know," she finished. "Promise me you'll hear her out if she should call or show up on your doorstep one day."

"Amy, don't meddle."

She shook his arms. "Promise me."

Bless her heart for trying to cheer him up. "She's not coming back, Amy. She's been wanting to get out of this town all her life. There's nothing here for her anymore."

"Garth," she said once more.

Easy promise to make. It wasn't going to happen. "I promise."

Chapter 31

SANDRA HAD MADE A LOT of progress in the past three months, thanks to Dr. Charles Anderson, although he had more faith in Sandra than she had in herself. When combined with her mother's diary, their discussions had helped Sandra see her family life through a different lens. Yes, she carried around a load of baggage, but now she could let go of her parents' baggage, including the guilt that she caused the accident by making an immature decision.

Shifting the blame for the accident to Nick had been easy when he'd confessed to running her father off the road, but Sandra still regretted giving him the opportunity.

Amy's email telling Sandra she was pregnant had been fodder for two of Sandra's weekly therapy sessions. Funny how she hadn't realized she'd mentioned wishing she wasn't so afraid to be a mother so Amy's children could have cousins. Dr. Anderson took the opportunity to point out her unresolved feelings for Garth, and now she had her assignment—to go back and face her tangle of emotions.

He still needs a bookkeeper, Amy had written. *Don't suppose you know anyone who wants a job? I've been filling in, but I'll only be working another six months.*

Because Amy was pregnant, and she and Kevin were over-the-moon happy to be starting a family.

So many of Sandra's sessions had centered on Garth, but was that because he was her first lover? Because he'd saved her life?

Dr. Anderson had given her the tools to see inside herself. She was able to face most of the "if onlys," but one thing she had yet to face.

Her feelings for Garth.

Which was why she was driving to Edgarville.

Sandra exited the highway, and within a block she was under a canopy of colorful leaves. Reds and browns and oranges.

Home.

A sense of calm surrounded her and she turned the radio off to absorb it. Without thinking, she turned onto Greenleaf Avenue and pulled into the driveway of the home where she'd grown up.

Home.

Yes, her mother had worked long hours. Yes, her father drove his truck over the road and was gone for days at a time, but as she turned the engine off, she remembered picnics in the yard. Playing Frisbee with her dad. Decorating for Christmas. Her Grandmother Meyer knitting colorful stocking caps and scarves, more than any of them could ever wear. *Isn't that a piece of cherry pie!*

"This is it," she said to the cat, who looked up from where it lay curled in the back seat.

Sandra gathered the cat in her arms and got out of the car. She let herself in the back door, the way she'd done a million times before. Now, instead of remembering the way her parents refused to look at one another, she remembered sly smiles over a cup of coffee. Flirty glances over the shoulder. A little girl gathered up in her father's arms and swung around while her mother laughed and scolded him that someone would get hurt.

She remembered sitting at the kitchen table decorating cut-out cookies with her mother and grandmother, and then boxing them up to give to shut-ins. Long nights at that same kitchen table when her mother would come home from the real estate office exhausted, and still spend the time to help Sandra with her algebra.

Love isn't about the things you say, it's in the things you do.

That Garth Benson was a wise man.

Sandra bounced on her toes, anxious to see him. Would he still set her heart racing?

The better question was if he would speak to her at all. She had to consider the possibility he'd want nothing to do with her. He'd fulfilled his role as protector. Even if he'd done it out of love the way he'd intimated he had, she hadn't responded well.

No time like the present. According to Amy, he spent most of his time at the trophy shop these days.

"I'll be back," she promised the cat, and walked out of the house. She slid into her car, and drove the five miles into town.

No expectations, Dr. Anderson had told her. *Say hello and see where the conversation leads you. No practicing conversations.* He had given her permission to apologize, and she'd been practicing *that* speech ever since.

Sandra parked in front of the café, glanced to the next block at the trophy shop across the street…

and walked into the café.

Chicken.

"Sandra!" Vicki squealed. She ran from behind the counter and gave Sandra a hug.

The kitchen door swung open and Darrell stepped out wearing a big grin. "There she is."

"Hi," she said sheepishly. "Wasn't sure if you'd be so happy to see me after I ran out on you."

"Big shoes to fill, but we've been limping along," he said. "How are you doing?"

"A lot better."

"Coming back to work?" he asked, giving her his best puppy dog eyes.

Sandra laughed. "I might be persuaded."

"Let me get you a cup of coffee," Vicki said, rushing behind the counter.

Sandra held up a hand. "No, not right now. I have somewhere else to stop, but I wanted to say hello."

Darrell cocked his head toward the door. "Been a tough couple of months, but I think he'll be happy to see you."

Small town life. Nothing like it. She chuffed. "Should I ask who you're referring to?"

"You know damn well who I'm referring to, same as I know where else you have to stop." Darrell threw an arm across her shoulders and squeezed. "Good to see you back in town. You'll let me know how things turn out?"

Sandra gave him a wink. "Soon as I know."

Darrell put his hands on her shoulder and walked her to the door. "Good luck."

Family. More than her mother and her father, the community she'd grown up in was as much her family as the one she'd been born into. Darrell as her older brother, Vicki as her sister. Everyone at the real estate office knew her life story. Leo at the service station fit in there somewhere. Center Street filled her with as much wistfulness as walking into her mother's home.

Sandra laughed as she crossed the street. She'd only been gone three months. Where was all this nostalgia coming from?

She'd missed Edgarville. Missed the sense of community. The sense of home.

She stopped before she reached the trophy shop window, took a moment to compose herself. Her chest fluttered like the autumn leaves in the breeze. This was it. The moment of truth.

She took the steps forward, bowed her head and pushed through the door.

A woman giggled.

Sandra raised her head. Garth was leaning over the counter, a playful smile on his face, one she'd seen every time he'd come into the coffee shop. A woman striking a pose flipped her hair and giggled again.

He'd moved on. Sandra's throat closed, but she continued into the shop. She'd come to apologize, if nothing else. The fact she wanted to cry wasn't going to stop her.

Garth straightened. My, but she'd forgotten how tall he was—and how broad. His honey-brown eyes fixed on her, but he didn't say a word. Was he happy to see her? Angry?

Her insides melted like lava cake, but the as yet unidentified woman giggling with him reminded her she'd walked away from Garth. If he wasn't happy to see her, she couldn't blame him. If he'd moved on, she'd have to find a way to do the same.

"I guess I'd better leave you to your business," the woman said. She reached for Garth's hand, squeezed it and walked toward the door, sending a big smile Sandra's way as she passed. A glint of light flashed off the woman's hand—a big fat diamond ring.

Sandra drew a deep breath to calm herself.

Her voice squeaked when she spoke. "Hi."

"Hi." He folded his arms.

Nope, he wasn't going to make this easy. Might as well apologize. Sorry, Dr. Anderson. The conversation didn't look like it was going to go anywhere.

"Listen, I wanted to thank you for everything you did for me. I realize I was screwed up, and you'll be happy to know I've been getting help. I'm in therapy…" Her voice trailed off. The next line was supposed to be how she hoped he'd forgive her, how she wanted him in her life, but somehow that seemed like the wrong thing to say right now. Sandra cast a glance at the door the other woman had walked through. "I stopped to say I'm sorry. And I'm sorry I stole your cat."

Not anywhere near what she'd intended to say.

~ ~ ~

She looked so damn good, and yet so damn unobtainable. No point being happy to see her when she was probably going to be gone again before the end of the day.

"I didn't know I had a cat to steal," Garth said.

She motioned with her hands. "The stray. The one you fed at the back door. He looked so skinny." Sandra shook her head and grimaced. "He's at my mother's house if you want him back, or if his owners reported him missing. He looked so forlorn. I couldn't leave him behind."

"Don't think he had a home. I sorta figured he'd gotten caught up in the circle of life, you know, run across a bigger critter." He wanted to laugh. He wanted to take her in his arms and tell her how much he'd missed her, but she had that Bambi look in her eyes again, like she was ready to run. "It's good to see you. How long are you in town?" Did he sound angry? Probably, but then he was. Angry. At himself.

"I figured it was time to either sell my mother's place or move back in."

And his guess was she wasn't staying. "I'm sure Staley Real Estate would be happy to help you sell it. You finally got your wish. Nothing tying you down to Edgarville anymore. So where are you off to?"

"One twelve Greenleaf Avenue."

Her mother's address. "I mean after you sell her place."

"I'm not selling it."

Garth put his hands on the counter. "Oh, I get it. You want to fix it up first? If you need any help, Brian can give you a hand. He's good with that kind of stuff."

"No," she said meeting his gaze. "I'm not selling it. I'm moving back to Edgarville."

Not what he expected to hear. "What was it your grandmother always used to say? Isn't that a piece of cherry pie?"

Sandra laughed. "Well, yeah, but that generally meant too much of a good thing in a negative way. Don't worry, you don't need to make room for dessert. I won't ruin you plans. She's cute, by the way."

Plans? "What are you talking about?"

Her nostrils flared and she looked less sure of herself. "I mean, it isn't good for my ego to see you've found someone new so quickly, but I suppose once we got it out of our systems, it was probably easier to move on."

Garth checked the door, then looked at Sandra. He fought to keep from laughing out loud. "Are you referring to Felicity?"

"The woman who left a moment ago? I don't know her name."

Garth walked around the counter, head down so she couldn't see him grinning like an idiot. He stopped in front of her. "First. I haven't gotten 'it' out of my system."

Sandra took a step back with a near-silent, "oh."

"Second, Felicity is engaged to Howard Greenbaum, Jordan's little brother. You might remember him. Not quite as big a douche as Jordan. She stopped in to order engraved flasks for the groomsmen but she's happy to show off the ring to anyone who asks her about it."

Color flushed Sandra's cheeks, and her eyes shone like a summer lake. God, she was beautiful! But he wasn't going to get worked over again. When she'd left town, she'd taken his heart with him. He'd be damned if he'd let her stomp on it some more. "Why are you moving back to town? You couldn't wait to get out of here."

She took a measured breath, then raised her face to look at him. "I got homesick." She drew a finger over her heart. "God's honest truth. Who'da thought, huh? And then I remembered you mentioning a job." She swallowed hard. "Are you still hiring?"

What was she playing at? The time for casual flirtations had passed. She was either in, or she was out. "Sandra…"

"I love you." Her voice was little more than a whisper, but it slammed against his heart like a church bell.

She was coming home to him.

"You know, Old Man Watson always said this business was more of a mom and pop thing." His heart hammered, hoping he wasn't misreading her.

She took a step closer. "So what're you saying, you don't want me to be the mom part of the business?"

Damn it all to hell. He took hold of Sandra, lowered his head and kissed her. She melted into him, as sweet as he remembered. "Still not getting old," he whispered against her lips.

"Not even a little," she replied.

"If you want the job, you might have to marry me."

A sly grin creased her lips. "That might be considered sexual harassment, those kind of conditions for employment."

"Only if its unwelcome. You going to make me sleep in a tree on our wedding night?"

"Not unless I can sleep out there with you, but we'd probably be more comfortable in a bed."

"Bed? Where's a bed?" He glanced around the shop. "Right now, I'm thinking my work table would work just fine. I could lock the door, turn the closed sign out…"

She stepped back. "Are you asking me to marry you?"

"Only if you say yes."

"More conditions?"

Were they kidding? Sandra had a way of messing with his head. "Did I just propose?"

"You did a sloppy job of it, but sure sounded like it."

And yet she hadn't moved. Neither did he. This wasn't the way this was supposed to go. "No. I want a do over. I'm taking you to dinner tonight. Riccardo's. A glass of wine, soft music…"

"Garth. I'm teasing you. I was pretty screwed up when I left town, but one of the reasons I came back was because there was one thing I knew I couldn't walk away from." She pressed her palm to his chest. "I want you in my life, for as long as you'll have me, whether we live in Edgarville or Galena or Paris, France."

"Then you don't want to miss dinner tonight. I have it on good authority that lunkhead you just said I love you to wants to impress you."

"That big lunkhead already has impressed me."

He held her close. "Are you sure?"

Her head bobbed against his chest. "That doesn't mean you can't still take me to dinner."

He raised his head and laughed, his eyes filled with tears. "Okay, but first…" He cleared his throat, took a step back and dropped to one knee. "To make it official. I want to make sure there's no misunderstanding." He cleared his throat a second time and laughed nervously.

"Sandra Meyer, I have loved you for as long as I've known you." Now that he'd asked for the stage, he was at a loss for words. He glanced around the trophy shop, at the freshly painted walls. "Will you be the mom to my pop? Help me make this business a success by day and warm my bed by night? Will you take my name and bear my children and stay with me until we're both old and feeble and don't remember each other's names?"

She laughed. "That's an awful lot to ask of a girl. I have a few conditions of my own."

"Such as?"

She pulled him to his feet. "I can't tell you when I fell in love with you, but I can't remember a time when I didn't want you in my life. I didn't know what love was until you weren't there anymore, and then I knew what I was missing. Did I mention I had to have my head examined?" She took his hand and bowed her head. "Will you go on adventures with me? Take me skiing in the winter or sailing in the summer and, most importantly, will you promise to bring me home after? To Edgarville?"

He cupped her face so she looked at him again and smiled so she'd know he was glad to have her joking with him again. "Does a paddleboat in Dubuque qualify as sailing?"

She smiled. "Yeah. And I should warn you, I plan to two-time you."

He took a step back, not sure he'd heard right.

"I'll be the mom to your pop, but I want to keep my job at the café, too. Are you willing to share me?"

He clutched her hands to his chest. "Damn, woman, you nearly gave me a heart attack. As long as you come home to me every night."

"Did you say something about your work table in the back?" she asked, wagging her eyebrows.

He crossed to the door, locked it and turned the closed sign out. "Still not getting old," he said. He growled and lunged toward her. Sandra giggled and ran to the back room.

No, loving Sandra would never get old.

Dear Reader:

Thanks so much for reading this book. If you enjoyed the story, I hope you will encourage others by "liking" my books on Goodreads and everywhere the option is offered, and by posting an honest review to the site where you bought this book and/or at other book blogs/reading sites so you can help other readers decide whether it's worth their time. Authors like and need to get feedback to make each new book as good as it can be.

—Karla Brandenburg